# The Madwoman of Melun
# & Other Plays
# of Murder & Mayhem

# FROM THE SAME AUTHOR

*Lord Ruthven the Vampyre* (2004)
*The Return of Lord Ruthven* (2004)
*Arsène Lupin vs. Sherlock Holmes: The Stage Play* (2005)
*Frankenstein Meets the Hunchback of Notre-Dame* (2005)
*Sherlock Holmes: The Grand Horizontals* (2006)
*Rocambole* (2006)
*Gentlemen of the Night & Captain Phantom* (2007)
*Nick Carter vs. Fantômas* (2007),
*Chéri-Bibi* (2008)
*Sherlock Holmes vs. Fantômas* (2009)
*Lord Ruthven Begins* (2010)
*Sherlock Holmes vs. Jack the Ripper* (2011)
*Sherlock Holmes, Fantômas, Lupin, Raffles and More: The Spanish Plays* (2017)
*Vidocq and the Lemonade Girl & Other Plays of Murder & Vengeance* (2020)

# The Madwoman of Melun & Other Plays of Murder & Mayhem

Plays by
**Jules Mary, Xavier de Montépin
& Jules Dornay**

Adapted by
**Frank J. Morlock**

A Black Coat Press Book

Visit our website at www.blackcoatpress.com

ISBN 978-1-64932-080-3. First Printing: October 2021. Published by Black Coat Press, an imprint of Hollywood Comics.com, LLC, P.O. Box 17270, Encino, CA 91416. All rights reserved. Except for review purposes, no part of this book may be reproduced or transmitted in any form or by any means, electronic or mechanical, including photocopying, recording, or by any information storage and retrieval system, without permission in writing from the publisher. The stories and characters depicted in this novel are entirely fictional. Printed in the United States of America.

# TABLE OF CONTENTS

*Xavier-Henry Aymon de Montépin was born in 1823 and passed away in 1902. He was a very famous popular novelist and journalist.* His most famous work was the best-selling La Porteuse de Pain *[The Bread Peddler], published in* feuilleton *in* Le Petit Journal *between 1884 and 1889. It was later adapted as a five-act stage play by Jules Dornay, and first performed at the Théâtre de l'Ambigu on 11 January 1889. An English translation by Frank Morlock was published in our previous collection,* Vidocq and The Lemonade Girl.

*Constant Jules Alexandre Lacroix, a.k.a. Jules Dornay, was born in 1829 and passed away in 1906. He was a famous playwright who often collaborated with Montépin, adapting the former's novels into plays. Black Coast Press has previously published a translation of his 1868 play* Douglas the Vampyre *under the title* Lord Ruthven Begins.

La Policière, *translated here as* The Police Agent, *was a play in six acts that was first performed at the Théâtre de l'Ambigu in Paris in 1889 with Montal as Pierre Lartigues, and Emilie Lerou as Aimée Joubert. It is loosely based on* Simone et Marie, *a melodramatic* feuilleton *by Montépin, collected and published in four volumes entitled* La Nuit Sanglante I & II *[The Bloody Night] and* L'Oeil du Chat I & II *[The Cat's Eye] by E. Dentu in 1883.*

# THE POLICE AGENT, or, THE CAT'S EYE
*by Xavier de Montépin & Jules Dornay.*

## CHARACTERS
*in order of appearance*

GABRIEL SERVET, a famous artist
ALBERT DE GIBRAY, his student
MARIE DE BRESSOLLES
LUDOVIC DE BRESSOLLES, her father

SIMONE (D'HARVILLE)
GUY D'ARFEUILLES, a socialite
YVAN SAMOILOFF, a Russian Count
BARON LANDELLY DE LANDILLY, a *bon vivant*
MAURICE VASSEUR
ALPHONSE MASSE, Commissioner of the Sûreté
LETELLIER, a shopkeeper at the Père Lachaise
AIMÉE JOUBERT, a.k.a. The Cat's Eye
MARIANNE, her maid
PAUL DE GIBRAY, Albert's uncle, an Investigating Magistrate
PIERRE LARTIGUES (a.k.a. Jules Théroux)
VICTOIRE, a maid
GASTON VERDIER (a.k.a. Abbé Meyris, Captain Ratier)
CADET, a coachman
BAUDOIN, another coachman
PACARD, another coachman
FRANÇOIS, a groom
SYLVIE, a servant
MONSIEUR BINET, the owner of a carriage rental company
GALOUBERT, a thief
LA GRENOUILLE, another thief
VALENTINE DE BRESSOLLES née D'HARVILLE, Marie's mother
JODELET, Aimée's secretary
DOMINIQUE, a concierge
LA BELLE OCTAVIA, a courtesan
MESNIL, a Postmaster
BARDOUX, a Postal clerk
JULIEN, another postal clerk
RINGARD, another Postal clerk
DÉSIRÉE, a lady customer at the Post Office
POLICEMEN, SERVANTS, GUESTS AT A BALL, OTHER CUSTOMERS AT THE POST OFFICE

# ACT I
## SCENE I

The workshop of the painter Gabriel Servet. There is a door at the back which remains closed during the scene, and side doors. To the right, at the back, an easel on which is a portrait of Simone, at whose bedside watches a Sister of Charity. To the left, there is a small bed on which is another easel with an empty picture. To the right, yet another easel with an unfinished portrait of Marie Bressolles. Near the audience, there is a small desk with all the necessary writing implements. To the left, there is a stairway leading to the apartments above.

AT RISE, Gabriel is before the easel holding the picture of Simone. Albert de Gibray, seated before the easel at the left, is painting. Suddenly, he stops.

ALBERT: It seems to me that he's late. Isn't Mademoiselle Bressolles coming today?

GABRIEL (*smiling*): It's barely ten o'clock.

ALBERT: Really?

GABRIEL: The desire to see my adorable model makes you feel the hours are long, my dear Albert.

ALBERT: That's true.

GABRIEL (*laughing*): Ah-ha! In that case, it's dangerous.

ALBERT: How?

GABRIEL: I mean, for you, by Jove!

ALBERT: For me? Where's the danger? Is there a problem between her and me? I'm the son of General de Gibray, who died in battle, the nephew of a judge, my tutor and adoptive father, so can't I pretend to the hand of Mademoiselle de Bressolles?

GABRIEL: It's true that both your uncle and Monsieur de Bressolles are rich and honorable, but Marie is barely out of school, and as for you, you're just an overgrown kid.

ALBERT (*smiling*): Is that all?

GABRIEL: Also, to get married, it takes two. You love her,

but there's no evidence that he loves you in return.
ALBERT (*sighing*): That's true.

(*A bell rings outside*)

GABRIEL: There she is!
ALBERT (*joyful*): At last!
GABRIEL (*aside*): The boy is more smitten than I thought. I've got to give him a good rap on the shoulder. (*rising to greet the visitors*)

*Marie enters with Ludovic, her father.*

MARIE: Monsieur Servet, we've made you wait at least ten minutes. But it was my father who's at fault. (*to Albert*) Bonjour, Monsieur de Gibray!
ALBERT: Mademoiselle.
LUDOVIC (*taking Gabriel's hand*): It's always my fault.
GABRIEL: In that case, I should punish you.
LUDOVIC: By keeping Marie ten minutes longer?
GABRIEL: For a father, this punishment would be doleful indeed, but not sufficiently stern. I have another in store for you.
MARIE: My God, what's that?
GABRIEL: Your father has trusted me with a great favor, Mademoiselle. He's promised me to come with you and your mother at an intimate soirée I'm giving here on the 31st of the month. My students will put on an exhibit of the studio's work. All our friends will be featured in it.
MARIE: And tell me there'll be dancing, too! Ah, how nice! Papa, Mama and I will gladly accept your invitation.
LUDOVIC: Indeed; it will be our pleasure!
GABRIEL: Truly? So now you enjoy balls?
LUDOVIC: No more than ever, but I am sacrificing myself, because I've met Monsieur Vasseur...
GABRIEL: Ah.
LUDOVIC: You know him, too?

GABRIEL: I should say so. A do-everything sort who has the precious gift of opening all doors. He began as a painter, then became a stock broker, then he turned to the theater, and to-day, if I'm not too far out of date, he dabbles in journalism.

MARIE: Oh! So you do know him!

GABRIEL: And he remains a very likable bachelor. Carefree and modern.

LUDOVIC: Well, since we met him, my wife has only one idea: to put our daughter into society, and Monsieur Vasseur seems to have become the organizer of all festivities. He's turning our home topsy-turvy, for it seems he's also an interior decorator. So I left. I've done my part. I simply obey my wife.

GABRIEL: You've done the right thing, because Mademoiselle Marie is of an age to be married.

MARIE (*upset*): Who, me?

GABRIEL: And your duty is to find a husband worthy of her.

ALBERT (*aside*): I'll marry her!

GABRIEL: Seek, and ye shall find, Monsieur de Bressolles. Albert, will you bring your uncle to the soirée?

ALBERT: Bringing a magistrate to a ball? What are you thinking about?

LUDOVIC: He'll do as I do; he'll sacrifice himself.

GABRIEL: He'll want to come, I'm sure of that. (*low to Albert*) He has to meet Marie, right?

ALBERT: Ah, yes, thank you.

*Marie removes her cap and coat, and finds herself looking at the picture of Simone.*

MARIE: Ah!

ALL: What's the matter?

MARIE: Don't be alarmed. It was just a cry of admiration. (*pointing to the picture*) Look at it, Papa! I've never seen it before.

GABRIEL: It was always covered up before. I was working on it just before you came. It's been my main work for this year.

11

LUDOVIC: I predict it will be a great success.

MARIE: Ah, yes, it's beautiful, very beautiful. But how sad she is… It's heartbreaking.

GABRIEL: Like truth itself.

MARIE: Such a sweet face. Suffering and resigned. Is it actually a portrait?

GABRIEL: Yes, Mademoiselle. I used a very sick girl as my model. Today, happily, she's out of danger. She's been cured completely, thank God, but she still needs a lot of care.

MARIE: Would you explain, please? What does she need?

ALBERT: A little coddling—and hope for the future.

MARIE: Is she a worker?

GABRIEL: Yes, she does needlework. She's very industrious.

MARIE: Poor girl!

LUDOVIC: How old is she?

GABRIEL: Twenty -two or twenty-three.

MARIE: Her family cannot help her?

GABRIEL: She has no family.

LUDOVIC (*pulls out a bank note*): Please give her this.

GABRIEL: She won't take it, Monsieur.

MARIE: But we can't let her struggle in poverty!

ALBERT: There's a way to help her.

MARIE: What is it?

ALBERT: Give her some work. Just knowing she has work will give her strength.

MARIE: That's a nice thought. We'll give her some work, won't we, Papa?

LUDOVIC: Certainly.

MARIE: I've got an ever better idea…

*Suddenly, Simone appears in the doorway, a small package in her hand.*

SIMONE: Monsieur Servet?

ALBERT & GABRIEL: Simone!

MARIE: Why, it's your protégée, Monsieur Servet.

GABRIEL: Indeed, it is! Luck has sent her to us at a very appropriate time.... (*to Simone*) Come in, Simone, come in, child... I must scold you....

SIMONE (*bowing to everyone*): Scold me?

GABRIEL: Yes, what are you doing out, weak as you are?

SIMONE: Monsieur Albert gave me a dozen handkerchiefs to embroider with his initials, and now that I'm done, I came to return them to him.

ALBERT (*taking them*): Thank you!

GABRIEL (*pointing to a chair*): Sit down. Despite your recklessness, I'm happy that you have come. We were all concerned about you.

SIMONE: Concerned about me?

MARIE: Yes, Mademoiselle. While we were admiring your portrait, Monsieur Servet told us all about you, and we were seeking a way to improve your life.

SIMONE: I thank you from the bottom of my heart! (*fearfully*) It's true that I've been very ill. Sometimes, I thought that the will to live was going to leave me...

LUDOVIC (*to Albert*): The poor child!

SIMONE: But it's over now. My health is coming back. I can work.

MARIE: Would you accept a respectable position?

SIMONE: Oh, yes!

MARIE: Then, this very day, we will talk to a friend of ours— Madame Dubief. She has a position open—but that might change, right, father?

LUDOVIC: Well said, my girl.

ALBERT (*to Gabriel*): How not to love her?

SIMONE: Ah, Mademoiselle, my heart overflows with gratitude.

LUDOVIC: Well, then, it's agreed. After we leave here, we'll go straight to talk to our friend.

SIMONE: May you succeed, Monsieur! I'll be grateful to you all my life.

LUDOVIC: Tell me your name for Madame Dubief.

SIMONE: Simone.

LUDOVIC: Your last name?

SIMONE (*tearfully*): I don't have one, Monsieur.

MARIE: Don't cry. Happiness will come to you.

SIMONE: Thank you with all my heart.

MARIE: Count on us absolutely, and if that position has been filled, we will find another.

GABRIEL: And you will live in peace and security.

SIMONE (*emotionally*): Mademoiselle... Monsieur... I don't know what to say...

ALBERT: Good-bye, Simone.

SIMONE: Ah, you are so good!

(*Simone leaves, crying*)

GABRIEL: You can give her a strong recommendation. I'll vouch for her.

ALBERT: What a good deed you are doing.

(*The bell rings again*)

LUDOVIC: Another unexpected visitor?

ALBERT (*jocularly*): This seems to be the day for it!

(*Guy d'Arfeuilles enters, followed by Count Yvan Samoiloff*)

MARIE: Ah, Monsieur d'Arfeuilles.

(*she offers her hand, Gabriel and Albert go to shake the Count's hand*)

GUY (*taking Marie's hand*): Mademoiselle. (*bowing to the other men*) Messieurs.

GABRIEL (*to Yvan*): My friend!

YVAN (*to Gabriel, shaking his hand*): Coming here is like coming to a party, my dear Gabriel!

GABRIEL: It's the way it is! (*to Marie*) Mademoiselle (*to Ludovic*) Monsieur de Bressolles, allow me to present my friend, Count Yvan Samoiloff who just arrived in Paris two weeks ago.

LUDOVIC & MARIE (*bowing*): Monsieur le Comte.

GABRIEL (*presenting Marie*): Mademoiselle Marie de Bressolles, whose unfinished portrait you've seen on my easel. Her Father, Monsieur Ludovic de Bressolles.

YVAN (*bowing*): I am delighted to be introduced by our great artist, one of my dearest friends.

LUDOVIC: Are you staying in Paris long?

YVAN (*a bit embarrassed*): For a few days, only, at least, I think so.

GABRIEL: To my regret, he won't remain for longer.

YVAN (*aside, darkly*): Who knows?

GABRIEL: I wish you'd stay forever, Yvan. Our friendship goes back fifteen years. I could be his father.

YVAN (*taking his hand*): My dear Gabriel!

(*We hear a voice outside*)

LANDELLY (*outside*): No, really, it's very chic!

GUY: Why, that's Landelly's voice!

YVAN (*laughing*):The little Baron de Landelly!

GUY: A most annoying chap!

GABRIEL (*laughing*): Say what you will, he amuses me!

(*Landelly enters*)

LANDELLY: A true saying, my good friend. His success is stupefying... (*to Maurice Vasseur, still outside*) Enter, will you, old boy!

(*Maurice Vasseur enters*)

MARIE: Monsieur Vasseur!

(*Maurice bows and shakes the hands of Gabriel, Monsieur de Bressolles, Guy and Ivan*)

MARIE: Messieurs, may I introduce to you Monsieur Maurice

15

Vasseur, one of our friends, a journalist.

MAURICE: A journalist! Oh, no, not yet, merely a reporter.

MARIE (*to Maurice*): This is Count Yvan Samoiloff.

(*Maurice bows*)

LANDELLY: Mademoiselle, would you kindly agree (*coughing*) Cough! Cough! My dear great painter, no, truly, you know… The entrance to your house… Your workshop is dazzling. (*coughing*) Cough! Cough!

GABRIEL Still a bit of a cough, Baron? You must take better care of it.

LANDELLY: Not at all. Iron constitution! Cough! (*to Yvan*) Ah, my good friend, in your northern steppes, you don't know what it is to be sick! You are all so healthy. Cough!

MARIE (*aside, to Albert*): Why, he's half dead already!

ALBERT: He's quite a character.

MARIE (*chuckling*): Made of iron, apparently.

LANDELLY (*noticing Marie's portrait*): Ah, yes! Bravo! Bravo! Mademoiselle, you've got style. (*All laugh. He examines the picture*)

GABRIEL (*to Yvan, pulling him aside*): Why didn't I see you yesterday, dear friend?

YVAN: I went to deposit a wreath.

GABRIEL: At the tomb of Kouravieff? At night, surely?

YVAN: I dined with the beautiful Octavia, then waited for a friend who'd returned from Switzerland that morning.

GABRIEL: The beautiful Octavia who is still counting on calling herself Countess Samoiloff?

YVAN (*laughing*): The same!

GABRIEL: Have you heard from Pierre Lartigues?

YVAN: Nothing yet.

MAURICE (*to Gabriel*): My dear maestro, my visit is selfish. I only accompanied the Baron in order to ask you for the title of the painting you plan to exhibit this year. I want to be the first to announce it.

GABRIEL: The Sister of Charity.

LANDELLY: Stupendous! One would swear it's a dime novel.

MAURICE: (*writing in his notebook*): The Sister of Charity. Thank you. (*continuing to write*)

LANDELLY: Still the first to want to know, my friend Maurice. He'll be the head of his company, and deservedly so. He's got no equal in getting news, and not ordinary stuff either—sensational news, if you please. For example, what he was telling me as we came...

GUY: News about...?

LANDELLY: No, nothing of the sort. Not at all.

MARIE: What are you talking about?

LANDELLY: A crime, Mademoiselle. Actually, two crimes. Enough to give you goose bumps.

MAURICE: I was at the Sûreté and I learned of a rather strange murder...

ALL: A murder!

LANDELLY: Yes. All quite unheard of. Stupefying. Hypnotizing. Read this, Maurice...

MAURICE: No, I don't think it's a good idea...

LANDELLY: He's having an attack of good manners. (*reading over his shoulder*) Murder at the Père Lachaise...[1]

YVAN (*aside*): At the Père Lachaise?

LANDELLY: A double murder!

MAURICE (*closing his notebook*): You're insupportable!

MARIE: Why so much discretion about a news that the whole world will discover tomorrow?

MAURICE: You are right, Mademoiselle. (*opening his notebook, and reading*) "This morning at the Père Lachaise cemetery, a stream of blood oozed under the bronze door of a tomb, attracting the attention of a workman. Workers forced the door open and discovered the body of a woman stabbed to death. At the same time, the groom at a local stable for carriages located

---

[1] The cemetery of the Père Lachaise opened in 1804 and takes its name from the confessor to Louis XIV, Père François de la Chaise (1624-1709), who lived in the Jesuit house rebuilt during 1682 on the same site. It is the largest cemetery in Paris (over 100 acres) with more than 3.5 million visitors annually.

Rue Ernestine found the body of a man murdered in one of the cabs..."

MARIE: Ah!

MAURICE (*continuing*): "The Police was informed and descended upon the two crime scenes immediately. The investigation soon revealed that the double murder was the work of the same hand. Vital clues have allowed the police to follow the trail of the murderer, who will soon be apprehended."

GUY: Really?

MAURICE (*carelessly*): No, but we always insert that.

MARIE: Why, that's horrible. A murder inside a tomb!

LANDELLY: It's shocking! But then, that is the case in all famous murder cases.

MAURICE: I'm running to file my article with enough juicy gossip to keep all the concierges in Paris jabbering for a whole month. My dear Maestro, a thousand thanks. Mademoiselle, Messieurs, please, no indiscretion. Don't prevent me from being the first to break the news.

LANDELLY: Never fear. I'm discretion personified.

MAURICE Goodbye!

(*he leaves*)

LANDELLY: Very resourceful young man, huh? What shocking news!

GUY: He's got a lot of flair.

LUDOVIC: Yes. He'll succeed.

LANDELLY: But a good chap at heart!

LUDOVIC: We liked him right away, my wife and I.

ALBERT (*to Marie*): And you like him too, Mademoiselle?

MARIE: He's just a distraction, nothing more.

LUDOVIC: We've got to go. We shall take our leave, gentlemen.

MARIE: (*taking her hat from Albert's hand*): Till tomorrow, in that case, Monsieur Servet. We won't waste time, like today.

GABRIEL: It was no waste at all. Till tomorrow, Mademoiselle.

(*Commissioner Masse and Letellier enter*)

GABRIEL (*surprised*): Who are you and what do you want, gentlemen?

MASSE: Are you Monsieur Gabriel Servet?

GABRIEL: Yes, Monsieur.

MASSE: Forgive me, Monsieur, for invading the home of such a well respected and great artist, but I am Commissioner Masse of the Sûreté. (*opening his wallet and displaying a tri-color card*)

GABRIEL: I bow to to your authority, Monsieur.

MASSE: I need to know which of these gentlemen is Count Samoiloff.

YVAN (*stepping forward*): I am, Monsieur.

LETELLIER (*low to Masse*): That's the one.

MASSE (*to Yvan*): Monsieur, I am arresting you in the name of the Law.

ALL: Ah!

YVAN: Arrest me? Why, that's crazy! By what right should you arrest me?

MASSE: By right of this warrant which I am carrying.

GABRIEL: Commissioner, no one respects the law and its officers more than I, but allow me to tell you that there must certainly be some kind of mistake.

GUY: Perhaps s similarity of name easy to clarify. Our friend here is above suspicion.

LANDELLY: He's a respected gentleman, and...

MASSE: Silence, Messieurs. I cannot discuss the case with you.

YVAN: But still, Commissioner, you must explain yourself.

MASSE: Out of respect for Monsieur Servet I shall ask you a question which, I am sure, will provide the explanations you all require. Count, did you go to the Père Lachaise cemetery yesterday?

ALL: Ah!

19

YVAN: Yes, I did.

MASSE: Carrying a wreath?

LETELLIER: Purchased from my shop.

YVAN: Yes, indeed.

MASSE: And you visited the tomb of the Kouravieff family?

YVAN: Yes, but so what? Is that a crime? I want to know of what I am being accused?

MASSE: The investigating magistrate will tell you. (*to Gabriel*) Unfortunately, he has no doubt.

YVAN: No doubt?

GABRIEL: Yvan!

YVAN (*with a shout*): Ah, that crime in a tomb… In the tomb of my… And I'm suspected of it?

ALL: Ah!

GABRIEL: Why, this is madness!

YVAN: Let it go, my friend. This monstrous error of which I am the victim won't last long. (*to Masse*) I am yours, Monsieur. (*to Gabriel*) Till later, my friend.

GABRIEL (*shaking his hands*): Yvan!

(*Yvan leaves, escorted by the Commissioner and Letellier*)

LANDELLY: This is a monumental mistake! Mark my word.

CURTAIN

## *SCENE II*

The stage is divided into two parts. The section on the left is a small office. The section on the right is a small salon at the rear of which is found a bay window opening onto a veranda decorated with flowers, with view over a garden.

AT RISE, Aimée Joubert is seated before a small table reading a newspaper.

AIMÉE (*lazily*): Yet another murder! You'd think the journalists invent them!

(*Marianne enters with a basket of preserves*)

AIMÉE: Ah, it's you, Marianne (*putting down her paper*)
What have you brought for dinner?
MARIANNE: Stew, Madame, like every Sunday, and then…
AIMÉE: And then?
MARIANNE: And then, it's been six days since Monsieur
Maurice's last visit. He's never remained away for so long,
and I thought…
AIMÉE (joyfully): You thought he'll come today! You are a
sweet girl, Marianne. Tell me quickly what you brought for
him, because I am indeed expecting him. Let's busy ourselves
about him and he'll come sooner.
MARIANNE: A small salmon, two partridges and two fish.
AIMÉE: That's all? (*ringing outside*) Ah, someone's ringing.
It could be him… (*rising and looking out from the veranda*) It
is him, Marianne! It's Maurice! Show him in.

(*Marianne leaves*)

AIMÉE: My son, my beloved son… When will I be able to
say that aloud?

(*Marianne returns with Maurice Vasseur*)

MARIANNE: Come in, come in, Monsieur Maurice.
MAURICE (*running to Aimée*): My dear friend!
AIMÉE: Dear child!
MARIANNE (*withdrawing*): Now she's happy!

(*She leaves*)

AIMÉE: I was no longer expecting to see you today. And I
was very pained. You haven't come in six days.
MAURICE: Auteuil is a long way away.

AIMÉE (*making him sit*): Ah, how long the time seems to me.
MAURICE: To me, too.
AIMÉE: Really?
MAURICE: I swear! I am so happy to see you. When I'm near you, I feel better.
AIMÉE: Better? So you feel bad when you're away from me?
MAURICE: Not really. (*taking her hands*) But I only truly feel good when I hold your hands in mine and when I embrace you. (*hugging her*)
AIMÉE: Then why didn't you come sooner?
MAURICE: Because it was impossible.
AIMÉE: Will you be spending the day with me?
MAURICE: I cannot, to my great regret.
AIMÉE: Why?
MAURICE: I am to be presented today to a wealthy foreign gentleman, who might actually hire me to be his secretary. That would be a safe position. I would be able to save some money.
AIMÉE: At least, you won't leave Paris!
MAURICE: No, except maybe a trip from time to time.
AIMÉE: Ah, you have me scared. You see, I love you as if you were my own child! The very idea of being away from you pains me.
MAURICE: Don't be afraid, my dear friend, it would be hard for me too to be away from you.
AIMÉE: Oh, my dear, dear child! (*controlling herself*) You say this now, but if you met a pretty girl to your taste... Ah, Maurice, the thought of it terrifies me.
MAURICE: But I am thinking no such thing. Anyway, I'm young and do not wish to bid goodbye to my bachelor life yet. Later, we'll see.
AIMÉE: Later, much later. Yes, and who knows, it might be much better for you.
MAURICE (*rising*): That's possible.
AIMÉE: What? You've hardly got here and you're leaving already?
MAURICE (*looking at his watch*): My dear friend, I really

shouldn't make the man who might make my fortune wait. In life, one must never miss the train.

AIMÉE: That's true. Your future above all. When will I see you again?

MAURICE: In two or three days, I promise you. Au revoir, my dear friend! (*hugging her*)

AIMÉE: My dear Maurice!

(*he leaves*)

AIMÉE: Yes, yes, much later. And I'd really like it to be never. If he marries, it will come out that his father, Pierre Lartigues, is a murderer, an escaped galley-slave, and that his mother gave birth to him in prison. To confess all that to him! My God, won't he despise me?

(*Marianne returns*)

MARIANNE: Madame, there are some gentlemen who wish to speak to you. Here are their cards.

AIMÉE: (*after looking at the cards, visibly upset*): Show them in.

(*Paul de Gibray, Commissioner Masse and Count Yvan Samoiloff enter, while Marianne departs*)

AIMÉE: Messieurs. (*the two men extend their hands, Yvan looks at Aimée with controlled emotion*)

PAUL: Dear Madame, we met two years ago. I'm happy to see you again.

MASSE: We went over our reports of the very fine work you did for us. We really miss you.

AIMÉE (*uneasily*): Miss me? Hush, please, Messieurs! (*she assures herself that Marianne has gone*) You understand that not everyone appreciate the work I've done for you in the past. So I've carefully hidden my past from those who surround me. Now, please sit down and tell me the purpose of your visit.

PAUL: First of all, Madame, know that you have our complete respect.

AIMÉE: Thank you again.

PAUL: I'll come straight to the point. Have you read the newspapers?

AIMÉE: Certainly.

PAUL: Then you are aware of the double murder?

AIMÉE: At the Père Lachaise?

PAUL: Yes.

AIMÉE: They say that you are on the trail of the perpetrator.

PAUL: They do, but unfortunately, we haven't made much progress. (*with an ironic glance at Masse*) However, that hasn't prevented the police from making an arrest.

MASSE: An unfortunate mistake.

PAUL: We at the Sûreté quickly recognized Count Samoiloff's innocence (*glancing at Yvan*) and set him free this morning.

MASSE: A case of mistaken identity... A remarkable resemblance that put us on a false trail.

PAUL: In short, we find ourselves confronted by unprecedented difficulties.

MASSE: Which is why we miss the old team—of which you were a part.

AIMÉE: You're too kind! But you still have Jodelet and Martel.

MASSE: But a dozen Jodelets and Martels don't add up to the Cat's Eye—and that was you!

PAUL: Madame, you read the description of the crime in the newspapers. What do you think? What, do you suppose, was the criminal's motive?

AIMÉE: A powerful family interest?

PAUL: We had the same idea. Which is why we need your help.

MASSE: Better yet, we'd like you to lead the investigation.

PAUL: Come on, what do you say?

AIMÉE: I'll say this: you know my motive in seeking employment in the old days.

PAUL: The desire for vengeance, yes.

AIMÉE: I was hoping to deliver Pierre Lartigues to you. He made me the unknowing accomplice of his crime, then seduced me, abandoning me with a child. My son is now grown up and I want to keep the whole sordid affair from him. So far, I've succeeded. He sees only Madame Joubert, his mother's best friend who's cared for him since his mother's unfortunate death. If I accept your offer, my peaceful existence would be at risk. And, as in the past, I'd be assailed by perpetual alarms and fear. No, no, you see plainly, it's impossible.

PAUL: You are greatly exaggerating the situation.

AIMÉE: I see it the way it is, and it scares me.

MASSE: Does your son live with you?

AIMÉE: No. That would be hard to justify. Maurice sees in me only an old friend of his mother.

MASSE: Then you are absolutely free.

PAUL (*urging her*): We will give you complete freedom of action. All precautions will be taken so your son will never suspect the change in your life.

MASSE: We won't insist that you return to your previous position. You will fight, not as a uniformed soldier, but as an irregular.

PAUL: In the interest of your child, please say yes. Then you can tell him the sacrifice you have made.

MASSE: You can be assured of the protection of the Sûreté and the State Prosecutor.

AIMÉE (*in tears*): I beg you, Messieurs, do not ask me further. It will be in vain.

PAUL: And yet, you must agree. Something tells me that you alone can solve this terrible crime. This double murder is as mysterious as it is frightening. Who knows if it's not related to the one of which you were the victim.

AIMÉE: Me? How?

PAUL: The woman murdered at the Père Lachaise was found in the Kouravieffs' tomb.

AIMÉE (*terrified*): In the Kouravieffs' tomb!

YVAN: In my mother's tomb, yes.

AIMÉE (*stupefied*): Ah. Count Yvan! (*tearfully*) You are the son of Countess Kouravieff, murdered by Pierre Lartigues.

PAUL: This is the son of your protectress, who has just asked you to give in to our pleas.

YVAN: Madame, your presence brings back cruel memories and revives the mourning of my life. It reopens a wound that has never healed. But I also recall that, in my childhood, you were a friend to me. I admire you and I am happy to see you again today. And I hope you will join me in the struggle against this lifelong enemy of my family.

AIMÉE (*with tears*): But how can I help? How does the crime at the Père Lachaise affect you? Our common enemy is Pierre Lartigues.

ALL: Pierre Lartigues!

AIMÉE: Yes. You recall that he was your mother's business manager and that he murdered her to cover up the theft of her fortune.

YVAN: Ah, if my father had lived, he'd have caught him. I was only a child then, but I swore to get him, no matter what.

AIMÉE: But twenty years have gone by, and…

YVAN: I am still pursuing Pierre Lartigues today, and I suspect that…

AIMÉE: I tracked him for twenty years—in vain! He's dead.

YVAN: No! Pierre Lartigues is alive!

AIMÉE: He is?

YVAN: I've seen him!

AIMÉE: Where? When?

YVAN: Three years ago, in Berlin. But I was unable to get him arrested then.

AIMÉE: And you've been on his trail ever since?

YVAN: Yes. Before—but especially since.

AIMÉE: You think that he's here—in Paris?

YVAN: Yes, I'm certain of it.

AIMÉE (*after a silence*): In that case, we will deliver the murderer on the tomb of his victim. (*thinking*) Why was this crime committed on a tomb? Why there?... Because the tomb belonged to foreigners, and therefore was unlikely to be visited...

But who knew that?... Lartigues assuredly planned it... Yes, I believe you... Pierre Lartigues is in Paris.... But he's not alone. He has accomplices. Who are they? I will find out! We will go together to the Kouravieffs' tomb. Then, I'll go to the Morgue to look at the bodies of the victims... And if I don't succeed in finding the key to this mystery, I am no longer worthy of my nickname—The Cat's Eye!

CURTAIN

# *ACT II*

## *SCENE III*

A small room in a seedy Parisian hotel. There are doors at the sides and the rear. It is furnished with as bed, a desk, chairs, etc.

AT RISE, Pierre Lartigues is standing before the open door at the back. Victoire stands in the doorway with a menu in her hands.

VICTOIRE: I am bringing Monsieur his lunch for today.
LARTIGUES: Fine. (*taking it*)
VICTOIRE: Monsieur is dining in his room this morning?
LARTIGUES: I don't know yet.
VICTOIRE: You have only to ring; I will take your order.

(*she leaves*)

LARTIGUES: Then go, you gossiper! (*tossing the menu away*) I'll go out to eat, that'll be better. Then I'll make a new visit to the Père Lachaise to see if the lock on that tomb was actually changed, or if it was only because of my clumsiness that I was unable to open it.

(*There is a knock at the back*)

LARTIGUES: A visit? Another agent from the Five perhaps?

(*he opens the door. Gaston Verdier, dressed as a Naval Officer, stands on the threshold. Lartigues takes a step back*)

LARTIGUES: Is this a mistake?
VERDIER: I don't think so, because I asked for Monsieur

Jules Théroux as instructed.

LARTIGUES (*taking Verdier by the hands*): Verdier!

VERDIER: Don't be imprudent! The name of Verdier must never be pronounced, just like that of Pierre Lartigues.

LARTIGUES: That's true, old boy, but what do you want? I'm used to seeing you only as a priest. Why are you no longer the Abbé Merys?

VERDIER (*low*): You don't know then?

LARTIGUES (*uneasily*): Don't know what?

VERDIER: Have you been to the Kouravieffs' tomb?

LARTIGUES: Yes, the day before yesterday, just before the cemetery closed.

VERDIER: Did you get inside the tomb?

LARTIGUES: No.

VERDIER: Why not?

LARTIGUES: My key no longer works. I thought you had changed it on orders from No. 1.

VERDIER: Did you notice anything unusual?

LARTIGUES: Nothing. The cemetery was deserted.

VERDIER: You haven't received a visit from No. 5 in the last two days?

LARTIGUES: That's Gustave Perrier, right?

VERDIER: A.k.a. Percival Clyde.

LARTIGUES: I have received no visits. But you're worrying me with all your questions. Look, old boy, what's going on?

VERDIER: Someone has discovered the place where we put our correspondence. Someone has discovered our secret.

LARTIGUES: A snitch? The Police?

VERDIER: No, worse than that—a rogue who would like to profit from it. That's why I've momentarily changed my disguise, and I advise you to do so as well.

LARTIGUES: Do we know who this man is?

VERDIER: All I know is that he didn't hesitate to murder Jenny, our courier, who was carrying a thousand pounds and all our correspondence from the Kouravieffs' tomb to London.

LARTIGUES: Curses! Was Jenny carrying important documents?

VERDIER: Yes.

LARTIGUES: And what about Perrier?

VERDIER: He was carrying on his person more documents pertaining to the inheritance of Arnould d'Herbille. He was supposed to arrive here on the night of the 20th at 1 a.m.

LARTIGUES: Two days ago… And you haven't seen him?

VERDIER: No.

LARTIGUES: In that case, what's become of him?

VERDIER: That's what worries me. He hasn't come here, nor has he written to me. Could Jenny's assassin have killed him, too?

LARTIGUES: Such a thought! It makes no sense!

VERDIER: Even less than you think. The note stolen from our poor Jenny was very detailed, and revealed the importance of that secret.

LARTIGUES: What about the murderer? Do we know who he is?

VERDIER: How could we?

LARTIGUES: The Sûreté is certain to send all its agents after him.

VERDIER: Good luck to them! His cleverness seems prodigious to me.

LARTIGUES: If he's caught and they find the stolen papers on him, our organization will be severely compromised. All our plans will be jeopardized. (*clutching*) Ah, if only I could get my hands on this man, it would soon be over.

VERDIER: Don't get worked up…

LARTIGUES: Why shouldn't I? There's twelve million at stake, dangling in front of our mugs. This should have been our last affair. After that, we could retire…

VERDIER: You're angry, and anger is a bad counselor. I know enough to remain cool and judge matters rationally. Let's remain on our guard, that's all. We cannot act intelligently without first knowing who our adversary is.

LARTIGUES: How can we find out?

VERDIER: Because, clever as he is, if he has learned our secret, he'll want to profit from it, thus exposing himself.

LARTIGUES: What if he's content himself with just the thousand pounds he stole and burns all the documents?

VERDIER: If he does that, then we have nothing more to fear from him.

LARTIGUES: Perhaps... Have you informed Brémont in London of what happened?

VERDIER: I will write him tonight so he can come up with a new plan.

LARTIGUES: Where is Jenny's body?

VERDIER: At the Morgue.

LARTIGUES: Can she be identified?

VERDIER: No. No one in Paris knew her.

(*A bell rings*)

VERDIER: Someone's at the door.

LARTIGUES: The waiter?

VERDIER (*checking his revolver*): We need to be sure.

LARTIGUES: I'm going to see.

VERDIER: Be careful.

LARTIGUES: What for? I've been unrecognizable for the last twenty years.

(*opening another door. Maurice Vasseur stands on the threshold*)

LARTIGUES: You must be mistaken, Monsieur...

MAURICE: Not at all—if this is room 17, and if I have the honor of speaking to Monsieur Jules Théroux.

(*Verdier is worried, Lartigues is surprised.*)

LARTIGUES: I am Jules Théroux.

MAURICE: Then I must speak to you, Monsieur, about a matter of some importance.

LARTIGUES: But I have no business in Paris. I'm traveling for pleasure. There must be some mistake.

MAURICE: Not in the least. You are precisely whom I am seeking, and I have come on behalf of one of your friends.

LARTIGUES: In that case, you must have a letter of introduction?

MAURICE: I'm afraid not, Monsieur.

LARTIGUES: In that case, I cannot…

MAURICE: Hold on, Monsieur. I'm here on behalf of No. 5.

LARTIGUES: Ah, I see! Please do come in, Monsieur! I'll be happy to listen to what you have to say.

(*Maurice enters but stops at the sight of Verdier*)

LARTIGUES: Don't be afraid. My friend is a friend of the person who sent you to me. I have nothing to hide from him—absolutely nothing.

MAURICE (*bowing to Verdier, who returns his bow, coldly*): Am I to conclude that the Captain is one of the Five?

VERDIER (*to Lartigues*): What did he say?

LARTIGUES (*to Verdier*) He's been sent by No. 5.

VERDIER (*to Maurice*): Five is in Paris?

MAURICE (coldly): Yes.

VERDIER: You've seen him.

MAURICE: I have.

VERDIER: Then why didn't he come himself?

MAURICE: Because it's impossible for him to come.

VERDIER: Impossible?

LARTIGUES: Why?

MAURICE: For the best reason of all: Gustave Perrier, a.k.a. Percival Clyde, a.k.a. No. 5, is dead.

VERDIER AND LARTIGUES: Dead!

LARTIGUES: How did he die?

MAURICE: Murdered.

LARTIGUES: Murdered!

VERDIER: Ah, I had a foreboding… (*abruptly striding towards Maurice*) Do you know the identity of the murderer?

MAURICE (*ice cold*): I do. It is I.

VERDIER: You!

MAURICE: Precisely.

VERDIER AND LARTIGUES (*threatening Maurice with*

*their revolvers*): You, wretch!

MAURICE (*calmly, shrugging*): Are you trying to frighten me? I know very well that you won't be stupid enough to kill me. First, you'd be terribly embarrassed to dispose of my body. Besides, you would never risk Brémont's reproaches.

VERDIER: So you know all our secrets?

MAURICE: Only those pertaining to the inheritance of Arnould d'Harville, the banker.

LARTIGUES: And you came to throw yourself into our hands?

MAURICE: Unhesitatingly, gentlemen. I'm quite certain you will listen to me, and the proof of it is that you want to question me.

LARTIGUES: This joker is really charming.

VERDIER: Shut up!

MAURICE: It's natural enough. You need to know what Brémont was sending you by courier.

(*Verdier and Lartigues react*)

VERDIER: Speak!

MAURICE: In a bit. First, allow me to tell you about myself. Every man in his life is placed must choose between two paths: that of vice, and that of virtue. It's a cliché, but it's also true. And once he's chosen, he must go forward bravely.

LARTIGUES (*to himself*): He has style.

MAURICE: The brave woman who replaced my mother gave me funds insufficient to my tastes. I wasn't naive enough to ask for serious work or to compromise myself in gambling or playing the stock market. What I was waiting for was a great operation that would enrich me in a single stroke—to make my fortune once and for all. But please, sit down, gentlemen. To acquire this fortune, it was necessary to sacrifice a man and a woman. I didn't hesitate. That's why I'm here.

LARTIGUES: By my word!

VERDIER: Who put you on the trail of our association?

MAURICE: You.

VERDIER: Me?

MAURICE: A week ago, you were strolling in the Bois de

33

Boulogne...

VERDIER: You're mistaken.

MAURICE: Oh, not at all, Captain. I'm a physiognomist. I always notice the eyes. That day, you were dressed as a priest. You read a letter, tore it in small pieces, which I then picked up and put back together with great patience. Ecclesiastical secrets always interest me.

VERDIER: But that letter was insignificant.

MAURICE: So much so that I became convinced that it was insignificant only in appearance.

VERDIER: You must be joking!

MAURICE: Not at all! I have the most complete collection of secret codes that you could imagine.

LARTIGUES: What?

(*Verdier gestures him to stay quiet*)

MAURICE: So I tried all sorts of combinations, and finally broke your code. That's how I discovered your mail drip at the Père Lachaise.

LARTIGUES: He's got us!

VERDIER: Listen, will you!

MAURICE: I also have a gift for disguises. I assumed the appearance of a Russian gentleman whom I'd seen in society and went to the tomb of the Kouravieffs. Gentlemen, the luck I was waiting for finally presented itself. I profited by it. (*pulling out a sheath of bank notes*) Let's proceed in an orderly fashion. First of all, I am returning the thousand pounds in bank notes to Jules Théroux... (*tossing the money on the table*) Not a penny missing.

VERDIER: Who is this bloke?

MAURICE (*opening his briefcase and taking out papers*): Now here's the important thing you were waiting for—the motive for your visit to Paris—a copy of Arnould d'Harville's will. Gustave Perrier was supposed to deliver it to you, but I am doing that for him, in view of his permanent incapacity. (reading) "My only relative is my sister Valentine. She was married in 1866 to Monsieur Ludovic de Bressolles..."

LARTIGUES AND VERDIER: Ludovic de Bressolles!

MAURICE (*continue reading*): "From this marriage was born a daughter named Marie..." blah, blah blah... "Michel Brémont, my friend for the last fifteen years, shall be my executor, and is hereby instructed to divide my estate equally between Marie de Bressolles, the legitimate daughter of my sister Valentine, wife or widow of the aforesaid Ludovic de Bressolles, and Simone d'Harville, the natural daughter..."

VERDIER: Ah-ha! So he had an illegitimate daughter!

MAURICE: No, he didn't. (*continue reading*) "...the natural daughter of Valentine and Monsieur Paul de Gibray. The remainder of my fortune shall go to my executor, Michel Brémont..." blah, blah, blah, etc. etc."

LARTIGUES: Twelve millions!

MAURICE: Ah, Brémont is a clever man!

VERDIER: Is there more?

MAURICE: Yes. Simone d'Harville's birth was registered at the Mairie of the 3rd Arrondissement in Paris as the natural child of Valentine d'Harville, father unknown. She was entrusted to a nurse, Claudine Charret, who lived in Gif-sur-Yvette. Then there is this further note from Michel Brémont: "Arnaud d'Harville passed away on November 25, 1886; if the two children die without issue, his entire fortune shall pass on to me, and will be shared equally with the rest of the Five. Act as your interest dictates in watching over them."

LARTIGUES: Ha, ha!

MAURICE: The idea is not bad, but there's a danger.

LARTIGUES: What?

MAURICE: A stranger with a mercenary mind might be clever and discover the reasons for disposing of Valentine's two children. If he learns those, he becomes your master and not your instrument. He could then demand a portion of the inheritance

LARTIGUES: Don't beat about the bush, my lad. What do you want

MAURICE: May I continue, please?

VERDIER: Yes. Go on.

MAURICE: If you refuse, I have two choices. I could expose

your scheme and denounce you, or, for a price, help the d'Harville children get what is rightfully theirs.

LARTIGUES: What about the two murders you've already committed? Don't take us for fools, friend. You're bold, yes, and very clever, too, we recognize that. Truthfully, you enchant me. You are just what I was at your age. But we aren't going to play the fools for a kid, even one of your caliber. The notion of sharing that inheritance with you makes me smile.

MAURICE: On the other hand, I could be just the man you need under the circumstances—but on the condition of replacing the late Monsieur Perrier in your organization.

LARTIGUES: I see. Not bad, kid.

VERDIER: So you would undertake to find and eliminate the two daughters of Valentine d'Harville?

LARTIGUES: And render the succession... er, vacant?

MAURICE: By getting rid of the legitimate heirs, yes.

VERDIER: What's your name?

MAURICE: Maurice Vasseur.

VERDIER: Are you certain you left no evidence connecting you to...?

MAURICE: None whatsoever.

VERDIER: The clothes you were wearing?

MAURICE: All burned.

LARTIGUES: Fine.

VERDIER: Have you got any mistresses?

MAURICE: Only two. The one that all Paris calls La Belle Octavia, who is trying to get herself married to a Russian Prince—the very same man whose appearance I stole to commit my crimes. I shall gladly leave La Belle Octavia for you. The other—and you will see how luck smiles on us—is the mother of our two heiresses...

LARTIGUES AND VERDIER: Valentine d'Harville?

MAURICE: A.k.a. Madame de Bressolles.

VERDIER: And you know the two girls?

MAURICE: I only know Marie, who is greatly smitten with a certain Albert de Gibray, who is Paul's nephew. Paul is the father of the second heir, Simone. He's also an Investigating

Magistrate.

LARTIGUES: Marvelous!

MAURICE: I think that now you can see how indispensable I am.

VERDIER (*looking at the documents*): These are copies. What happened to the originals?

MAURICE: I'm keeping them.

LARTIGUES: You are suspicious of us?

MAURICE: Knowing you, it's quite natural.

LARTIGUES: Ah, if you attempt to betray us, beware!

MAURICE: I shall act quite transparently; just do the same.

CADET (*from outside*) Monsieur Théroux? Yes, yes, that's fine. I understand.

(*The three men listen*)

VERDIER: He's asking for you?

CADET (*from outside*): Number 17.

LARTIGUES: He's coming here.

(*ringing. Lartigues hesitates to open*)

MAURICE: Are you afraid?

(*more ringing*)

VERDIER (*to Lartigues*): Go open. There's no danger. He's a coachman who's bringing me a new wallet.

LARTIGUES: A new wallet?

VERDIER: Yes. Each time I change my name, I am careful to get a new wallet with my new identity imprinted on it. This isn't a useless precaution.

LARTIGUES: The Devil!

(*more ringing*)

VERDIER: Will you go!

(*Lartigues opens. Cadet, wallet in hand, stands in the door-*

*way*)

CADET: Excuse me, Monsieur, but I was coming…
MAURICE (*aside, uneasily*): Ah, that man…
CADET (*seeing Verdier*): Ah, it's you I was looking for, Captain.
VERDIER: Truly?
CADET: You don't recognize me? I drove you here. You left your wallet in my cab, My number is 813.
VERDIER: Ah, thank you, my friend. (*fumbling in his pocket*) Here's a tip for you!
CADET: Oh, I was only doing my duty. But, because it's you…
MAURICE (*aside*): What a strange coincidence….
CADET: If it's all the same, I'll spare you the trouble of reporting the loss to the police. Because, you see, I have to go and talk to them...
MAURICE: You've committed an offense?
CADET: Oh, no. I've been summoned on account of a criminal who cooled a passenger in my cab.
LARTIGUES AND VERDIER: Ah!
CADET: Several nights ago. I didn't hear a thing.
MAURICE (*staring at him*): You mean the crime at the Père Lachaise?
CADET: Or elsewhere. I don't know.
MAURICE: Have they caught the murderer?
CADET: I have no idea. They say they have a suspect.
MAURICE: And who is this wretch?
CADET: A Russian Count, or Prince, by the name of Sokoloff, Malakoff, Jabloskoff... It ends in "off." My poor cab's been impounded by the Police until there's a conviction. Until then, I'm driving an old hack that sounds as if the wheels are gonna fall off at any time. You must have heard about it, Captain. Ah, the swine will pay me for all the trouble he's caused me.
MAURICE: And would you recognize this man?
CADET: You bet! I'll fix him good. I gotta go now. Thanks

for the tip.

(*Cadet leaves*)

MAURICE: Well, gentlemen, are you convinced that the measures I took to not be recognized were well taken?
VERDIER: You were the man in that cab?
MAURICE: Yes. That's where I killed Perrier.
LARTIGUES (*enthusiastically*): Ah, if I had a son, I'd want him to be just like you!

CURTAIN

## SCENE IV

The Carriage Rental offices of Monsieur Binet, Rue Ernestine. To the right, there is the entrance to the Binets' home. At street level, windows that can be used. Further back, there is a large shed in which Cab 813 is being kept; its doors are sealed. To the left, there is a stable with a grain towers overhead, accessed by a movable ladder on wheels. In the middle of the stables, there is a closed vault with a door opening on a second, but unseen, courtyard.

AT RISE, François is grooming a horse; Sylvie, a servant, brings in a bucket of hay, then sweeps the chaff. Three coachmen, Baudoin, Pacard and Cadet, are seated at the left, on stools, chatting.

BAUDOUIN:(to the other coachmen): The rest of you are making me sick talking like that about the Police. If ever they catch the murderer who killed a man in Cadet's carriage, well, I'll buy him a pair of gold-plated eyeglasses.
PACARD (*his mouth stuffed with food*): It's not eyeglasses they need, it's a telescope.!
CADET: Damned right they do! I'm mad as hell! Someone kills a man in my cab, and I don't see a thing! I said a Russian

was the killer, so they arrested a Russian. But now, it turns out, he's not the killer. So I look like an idiot, a drunken idiot! I swear, I'll never drink anything but water anymore.

BAUDOIN (*gasping*): Drinking only water?

CADET: Yes! Mark my words, I will!

BAUDOIN: You won't last three weeks.

CADET: We'll see about that!

(*Monsieur Binet enters*)

BINET: Hey, guys, shut the doors, quick! The Magistrate is coming!

CADET: They're gonna start all over again with their questions.

(*They shut the doors; Paul de Gibray enters, followed by Commissioner Masse, Count Yvan Samoiloff, Aimée Gilbert and two Policemen*)

BINET (*to Paul*). You can go into the courtyards, Your Honor. You won't be disturbed.

PAUL: We are the one who are disturbing you, Monsieur Binet, but, I hope, for the last time. We need to see the carriage again.

BINET: Hey, Cadet, bring Cab 813 out.

CADET: Yes, boss. (to François) Give me a hand.

(*they pull the carriage out of the shed*)

AIMÉE (to a Policeman): Get rid of this crowd.

CADET (*as he's pulling the carriage*) Who's that broad?

PAUL (to Binet): Can you please ask your employees to withdraw?

AIMÉE: Only Cadet and the groom should stay.

FRANÇOIS: I?

BINET (*to all the others*): Go on, my friends, go.

(*Everyone leaves and they close the doors*)

AIMÉE: Have the men keep watch outside.

(*The Policemen leave*)

CADET (*aside*): She must be a cop!
MASSE: Shall I break the seals?
PAUL: Yes.

(*The Commissioner breaks the seals on the cab*)

YVAN: Is this the cab in which the second murder was committed?
CADET: Yes, Count. The old coach that I was using that very night.
YVAN (*to Aimée*): What do you hope to discover here?
AIMÉE: At the Père Lachaise, an hour ago, we found a turquoise in the tomb of your mother which may yet prove to be a valuable clue. That stone, detached from a piece of jewelry must have belonged to the first victim.
YVAN: Ah, Madame Gilbert, you do the impossible! If thanks to you, I can avenge my mother, I will give your son five hundred thousand francs.
AIMÉE: I will do the impossible, Count.
PAUL: I'm giving you carte blanche.
AIMÉE (*approaching the cab*): Everything is in the same condition as it was when the body was found?
MASSE: Exactly the same.
AIMÉE: Have you looked under the cushions?
MASS: Everywhere.
AIMÉE: Let's take a look (*she climbs into the cab and examines it on all sides*)
CADET: Did that rascal fix my carriage up! All the cushions were brand new!
MASSE: My dear lady, my men inspected it thoroughly and found nothing.
AIMÉE (*smiling*): Commissioner, your men also visited the tomb and yet I found something there that they'd missed.

CADET (*aside*): She's a smart cop!

AIMÉE (*pulling back the cushions then looking under the floor*): Ah!

YVAN: Well?

AIMÉE: Nothing! I don't see a thing. (*to Cadet*) You are the coachman--Monsieur Cadet?

CADET: Yes, Claude Leonard Carré, also known as Cadet, orphan and bachelor. I pick my nose too much, it's true, but I've sworn that I didn't have more than a drop that night.

AIMÉE: I'd like to ask you a few questions.

CADET: Fair enough. You're in the driver's seat, as it were.

AIMÉE: Where did you pick up your fare?

CADET: At Saint-Maur.

AIMÉE: What time was it?

CADET: Around midnight.

AIMÉE: Where did you take your passenger?

CADET: To the Gare du Nord. I drove fast 'cause he said he was in a hurry to meet a friend who was arriving in an hour.

AIMÉE: Was he well dressed?

CADET: Very fashionably. I took him for the Count, here.

AIMÉE: Did he resemble him greatly?

CADET: Like two halves of the same cheese.

AIMÉE (*to the others*): Our suspect was disguised, gentlemen, there's no doubt about it. (*back to Cadet*) Once at the station, what did your passenger do?

CADET: He went into the waiting room. An hour later, I heard the train's whistle. Then, he returned with another man. They both climbed into my carriage.

AIMÉE: Was it him who ordered you to go to the Rue Montorgueil?

CADET: Yes. And not to spare the horse.

AIMÉE: And once there, he rang for you to stop?

CADET: Yes, just in front of that hotel.

AIMÉE: What happened next?

CADET: He got out and told the other fella inside to wait, and he offered me a fifty-franc note. He said to keep ten and only give him back forty in change. That was generous, but I didn't have forty francs change. So I went to get change at a shop that was still open. When I returned, the guy was waiting for me outside. I counted out his change and I asked him why his friend hadn't gotten out. He replied that, on the contrary, his friend had gotten out long ago. Then he went into the hotel and vanished.

AIMÉE (*to herself*): There were no traces at that hotel... (*to Cadet*) So somewhere between the Gare du Nord and the Rue Montorgueil, a man was killed in your carriage, but you heard nothing.

CADET: There was a lot of traffic...

AIMÉE: And returning here at night, you still didn't notice anything?

CADET: It was François who, opening the carriage in the morning, first noticed the body.

FRANÇOIS: Cadet had forgotten to pull the straw mat back, and it was when I did it that I saw the stiff.

MASSE: It was the same man you saw again at the Morgue?

CADET AND FRANÇOIS: Yes.

AIMÉE (*to Paul*): Neither the man, nor the woman, have yet been identified?

PAUL: No.

AIMÉE (*to Masse*): There was no identification on them?

MASSE: Not on the woman, but the man had a tattoo of two crossed sabers on his right arm, and a date: 1867.

AIMÉE: Hm. An old sailor or soldier. What about their clothes?

MASS: No identifying marks.

AIMÉE: For sure, we're dealing with an organized gang. The killer wouldn't have time to remove such marks from the clothes of his victims. But, if the victims were part of some kind of gang, which one? That's incomprehensible! Still, we must keep looking... (*she goes to the back of the carriage and leans over*)

CADET (*aside*): She's really taking this to heart.

PAUL: Monsieur Binet, after we're done here, you may use that carriage again.

BINET: Thank you, I need it.

CADET: Ah! I've got my carriage back! None too soon!

AIMÉE (*leaning over a floorboard*): Ah-ha!

ALL: What is it?

AIMÉE: A hole in the floor and I found something in it that I believe is very interesting... (to Masse) ...And which seems to have escaped your investigators, Commissioner.

CADET: What an eye!

AIMÉE (*rising and showing a metal button*): Look, gentlemen!

PAUL: A gold cufflink!

AIMÉE: Representing a locomotive, with six turquoises as nails.

MASSE: That cannot belong to the victim.

AIMÉE: But it may belong to the murderer, and the proof is that one turquoise is missing, which must be the same one I found on the steps of the Kouravieffs' tomb. (*pulling the turquoise from her purse*) Look how well it fits.

ALL: It's true!

AIMÉE: Yes, it is! But the evidence I've just recovered, instead of helping us solve our case, derails it completely.

PAUL: Why?

AIMÉE: Because this cufflink is valuable; it must belong to a rich man. And that was not the way we'd pictured our murderer so far.

PAUL: That doesn't matter. It's still a clue.

AIMÉE: I hope so. We must have this cufflink photographed and the photo sent to all the jewelers in Paris. But tell them only that we're looking at a theft.

CADET: Ah, if they could nab the buyer...

(*The door at the rear opens and a policeman appears*)

POLICEMAN (*to Masse*): Commissioner?

MASSE: Yes? What is it?

POLICEMAN: Baron Landelly is here.

MASSE: Let him in.

44

*(The Policeman gestures. Baron Landelly de Landilly enters, followed by Galoubert and La Grenouille. Meanwhile, the grooms put the carriage back in its shed)*

LANDELLY: Ah, gentlemen, I've found you at last! What a race! From the Prefecture to the Père Lachaise to here. Luckily, I have nerves of steel. I was born to be a detective. (*to Yvan*) My dear Count, he's been identified.
YVAN: Identified? Who?
LANDELLY: The victim, by Jove!
PAUL: You recognized him?
LANDELLY: No, not me! I had gone to the Morgue. There was a crowd. I heard two good people whispering to themselves. I leaned over and noticed this gentleman and that lady... (*pointing to Galoubert and La Grenouille*)
LA GRENOUILLE (*to Galoubert*): Bow, will you, dummy! (*they bow*)
LANDELLY: So I told the police what I'd heard.
CADET (*aside*): Now there's a clown.
LA GRENOUILLE (*aside*): Monkey brain!
PAUL (*to Landelly*) But who are these people?
LA GRENOUILLE: We're good people! (*pointing to Landelly*) He said so, so you must believe him.
LANDELLY: They're two recidivists.
AIMÉE: I recognize them. (*pointing to Galoubert*) That's a notorious thief, Ernest Sicre, nicknamed Galoubert.
GALOUBERT: A nickname I got because of my dazzling attires.[2]
AIMÉE: Did five years at Poissy, three at Clairvaux, two at La Roquette.[3] Have I forgotten anything?
LA GRENOUILLE He never had any luck.

---

[2] From the Occitan *galaubar* (to play beautifully of an instrument), akin to *galaubier* (elegant, graceful, magnificent) and *galaubey* (pomp, display).
[3] Nams of various prisons.

AIMÉE (*pointing to La Grenouille*) : And that's Sophie Besson, called La Grenouille...

GALOUBERT: A little lamb.

AIMÉE: ...Who's done even more time than her companion.

LA GRENOUILLE: Ah! You are the Cat's Eye!

GALOUBERT: All that doesn't prevent her from being a good woman all the same, my legitimate, my true legitimate.

MASSE: You're married?

GALOUBERT: Married for love! I had a leech for her.

LA GRENOUILLE: And I had a leech for him. In those days he was thin. I suited him, he suited me.

GALOUBERT: A marriage full of tenderness.

LA GRENOUILLE: We're not posing for any virtue prize, but we still have feelings. If we could get some work that didn't require much effort...

GALOUBERT: We might become industrious.

PAUL: Answer my questions and I'll see what we can do.

GALOUBERT: Oh, yes! Anything for justice.

LA GRENOUILLE We'll be happy to answer your questions.

GALOUBERT To sing a little.

LA GRENOUILLE: If it brought us some small benefits.

GALOUBERT: 'Cause times are so tough.

LA GRENOUILLE: We sell chicken feet at the market but business isn't so good any more.

GALOUBERT: We could be very useful to you. We know so many rogues.

LA GRENOUILLE: Who are idle in Paris.

PAUL: You recognized a body.

LA GRENOUILLE (*pointing to Galoubert*): He's the one who recognized him. He's got an eye for faces.

PAUL: Where'd you meet him?

GALOUBERT: At Poissy, where I pulled five long years.

LA GRENOUILLE: My poor darling!

LANDELLY: Five long years. Monumental!

AIMÉE: When was that man at Poissy?

GALOUBERT: In 1867. I'm the one who tattooed his arm. Two sabers and a cross. I also recognized his ear. Another prisoner took a bite out of it.

PAUL: The name of the deceased?

GALOUBERT: Gustave Perrier.

AIMÉE: Did he have any friends?

GALOUBERT: Michel Brémont.

LA GRENOUILLE: An educated slob who spoke several languages.

GALOUBERT: They were both part of a gang.

PAUL: A gang?

GALOUBERT: Yes, there were five of them.

AIMÉE: Five?

GALOUBERT: Just five. I heard 'em talking when they thought no one was around. I know their names.

AIMÉE: Well, you've mentioned two names. Who are the others?

GALOUBERT: Can we count on your protection?

MASSE: Let's hear the names first.

LA GRENOUILLE: Since these gentlemen invite you to diner, eat idiot! And try to be clever!

GALOUBERT: Well, the other three… Let's see, there was Verdier, also known as Captain Ratier.

CADET: Huh?

GALOUBERT: 'Cause he dresses up as a Navy Captain, and also sometimes as a priest. Then a man named Chauvin, and another nicknamed Curly.

AIMÉE: Pierre Lartigues, perhaps?

GALOUBERT: Yeah, that's the one—Pierre Lartigues.

CADET: Damn it I know both of 'em!

AIMÉE: You know them, Monsieur Cadet?

CADET: A week ago, I met a Navy Captain in a room rented by a Monsieur Jules Théroux at the Hotel des Pays-Bas in the 18th arrondissement.

AIMÉE: Really?

CADET: I brought him his wallet he'd forgotten in my cab. The name 'Ratier' was on it.

LANDELLY: Splendid!

GALOUBERT: That must be him 'cause we recognized him

two weeks ago dressed in a priest outfit at the Bois de Boulogne.

LA GRENOUILLE: We went there to pick mushrooms.

CADET: And there were three of them.

ALL: Three!

CADET: Two older men and a young guy who seemed nervous.

AIMÉE: Ah, we've got them! I wasn't mistaken. The gang of Five exists. The man at the Morgue was one of them. He must have been killed by other members of the gang. They're probably plotting new crimes as we speak. They must be arrested! (*to La Grenouille*) You knew Michel Brémont and that Verdier character?

LA GRENOUILLE AND GALOUBERT: Yes.

AIMÉE: And Pierre Lartigues?

GALOUBERT: No, him we don't know.

CADET: I bet I do. It's Jules Théroux, and the priest-captain is Verdier.

AIMÉE (*to Paul de Gibray*): Monsieur the Magistrate, Monsieur Sicre, a.k.a. Galoubert, Madame Bisson, a.k.a. La Grenouille, and Monsieur Cadet the coachman must become my assistants.

GRENOUILLE AND GALOUBERT (*joyfully*): Your assistants!

CADET (*apprehensively*): Me?

AIMÉE: They must help me in my investigation.

CADET: There's no dishonor in working with honest men. (*to Aimée*) But how can I help? On foot or on a horse?

AIMÉE: I want your carriage, every day, at my command. Let's start tomorrow at 9 a.m. sharp in front of the Prefecture. I'll tell you what you have to do.

CADET: Fine by me!

BINET: But…

PAUL: You'll be properly compensated, Monsieur Binet.

YVAN (*to Paul*): I'll pay for Madame Gilbert's assistants.

LANDELLY (*giving an envelope to Paul*): Before I forget, the clerk at the Morgue also asked me to deliver to you this paper that he found inside the jacket of the man at the Morgue.

PAUL (*unfolding the paper*): It's written in code.

AIMÉE: Let me see… Yes... Our trail is hot. Lartigues is at that hotel under the name of Jules Théroux. He thinks no one knows or threatens him.

GALOUBERT: Well, that's that then.

LA GRENOUILLE: We are there!

CURTAIN

# ACT III

## SCENE V

The set is the same as in Scene I, except that all the easels and unfinished works have been removed and replaced. The workshop is brilliantly lit. In the rear there is a second workshop, also brilliantly lit.

GUESTS (*in the distance*): Bravo! Bravo! (*applause*)

VERDIER: I am charmed to be presented to a man of talents as admirable as yours.

GABRIEL: Be welcome, gentlemen. Monsieur Vasseur appears only at the second act. He will have plenty of time to show you what he dubs my masterpieces. I commend the small salon above to you. It is filled with marvels that are not mine.

LARTIGUES: Thank you for your gracious greeting.

GABRIEL: Consider yourself at home.

(*A Servant enters running*)

SERVANT: Dear Master, dear Master, they are asking for you on stage.

GABRIEL: I'll be there shortly. (*bowing*) Gentlemen, allow me to work with my actors.

VERDIER AND LARTIGUES (*bowing*): Monsieur.

(*Gabriel leaves with the Servant; Maurice Vasseur enters*)

MAURICE: So we're in the home of Gabriel Servet. Why did you insist on coming here? In my opinion, it's imprudent.

LARTIGUES: We have our reasons.

VERDIER: My dear boy, up to now, you haven't found a way

to, er, free up the inheritance of Marie de Bressolles.

MAURICE: I'm still thinking about it.

VERDIER: Well, she's coming here this evening with her mother. Perhaps, we'll find a way.

LARTIGUES: Shouldn't we help you with our advice?

MAURICE: Hum.

VERDIER: I've got a plan. I'll tell you about it after we've seen Madame de Bressolles and her daughter.

MAURICE: Fine by me.

LARTIGUES: Don't forget that you're leaving tomorrow for Gif-sur-Yvette to learn from Claudine Charret what's become of Simone.

MAURICE: I haven't forgotten.

GUESTS (*in the distance*): Bravo! Bravo! (*applause*)

SERVANT (*outside, announcing*): Monsieur Ludovic de Bressolles, Madame Valentine de Bressolles, Mademoiselle Marie de Bressolles.

(*The trio enters ; Gabriel returns, crossing the stage to greet them*)

GABRIEL: They're announcing some of your old friends, Monsieur Vasseur!

LUDOVIC: My dear Master! (*presenting Valentine who's glancing at Maurice*) This is wife, Valentine..

GABRIEL (*bowing*): Madame, allow me to thank you for doing me the honor of being present at this ball.

VALENTINE: My husband and my daughter have often spoken of you, Monsieur. And I've been remiss in forgetting to to thank you for the stunning portrait you've done of my daughter.

GABRIEL: I've tried my best, Madame.

MARIE: I'll show it to you, Mother.

VALENTINE (*going to Maurice and extending her hand to him*) Monsieur Vasseur.

MAURICE: Madame.

(*Several women guests come in and surround Madame de Bressolles*)

MARIE: Ah, Mr. Servet…
GABRIEL: Mademoiselle?
MARIE: Do you have news of your protégée?
GABRIEL: Simone?

(*Verdier, Lartigues and Maurice hear the name and listen attentively*)

MAURICE (*aside*): Simone!
VALENTINE (*returning*): What protégée?
MARIE: That young orphan I've told you about, Mother.
VALENTINE: The one raised at Gif-sur-Yvette?
MAURICE (*aside*): Gif-sur-Yvette!
MARIE: And that father recommended for a job.
VALENTINE: Ah, yes! I remember now! As a seamstress.
GABRIEL: She's been working at it for a week in a workshop Rue de Miromesnil.
LARTIGUES (aside): Rue de Miromesnil!
GABRIEL: She hasn't yet had the courage to present herself to you to thank you.
MARIE: I will go see her and thank Madame Dubief.
MAURICE (*aside*): Dubief!
LUDOVIC (*to Gabriel*): Have you had more news about her?
GABRIEL: I've learned that she was raised by a woman named Claudine Charret.
MAURICE (*aside*): Claudine Charret!
GABRIEL: She was actually an orphaned child.
VALENTINE: There are so many children like that!
LARTIGUES (*aside*): And she's yours.
MARIE (*to Gabriel*): Is Monsieur Albert coming, Monsieur Servet?
GABRIEL: Certainly, Mademoiselle.
MARIE: With his uncle?
GABRIEL: Very probably.

LARTIGUES (*aside*): Ah!

MARIE (*shaking Gabriel's hand*): Thank you, Monsieur Servet.

GABRIEL (*aside*): Dear sweet girl.

MARIE (*to Maurice*) Ah, Monsieur Vasseur, do you waltz?

MAURICE: Of course, Mademoiselle.

MARIE: Then I'll put you down for a waltz. (*to Gabriel*) Because you can't dance, can you?

GABRIEL: Oh, during the intermission… (*to Valentine*) Allow me to offer you my arm…

(*They leave followed by the guests.*)

LARTIGUES (*to Maurice, sarcastic*): Well, here you are, already back from Gif-sur-Yvette, old boy.

MAURICE: Yes, Simone appears to be in Paris.

VERDIER: A seamstress working at the workshop of Madame Dubief, Rue de Miromesnil.

LARTIGUES: And next door to where I'm living, in the rue d'Argenson.

MAURICE: To think that it's her sister who delivered her to us!

VERDIER: That Marie is a charming child. It will be a shame to sacrifice her like Simone.

MAURICE: What?

VERDIER: We've only got a moment. I told you I had a plan.

MAURICE: What is it?

VERDIER: Why shorten the life of that young girl? Make her your wife instead.

MAURICE: My wife!

VERDIER: Yes! If you marry her, Arnould d'Harville's millions will become yours.

LARTIGUES: And then, sharing then will be easy.

MAURICE: What about her family?

LARTIGUES: It was a stroke of genius befriending her mother like that.

VERDIER: Yes. Your influence over her will surely remove

all obstacles.

MAURICE: But Marie loves Albert de Gibray.

LARTIGUES: Bah! You will make her forget him.

VERDIER: Besides, once his uncle, the investigating magistrate, sees Madame de Bressolles, that love will be made to soon disappear.

LARTIGUES: I think we've said enough, Captain. Let's leave our friend to his reflections and go visit the marvels of Gabriel Servet.

VERDIER: I am with you, Monsieur Théroux.

(*More applause in the salon. They climb the stairs and disappear*)

MAURICE (*to himself*): Marry Marie... Who knows, perhaps they are right. But first, I need to convince Valentine... Ah! I hear the intermission!

(*Valentine de Bressolles enter; Maurice goes to her*)

VALENTINE: Ah, Maurice.

MAURICE: My dear Valentine.

VALENTINE: I was looking for you.

MAURICE: I'm at your command.

VALENTINE: I suppose you don't cling to the promise you made to my daughter?

MAURICE: You mean, the promise to waltz?

VALENTINE: Precisely.

MAURICE: Would you be jealous of your own daughter?

VALENTINE: Jealous of her? No, for goodness' sake, she's much too insignificant. But she annoys me. Her father does everything she wants. She reigns in my place.

(*Lartigues and Verdier reappear, they listen*)

MAURICE: Like a younger sister, no more.

VALENTINE: Maurice, I was wrong to introduce you to my

daughter; you've seen her and you no longer love me.

MAURICE: That's not true at all! (*passionately*) I love you, Valentine! (*lowering his voice*) I love you like a fool!

(*Many guests enter from various sides, accompanying Gabriel, Guy d'Arfeuilles and the Baron de Landelly, dressed as a coachman*)

GUESTS: Bravo! Bravo, Landelly! What a success!

LANDELLY: It was monumental!

GUESTS: Quite a performance! He sings ravishingly! Like a soprano!

GUY: Where the Devil did you get that outfit?

GABRIEL: My dear Baron, my congratulations for your coachman's costume.

GUESTS: He's a natural! Very much so!

LANDELLY: Ladies and Gentlemen (*coughing, then assuming the tone of a charlatan*) Don't assume that the coachman I have the honor to impersonate before you is a coachman of fantasy. No, ladies and gentlemen, he exists, like you and me. He's my friend, this coachman, whom I met in circumstances that were completely melodramatic, stupefying. I liked him right away, and I said to myself, 'he's just the type I should play in the Revue,' so I've taken him on for three months. After that time, we'll never leave each other. (*coughing*) Ha, ha, ha, monumental! (*laughter*)

GABRIEL: I don't know your model, Baron, but you appear to possess the gift of mimicry to the highest degree.

LANDELLY: Quite so, old boy.

(*Marie enters*)

GABRIEL (*to Marie*): Please excuse, the Baron, Mademoiselle. He's an eccentric. We are doomed to submit to his follies because we've committed the sin of laughing at them. Still, I think you are going a bit far, Landelly.

MARIE: Oh, don't scold him. He'll think he's obliged to be

funereal.

GABRIEL: Landelly! I am sure your outfit bothers some here. In your place I would go change it.

LANDELLY (*scandalized*): In front of the ladies! Well, since you insist…. One, two, three… Presto! (*he removes his coachman's coat and is now dressed for the ball*)

ALL (laughing): Bravo, Landelly!

LANDELLY: Mademoiselle de Bressolles, I humbly place my homages at your feet.

SERVANT (*announcing*): Count Yvan Samoiloff!

LARTIGUES (*aside*): Samoiloff!

SERVANT (*announcing*): Messieurs Paul and Albert de Gibray.

VALENTINE (*aside*): Paul de Gibray.

MARIE (*aside*): Albert!

MAURICE (*to Valentine*): What's the matter?

VALENTINE: Nothing! Nothing!

LARTIGUES (*aside*): The pigeon's fallen into the trap.

VALENTINE (*aside*): Come on! I'll keep my head steady.

(*Count Samoiloff and the two De Gibrays enter*)

GABRIEL: Good evening, Count. You missed our dear Baron's latest eccentricity

YVAN (shaking his head): As you can see I'm inconsolable.

LANDELLY: I will endeavor to provide another opportunity.

LARTIGUES (*to Verdier*): Count Samoiloff is in Paris.

GABRIEL (*going to Paul*): Ah, my dear De Gibray.

VALENTINE (*aside*): It's really him! Will he recognize me? Oh, in front my daughter, he wouldn't dare…

ALBERT (*low to Paul*): There. She is down there.

PAUL (*to Gabriel, after looking at Marie*): I don't regret being unfrocked.

GABRIEL (*pulling him*): Thank you for coming. (*low*) I'm going to tell you why I insisted on your coming. My young student is seriously smitten…

PAUL: Albert's confessed as much to me.

GABRIEL: Ah, he did the right thing. As you know, I gave this little affair so you could meet Mademoiselle de Bressolles and her family on neutral ground.

PAUL: Thank you for your concern about my nephew. I've never married and I love him like my son. I've already noticed Mademoiselle de Bressolles, she seems quite charming to me. It remains for me to meet her family.

GABRIEL: Oh, they're most honorable. Marie is seated over there with her mother, and I'm not going to release you until the presentations have been made.

PAUL: So be it!

ALBERT: Ah, uncle, how happy you make me!

PAUL: Don't get too enthused. Remember all I told you about my sufferings.

ALBERT: Don't compare Marie to that evil woman you told me about.

VALENTINE (*worried*): Come, child, I feel tired, let's go find your father.

MARIE: Already? (*following her mother*)

GABRIEL (*stopping Valentine*): Ah, Madame de Bressolles... (*Valentine hesitates*) Pardon me, Madame, but I cannot resist the desire to introduce you to my oldest friend... (*leading her towards Paul*)

ALBERT: Madame de Bressolles, my uncle...

GABRIEL (continuing): ...Monsieur Paul de Gibray.

VALENTINE (*Paul reacts, seeing her*): Monsieur. (*aside*) He's recognized me.

GABRIEL: My dear De Gibray, this is Madame de Bressolles, the mother of the most charming young girl that I know.

VALENTINE (*with effort*): Monsieur, I'm happy to have the pleasure of meeting you.

LARTIGUES (*aside*): What a joker!

PAUL: As for me, Madame, I'm very honored to be presented to you.

GABRIEL (*presenting Albert to Valentine*): And this is Albert de Gibray, one of my students, who desired greatly to meet you.

VALENTINE: I am flattered.

(*sound of a Quadrille in the distance*)

MARIE (to Albert): Ah, Monsieur de Gibray, the dance I promised you. It will gives us time to talk...

(*Albert and Marie leave with other guests who want to dance*)

GABRIEL (*to Paul*): I shall leave Madame de Bressolles in your hands.

(*Gabriel leaves with Yvan. Dancing in the rear*)

VALENTINE (*bold*): Monsieur de Gibray, would you give me your arm?

PAUL: Gladly, Madame, but first of all, I want to be sure I'm not mistaken

VALENTINE: No, you're not mistaken,

PAUL: Madame?

VALENTINE: You showed enough composure to not betray yourself—or me—by recognizing me. And enough compassion not to ruin me. I know you are a gallant man. I beg you to forget the past. Promise me.

PAUL: What need have you of such a promise?

VALENTINE (*worried*): You refuse?

PAUL: Perhaps I'll agree, later. But first, you must answer a few questions.

VALENTINE: You wish to question me? But I'm not an accused.

PAUL (*meaningfully*): Not yet. (*reaction by Valentine*) I bow before all that is respectable. Certainly before a mother—if she is truly a mother. So, first of all, what did you do with our child?

VALENTINE: I?

PAUL: I can prove that a child was born.

VALENTINE (*with scorn*): Proof?

PAUL: Yes, a daughter.

VALENTINE (*seeing the game is up*): Three days after her

birth, she was taken from me by my brother who took her out of France.

PAUL: Allow me to doubt that.

VALENTINE: I swear to you that's what he told me.

PAUL: So be it! But your mother's heart, I suppose, would not rest until… (*reaction by Valentine*) Ah, I see I am mistaken. You never demanded your child back from your brother.

VALENTINE: My brother was a very hard man. I do not know where she is. I no longer see my brother. He no longer speaks to me.

PAUL: Well, you should have come to me. I would have helped you! (*Valentine shrugs*) You have no maternal feelings. You must give me proof that my child was actually carried off by your brother. Don't refuse, otherwise I will accuse you of having killed the baby.

VALENTINE: You would accuse me of infanticide! I dare you! What good would it do to you? Besides, it's a lie.

PAUL: What will remain of the universal esteem that surrounds you if I speak?

VALENTINE (*terrified*): Paul!

PAUL: If your husband had known this, would he have given you his name, his honor?

VALENTINE: Shut up!

PAUL: You have a daughter that is his, but you have one that belongs to me.

VALENTINE: Keep it down!

PAUL: If you didn't kill her, give her to me. I'll take care of her. I'll find your brother and force him to tell me the truth.

(*Gabriel and Albert appear at the back*)

GABRIEL: They're busy discussing your happiness.

PAUL: Now let's talk about what brought me here. My nephew is in love with your daughter.

VALENTINE (*sensing an opportunity*): You must understand that Albert shall not marry my daughter, even if he were to die of sorrow.

ALBERT (*in despair*): Ah!

PAUL (*who's seen Albert*): So be it then. I've shown you a way, a quite simple way, to assure you of my discretion. Don't be slow to use it. That's the best advice I can give you. Goodbye, Madame! (*to Albert*) Come, lad, come.

GABRIEL: Courage, Albert.

(*They leave*)

MAURICE (*to himself*): Well, well, Your Honor, if you find Simone, at least you'll have proof that she wasn't killed by her mother...

VALENTINE (*staring after Paul*): That man is implacable. He'll ruin me.

MAURICE (*coming forward*): But I will save you.

VALENTINE: You? (*bewildered*) Ah, what must be done?

(*Marie appears at the back*)

MAURICE: Cut short the hopes of Albert de Gibray.

VALENTINE: What do you mean?

MAURICE: Force your husband to give me Marie as my wife.

MARIE (who's overheard, shaking): Oh!

VALENTINE (*angry*): Ah, I was right! You love my daughter!

MAURICE: I want to save you, nothing more.

VALENTINE (*noticing Marie*): Hush!

LARTIGUES (*to Verdier*): So far, so good. Maurice will marry Marie de Bressolles.

(*Guy d'Arfeuilles returns, ringing a bell; the others come back*)

GUY: On stage for the second act! Maurice, this is yours.

PAUL (*aside*): Ah, my poor Albert! Why did you meet the daughter of that woman?

GUY (*ringing his bell*): On stage! On stage for the second act everyone!

C U R T A I N

## SCENE VI

The stage is divided into two unequal parts. The room at the right occupies three quarters of the stage. To the left, there is another, smaller room serves as an office.

AT RISE, Jodelet is in the office, seated, writing.

(*Aimée enters*)

AIMÉE: Jodelet, have you completed your report?
JODELET: Yes, Madame. Here it is. (*handing her a document*)
AIMÉE (*reading*): Hum. So, as for the last week, we have nothing new to report to Monsieur de Gibray.
JODELET: Absolutely nothing, Madame.
AIMÉE (*somewhat defeated*): Nothing… (*to Jodelet*) No information from the jewelers?
JODELET: Nothing.
AIMÉE: Ah, we're having a streak of bad luck! And that so-called Jules Théroux has escaped us as well.
JODELET: We only missed him by a couple of days.
AIMÉE: An inch is as good as a mile, Jodelet! He left us no track to follow.
JODELET: Patience, Madame! We've only been on the case for two weeks. He'll mess up sooner or later, or we'll get a tip.

(*rapping at the door to the left; Aimée goes to open the door; it is Cadet*)

AIMÉE: Monsieur Cadet!
CADET: Yes, Madame.

AIMÉE: What news do you bring?

CADET: I spotted Lartigues an hour ago.

AIMÉE AND JODELET: Lartigues!

CADET: Unfortunately, I couldn't arrest him or follow him.

AIMÉE: Where did you see him?

CADET: Rue de Faubourg Montmartre. I was turning a corner with my cab when I saw him. I stopped and tried to follow him, but he went down a narrow alley way that was too narrow for my carriage to follow. Damn it!

AIMÉE (*discouraged*): Another stroke of bad luck!

(*Enter Galoubert and La Grenouille*)

GALOUBERT: Can we come in?

AIMÉE: Yes, yes! Do you have news?

GALOUBERT: No such luck, boss.

CADET: Like me, damn it!

GALOUBERT: I saw one of our rascals though.

AIMÉE: Which one?

GALOUBERT: Verdier

LA GRENOUILLE: Disguised as a priest again. But we were on a train going in the opposite direction. Towards Paris.

AIMÉE: The opportunity will present itself again, I'm sure of it. Actually, all this isn't bad news really. I was worried they might have left France. Verdier must be living in Vincennes.

GRENOUILLE: That makes sense.

AIMÉE: We'll comb that town for him. (*to Cadet*) And you and Jodelet will search the Faubourg Montmartre. Lartigues must be hiding somewhere in that neighborhood.

JODELET: Yes, Madame.

AIMÉE: Now, let's take a break, my friends.

GRENOUILLE: And a drink.

AIMÉE: Tomorrow, we'll set to work again.

CADET: What shall I do with my cab?

AIMÉE: Keep it and come and get me this evening at nine.

CADET: Understood. I'll need to feed the horses.

(*Cadet, Galoubert and La Grenouille leave*)

AIMÉE: I wonder if I haven't over estimated my strength and my intelligence.

(*knocking at the door; it is Marianne*)

AIMÉE: What do you want, Marianne?
MARIANNE: It's Monsieur Maurice, Madame.
AIMÉE: Show him in.

(*Maurice enters; Marianne leaves*)

MAURICE: Good afternoon, my dear friend.
AIMÉE: Ah, Maurice, my child. Come so I can hug you. I never see you anymore.
MAURICE: That's why I've come to spend some time with you. I have lots to tell you.
AIMÉE: Ah?
MAURICE: And very serious business it is.
AIMÉE: Really? Speak! I'm listening.
MAURICE: Just recently, my dear friend, as you will recall, we spoke of my future.
AIMÉE: I do remember. you came to tell me that some wealthy foreign gentleman might actually hire you to be his secretary..
MAURICE: You've got a good memory, but before that.
AIMÉE: Before that? Are you alluding to your plans to marry?
MAURICE: You've got it!
AIMÉE: I thought we'd agreed that for you to marry too soon would be absurd.
MAURICE: It turns out that the absurdity was to speak of it that way.
AIMÉE (*shivering*): Ah! Sp, you've changed your mind?
MAURICE: I have.
AIMÉE: Don't even think of it. At your age, you're too much

in love with freedom to chain yourself to a woman!

MAURICE: That was because I didn't know the one I love.

AIMÉE: The one you love?

MAURICE: When you meet her, you'll understand.

AIMÉE (*emotionally*): Look, dear child, you haven't considered...

MAURICE: I'm a man, my dear friend, and in marrying the one I love, I'll find not only joy in my heart, but a brilliant position in the world, and a family.

AIMÉE: A family? What family?

MAURICE: That of Monsieur de Bressolles, a wealthy architect who'll provide his only daughter with a fine dowry.

AIMÉE: And you are hoping to marry this heiress?

MAURICE: I'm not hoping, I'm certain of it.

AIMÉE: Have you already asked for her hand?

MAURICE: No, but I've spoken to her mother. And I'm coming to beg you, you who raised me, you, my protectress, you, my mother, my true mother, to make the official demand for me.

AIMÉE: Me?

MAURICE: Why does such a simple act cause you such great agitation? You seem afraid...

AIMÉE: Afraid? Me? What for? I'm just astonished by this sudden development, and I ask myself if you are being reasonable.

MAURICE (*taking her hands*) Yes, I am, dear friend. Don't doubt it. A chance to assume an honorable place in society has to be grasped. Don't worry, you will be greeted warmly, and you'll obtain a favorable result.

AIMÉE (*aside*): My God...

MAURICE: Until today, I've let myself live without troubling myself about who I am, or where I came from, or even where I was going. But you must understand: that insouciance is out of season now. And I'll need papers establishing my identity.

AIMÉE (*stammering*): Papers...

MAURICE: I know that my name is Maurice Vasseur, but I have no birth certificate. No death certificates for my parents.

I must be of foreign origin So, dear friend, I come to beg you to give me my family papers, or if you don't have them, to tell me where I can get them.

AIMÉE (*after an emotional struggle*): Child, this marriage is impossible.

MAURICE: Impossible! Why?

AIMÉE: Don't ask me. I can only keep repeating the same thing: it's impossible.

MAURICE: That answer means nothing. It hides only a mystery that I have the right to solve, and I will!

AIMÉE: My God! My God! Ah, no! It's impossible!

MAURICE: Look, calm down, my dear friend. Your agitation troubles me. It means that the mystery of my birth is shameful, even criminal, perhaps. It makes me thing that my father was a wretch, or my mother an odious creature.

AIMÉE: Ah!

MAURICE: Why these tears? I don't need tears, I need an answer. Was my mother infamous to the degree that…

AIMÉE: Shut up, you wretch! Don't insult your mother!

MAURICE: If I'm insulting her, it's your fault. Your silence arouses my suspicions. Tell me who my mother was, and then maybe I'll understand why you keep insisting that my marriage is impossible.

AIMÉE (*terrified*): You want to know?

MAURICE: Yes, I insist!

AIMÉE: In that case listen to me and you will understand. Your mother was hired as a companion by Countess Kouravieff, a great lady from Russia. At the same time, a young man became the Countess' business manager…

MAURICE: Countess Kouravieff?

AIMÉE: Yes. This young man was very good looking, seductive in his manners, and he persuaded your mother, who was very young and naïve, that he wanted to marry her. She couldn't resist him and became his mistress.

MAURICE: His mistress…

AIMÉE (*wildly*): Yes. Keep listening. Soon thereafter, the Countess was found dead in her bed, stabbed to death. She was murdered by the same business manager who was embezzling her fortune. He disappeared, but left false evidence behind framing your mother as the murderess.

MAURICE: Ah!

AIMÉE: She was imprisoned, waiting for her trial, when she gave birth to a son.

MAURICE: Me?

AIMÉE: You!

MAURICE: Ah! I was predestined! What's my father's name? The murderer's?

AIMÉE: Pierre Lartigues!

MAURICE: Pierre Lartigues... And my mother. What became of her?

AIMÉE: She was acquitted.

MAURICE: What did she do afterward?

AIMÉE: She swore to avenge this infamy and... (*hesitating*) and...

MAURICE Avenge it... But how? By what means? What could she do?

AIMÉE: Alone, nothing, but working together with the Police, a great deal. She's been working with them for twenty years.

MAURICE: What difference does it make? She must be dead by now. No one will be concerned about who she was.

AIMÉE: No, she isn't dead.

MAURICE (*strangled*): what? My mother isn't dead?

AIMÉE: No. And she's still working with the Police. She's still pursuing Pierre Lartigues, who appears to be, if not himself the assassin, but at least an accomplice of the recent murders committed at the Père Lachaise.

MAURICE (*recoiling*): Ah!

AIMÉE: So don't go asking for the hand of that girl. How can you say: I am a bastard, born at the prison of Saint-Lazare, the son of the murderer Pierre Lartigues, still at large, and Aimée Joubert, his mistress who is now an undercover Police agent.

MAURICE (*stunned*): My mother... You?

AIMÉE (*sobbing*): Yes, I! I am your mother! Haven't you guessed already, seeing how much I love you?

MAURICE: And you work with the Police! And you want to send my father to the guillotine!

AIMÉE: Maurice!

MAURICE: Don't come near me, you wretch!

AIMÉE: Maurice!

MAURICE (*aside*): I'm lucky! If I had given myself away, she'd have given me up to the Law.

AIMÉE: Don't reject me! I love you! You're killing me!

MAURICE (*aside*): She loves me! So she won't give me up! Perhaps I have nothing to fear…

AIMÉE: Maurice, my son, my only child… Do you hate me!

MAURICE: Mother! Hate you? Never! Forgive my first reaction. Hate you! How could you imagine that's even possible? You're my mother!

AIMÉE: My son!

MAURICE (*drying her eyes*): Darling mother, today I understand all that you've suffered, and that suffering only increases my love for you. I worship you even more than I love you.

AIMÉE: Is it really true? You forgive me?

MAURICE: I have nothing to forgive you for. Your courage is heroic.

AIMÉE: What you are saying makes me so happy.

MAURICE (*hugging her*): My dear Mother... So you are still looking for my father?

AIMÉE: Yes.

MAURICE: Are you on his trail?

AIMÉE: I know he's still in Paris. He was spotted this very day.

MAURICE: And he committed that double murder?

AIMÉE: If not himself, at least he was an accomplice.

MAURICE: If he was, who would be the real killer?

AIMÉE: I don't know yet, but I soon will.

MAURICE: My father's name was Pierre Lartigues?

AIMÉE: He's using the alias of Jules Théroux. Anyway, you can now see why all ideas of marriage are out of the question.

MAURICE: I'm not of that opinion.

AIMÉE: What do you mean?

MAURICE: Your influence with the Police should suffice to remove all obstacles. Only one thing concerns me: your affiliation with them. Would you agree to give it up?

AIMÉE: Right now, it's not possible.

MAURICE: Why?

AIMÉE: I made a firm commitment. Besides, it's in your interest that I should persevere.

MAURICE: In my interest?

AIMÉE: Yes. Count Kouravieff has promised to give a fortune to my son if I catch Pierre Lartigues. So it's not only for myself that I'm pursuing him, it's for you too. I'll get him eventually. I won't rest until I see him guillotined. And you'll be happy too, my Maurice.

(*a silence, then a rap on the door*)

AIMÉE: I have to see another agent now.

MAURICE (*wiping away sweat with his hand*): then I'll leave you, my dear mother.

AIMÉE: I'll see you soon.

MAURICE: Yes, because we have a lot more to talk about.

AIMÉE: Hug your mother.

MAURICE: Till soon, Mother!

(*Maurice only pretends to leave; Aimée closes the door behind him, but doesn't see him return furtively*)

AIMÉE: Ah, he forgave me!

MAURICE (*aside*): I want to know who this visitor is, and what he has to say.

(*Marianne introduces Count Yvan. Maurice listens attentively*)

AIMÉE: Ah, Count, for you to come here, you must have something very serious to report.

YVAN: Indeed I have, Madame.

AIMÉE: Please explain.

YVAN (*pulling an object from his pocket*): Do you still have that turquoise button from the cufflink belonging to the assassin?

MAURICE: (*aside, showing noticeable alarm*): I know that voice.

AIMÉE: Yes. (*taking a key from her pocket, opening a drawer, and removing the object in question*) Here it is.

YVAN: There's no mistake, Madame. Look at them.

AIMÉE (*looking*): They're exactly alike.

YVAN: This time we're on the trail of the assassin.

MAURICE (*aside*): Ah!

AIMÉE: Where's you find this jewel?

YVAN: At the home of a courtesan called La Belle Octavia.

AIMÉE: Did you question this woman?

YVAN: I did press her, but she kept lying to me.

AIMÉE: She won't dare to do so before the Investigating Magistrate. I'll get her arrested.

MAURICE (*aside*): Arrested!

YVAN: Can you do it at once?

AIMÉE: No. It's too late to get a warrant. We'll have to do it tomorrow. La Belle Octavia doesn't suspect a thing, does she?

YVAN (shaking his head): Not a thing.

AIMÉE: Then she won't flee. We've got her!

YVAN: I don't think she's an accomplice, however.

AIMÉE: But clearly, she knows the identity of the murderer and can identify him as the owner of the cufflink.

(*Cadet returns, opening the door at the back*)

CADET: Boss, it's time.

AIMÉE: Yes. (*puts on her hat*)

CADET (*seeing Yvan*): Good evening, Count.

YVAN: Good evening.

CADET: Any news?

AIMÉE: We've got a good scent this time.

CADET: Damned! Where are we going?

AIMÉE: To the Sûreté! Come with us, Count. Now I truly feel

that we can say, God is with us!

MAURICE (*aside*): And the Guillotine for me. The Guillotine... No, never!

(*Maurice leaves shaking*)

CADET: Come on, Boss, let's go.

(*They leave*)

CURTAIN

## SCENE VII

A enclosed garden. On the right, there is a wall, three meters high, above which can be seen the gallery of Italian pavilion. That wall is covered with plants and climbers. To the left, the entrance to the pavilion, composed of a ground level and first floor. In the wall at the back, there is a door half-hidden by climbing vines. Above that wall, there are large shade trees that are part of Madame Dubief's workshop.

AT RISE, it is night. There's a table near the exit of the pavilion. On it, a lamp, that faintly lights the stage. Pierre Lartigues and Verdier stand on the gallery.

LARTIGUES: Maurice has given us a plan of Madame Dubief's workshop. The pavilion where I live belongs to the same owner.

VERDIER: What about this locked door?

LARTIGUES: It used to communicate between the two. I had it unlocked. There's no deadbolt on the side of the workshop; the door there is partially hidden behind all these vines. I've made a set of duplicate keys that allow me to enter the workshop t any time. Twice, during the night, I was able, without attracting any attention, to cross the garden to come here. It's a secure retreat in case we're surprised.

VERDIER: A good plan!

(*a clock strikes, then we hear the confused voices of young women.*)

LARTIGUES: Ah, classes are over.
VERDIER: Never mind about that. Let's speak of Simone.

(The voices of young girls get louder)

LARTIGUES: In a few days. she'll be dead. She lives in this pavilion. See for yourself how easy it will be to get rid of her.
VERDIER: So we're nearing our goal?
LARTIGUES: The girl's a lamb ready for the slaughter.

(*A balloon floats over the wall and lands at Lartigues's feet.*)

VOICE OF A YOUNG GIRL: My balloon!
LARTIGUES: The devil with these girls! Every day I get visits of this sort.
VERDIER: Never mind that. The presence of Count Kouravieff in Paris doesn't worry you?
LARTIGUES: Yes, a little. I'm sure he's looking for me.
VERDIER: Why don't you move?
LARTIGUES: To do so would be to renounce all the advantages that this place gives us—no more opportunities to get rid of Simone.
VERDIER: Let Maurice come and live here instead.
LARTIGUES: You're right, As of tomorrow, this will be Maurice's home.
VERDIER: Have you located Simone's birth certificate?
LARTIGUES: Yes. It will establish her identity after her death.

(*ringing outside*)

VERDIER: There's ringing.

LARTIGUES: Dominique won't open unless the caller is well known (*pouring a drink*) Have a drink, old boy.

(*Dominique enters*)

LARTIGUES: Who is it?
DOMINIQUE: A girl from Madame Dubief's who asking if a balloon hasn't landed here.
LARTIGUES: Yes, yes, hold on. (*going to get the balloon*)
VERDIER (*stopping him, to Dominique*): Show her in.

(*Dominique leaves*)

VERDIER: An employee of the workshop. It might be useful.

(*Simone enters*)

SIMONE: Apologies, Messieurs, I'm only here to get the balloon that one of our students clumsily tossed into your garden.
VERDIER (*giving her the balloon*): Here, girl!
SIMONE: Thank you, Monsieur.
YOUNG GIRL'S VOICE (*from the other side of the wall*): Simone! Simone!
VERDIER AND LARTIGUES (*reacting*): Simone?
YOUNG GIRL'S VOICE: Where are you, Simone?
SIMONE: I'm here!
YOUNG GIRL'S VOICE: And my balloon?
SIMONE: I've got it!
YOUNG GIRL'S VOICE: Quick, throw it back to me.!
SIMONE: Oh, the naughty girl! (with her back turned toward the two men, she tosses the balloon over the wall)
LARTIGUES (*taking a knife from the table*): How convenient.
VERDIER: Stop, you idiot! (*taking the knife away*)
SIMONE: Thank you again, Messieurs.
VERDIER: You work for Madame Dubief?
SIMONE: Yes. I'm a seamstress.
VERDIER: Have you been here long?

SIMONE: Almost a month. (*a bell rings*) Ah! That's the time for the students to go to the refectory. Excuse me, Messieurs, and thank you again.
VERDIER: *Au revoir*.

(*Simone leaves*)

LARTIGUES: We had her and you let her leave!
VERDIER: Idiot! To kill her here would ruin us. If I weren't here, you'd do stupid things.

(*Maurice, very pale, his features discomposed, enters*)

LARTIGUES: Maurice!
MAURICE (*in a strangled voice*): Yes, it's I!
LARTIGUES: What happened?
MAURICE: We are ruined!
VERDIER: Ruined?
MAURICE: Well, I am, at least.
VERDIER: Explain, quick.
MAURICE: Not before you've answered me one question.
LARTIGUES: What do you want to know?
MAURICE: I want to know which of the Five is Pierre Lartigues.
LARTIGUES (*about to speak when Verdier grasps his arm*): Pierre Lartigues?
MAURICE: Yes. Up to now, it wasn't important.
VERDIER: Pierre Lartigues no longer exists and you ought to know that better than anyone.
MAURICE: Better than anyone? What do you mean?
VERDIER: He was the man hiding under the name Gustave Perrier—the same man you killed.
MAURICE: I killed my father!
(*Lartigues and Verdier are shocked*)
LARTIGUES (*with terrible emotion*): Your father! Pierre Lartigues was your father! Ah!
VERDIER (*low*): Shut up!

73

LARTIGUES (*low*): But he's my son!

VERDIER: Say something, will you!

LARTIGUES: Who told you that?

MAURICE (*strangled voice*) Madame Aimée Joubert—my mother!

LARTIGUES (*stunned*): Aimée Joubert! Your mother! She's in Paris?

MAURICE: Yes. She works for the Police. And Count Yvan Samoiloff, the son of Countess Kouravieff, is in league with her to send us to the Guillotine.

LARTIGUES: She's still alive… and working with the Police!

VERDIER: This time, we are truly threatened.

LARTIGUES: We must rid ourselves of Aimée Joubert.

MAURICE: Rid ourselves of her… But how?

LARTIGUES: By killing her, by Jove!

MAURICE: That, you won't do!

VERDIER: What will stop us?

MAURICE: Me! I don't want her harmed!

LARTIGUES: Do you love her more than your freedom? Your life?

VERDIER: Enough talk. Until today, we've escaped her clutches. We shall be clever enough to escape her again. Jules Théroux will start by leaving this place. And tomorrow, you Maurice, will take his place.

MAURICE: But you don't know the half of it. Danger is even closer than you think. Tomorrow, La Belle Octavia will be arrested. If she identifies me, I'm lost.

VERDIER: La Belle Octavia!

LARTIGUES: What does this mean? Why?

MAURICE: The day of the murders, I was wearing two cuff-links decorated with turquoise stones. I lost one. I didn't realize it at the time. My mother found it in the carriage.

LARTIGUES: Ah!

VERDIER: Clumsy!

MAURICE: The other was found by Count Yvan at La Belle Octavia's, whose affections we both share.

LARTIGUES: Damnation! If she talks Maurice's goose is

cooked. He's got to leave Paris tonight.

VERDIER: That would simply confirm his guilt.

MAURICE: What do we do then?

LARTIGUES: Could you go and see Octavia tonight?

MAURICE: Yes.

LARTIGUES: In that case, you are saved.

MAURICE: How?

LARTIGUES: Because you'll kill her.

MAURICE: Kill that poor woman? No, never!

LARTIGUES: You've already killed twice, and your hide was not even at risk.

VERDIER: If she talks, it's the Guillotine for you.

MAURICE: The Guillotine!

VERDIER: It's your life, or hers!

MAURICE: So be it! La Belle Octavia shall be silenced.

(*he rushes out*)

LARTIGUES: He's indeed my son, Verdier. But why did you let him believe that he killed his own father?

VERDIER: It was the only way to stop his curiosity. Be patient, my tender soul. The time for your family reunion will still come—but only after we're in possession of that inheritance.

CURTAIN

75

# ACT IV
## SCENE VIII

The stage is divided in two horizontal sections. The upper half represents La Belle Octavia's bedroom, lit by a lamp hanging over the bed. There is a window that lets out onto the rooftops. The bottom half is her salon/greeting room filled with tacky furniture. A staircase connects the two.

AT RISE, La Belle Octavia is lying on her bed with her back turned toward the audience. There is great Silence.

(*Maurice enters furtively, face half-hidden behind a neckchief, listening.*

(*Cautiously, he goes up the stairs.*

(*After a moment, Galoubert enters, listens, and then signals for Aimée to join him.*

(*Aimée enters, followed by Jodelet, La Grenouille, Cadet, Commissioner Masse and two policemen.*

(*In the upstairs bedroom, Maurice appears to hesitates, but makes a terrible decision. He goes to the sleeping Octavia, hesitates again, then summoning up his courage, slits her throat with a dagger.*

(*Octavia utters a strangled "Ah" convulses and becomes motionless.*

(*Maurice hears noises below and stops.*

(*Instead of going back downstairs, he goes out of the window, which he closes behind him.*

(*Meanwhile, Aimée is heading upstairs. She goes towards Octavia's bed. When she sees the courtesan, she examines her and yells for help.*)

AIMÉE: Dead! She's dead!
GALOUBERT (*looking through the window*): I see someone's climbing on the roof.
AIMÉE: It's the murderer! He' s still here! He won't escape us!

(*The others rush in*)

C U R T A I N

## SCENE IX

The three floors of the house pass successively before the audience. The shutters of the first floor are closed. The windows of the second floor are lit as for an evening party. A piano playing a Quadrille from Offenbach's *Orpheus in Hell* can be heard . Then we come to the third floor, closed like the first. Finally one reaches the roof.

## SCENE X

Panorama of Paris at night. The rooftops. In the distance we can see the Pantheon Dome.

(*Maurice appears, emerging from behind a chimney, then slipping over the roofs from house to house with difficulty.*

(*Aimée appears at the window on the right. She sees Maurice and fires at him with her revolver.*

(*Maurice vanishes behind a chimney.*

77

(*Aimée fires again.*

(*Maurice falls into the void below*)

CURTAIN

# ACT V
## SCENE XI

A street. To the right, there a kiosk for people waiting for cabs. To the left, we see the facade of a Post and Telegraph Office with gaslights, the interior of which can be seen by the public at the far left.

AT RISE, inside the Post Office, the Postmaster, M. Mesnil, supervises several employees finishing their accounts and stamping letters.

MESNIL: It's almost nine o'clock, Messieurs. Hurry up. Bardoux, lock the door and close the shutters.
BARDOUX: Yes, Monsieur.

(*Bardoux goes out into the street and closes the shutters of the windows*)

MESNIL: Julien, secure all the letter after you're finished stamping them.

(Julien opens the safe and places letters inside)

MESNIL: Ringard, are you done with the accounts? I'm only waiting for you.
RINGARD: Almost finished, Monsieur Mesnil.
MESNIL: Hurry up, Messieurs!

(*At this moment a lady coming from the street tries to open the Post Office door*)

BARDOUX: We're closed.
LADY: But this is important.

BARDOUX: Sorry, but we're closed.
LADY: But it's barely nine....
BARDOUX (*yelling*): We're closed, I said! Come back tomorrow!

(*he goes back inside*)

LADY (*furious*): Closed! Closed! What a brute!

(*She leaves, muttering*)

RINGARD (*to Mesnil*): Everything is in order, Monsieur?
MESNIL: Yes, it's fine..
RINGARD: Then, good night, Monsieur Mesnil.

(*Ringard leaves. Outside, a gentleman comes in to drop a letter in the mail slot*)

JULIEN: Are we done, Monsieur?
MESNIL: Yes, you can go.

(*the workers leave*)

MESNIL (*to Bardoux*): Put out the gas.

(Bardoux does. Mesnil puts the money in a bag and the bank notes in a portfolio.

(*Outside, Aimée Joubert enters, a lantern in her hand, a bag across her shoulder, singing*)

AIMÉE (*approaching the kiosk*): It's closed. And Cadet isn't here as he was supposed to. Why aren't Galoubert and La Grenouille here either?

(*A policeman enters*)

POLICEMAN: What are you doing prowling around here, Lady?
AIMÉE: Nothing, nothing, sergeant.

(*She leaves, singing. The Policeman leaves too. Several characters pass by. A young man drops a letter in the mail slot*)

BARDOUX: Everything is in order, Monsieur Mesnil. See you tomorrow.
MESNIL: Goodnight, Bardoux.

(*Bardoux leaves, and right after him, Mesnil does too, carrying the money. At the same time, Cadet enters, drunk, staggering, supporting himself against the wall*)

CADET: Jesus Christ! The street is spinning. I said I'd be here at nine... (*seeing the clock on the kiosk*) and here it is, almost 9:30... Well, it's not my fault... So, I'm late, just a bit, that's all.

(*He takes out a key and, with difficulty, opens the door to the kiosk and enters. Once inside, he sits down and watches the street.*

(*Maurice and Verdier appear in the distance*)

VERDIER: My dear Maurice, the Cat's Eye is worrying us. We've got to take precautions.
MAURICE: Ah, my mother is tenacious. It's no fault of hers that I'm alive today. We're being very closely tracked. Me, especially. We need to get it over with.
VERDIER: That's my opinion as well.
MAURICE: I'm signing the marriage contract Saturday.
VERDIER: In four days? Bravo! But Simone must disappear at the same time.
MAURICE: Friday always brings me luck. She'll be gone on Friday.

VERDIER: Great! Meanwhile, as we agreed, in order to avoid showing myself again, you will come and pick up Brémont's final instructions at the *poste restante* here.

MAURICE: What's the box number?

VERDIER: L.J. K. 50. (*giving him an envelope*) Here's a letter you can show them if they ask you any questions.

MAURICE (*taking it*): That should do. There's nothing more for us to say?

VERDIER: Nothing more. Good night.

MAURICE: Till tomorrow then.

(*he leaves; Verdier drops a letter in the mail slot*)

CADET (*rising*): Damn it! That's him! I recognize him! It's my phony Captain!

(*Cadet rushes out of the kiosk to nab Verdier, but stumbles and falls. By the time he gets up, Verdier is gone*)

CADET (looking in every direction): Where's he gone? Which way? Which street? Missed him again, damn it!

(*Aimée returns, with La Grenouille and Galoubert*)

ALL: Cadet!

AIMÉE: Why are you yelling?

CADET: I saw him! It was him! The phony Priest, the false Captain!

GALOUBERT: Here?

LA GRENOUILLE: Still disguised as a Captain?

CADET (*nodding*): Yes! He walked by the kiosk, and I didn't recognize him soon enough. He took a cab while I fell down, drunk that I am.

AIMÉE: Cadet, you promised me not to drink anymore!

CADET: One gets carried away, Madame. But there's still a way to save the day.

AIMÉE: What do you mean?

CADET: He slipped a letter in that mailbox.
GALOUBERT: Boss, if we had that letter…
AIMÉE: That's a good idea! Galoubert, quick, find a pharmacy and buy a pot of glue.

(*Aimée approaches the mailbox; the Policeman returns*)

POLICEMAN: What are you doing now?
AIMÉE (*presenting an id*): I'm an agent of the Sûreté.
POLICEMAN (*impressed*): How can I help you, Madame?
AIMÉE: Just leave us alone. We don't want to be disturbed.

(*The Policeman leaves.*

(*Galoubert returns with a pot of glue. Aimée opens it, dips a broom feather in it, and inserts it into the mailbox*)

LA GRENOUILLE: What a trick!
GALOUBERT: Before I became an honest man, that's how I robbed the church box.
LA GRENOUILLE: You always were a genius.
AIMÉE: I don't feel anything in here.
GALOUBERT: Maybe Cadet was mistaken?
CADET: Never in my life!
AIMÉE: Ah! I've got something. (*pulling out letter sticking to the feather, then reading the address*) It's addressed to Michel Brémont.
GALOUBERT: That's our man!
AIMÉE: Let's see. I can't open it without tearing it. All right, let's do that and we'll slip it back in another envelope. I can imitate the handwriting. (*she tears the envelope open and starts reading*)
CADET: My hair's standing on end!
AIMÉE: The letter is in code. (*she pulls out a decoding device*) Ah, I think I've got it.
GALOUBERT: Well, Boss?
AIMÉE: Silence! I'm almost there… (*reading*) "At the end of

the week, it will all be done. We've got the birth certificate. The Cat's Eye is harassing us ceaselessly. I await your response *poste restante*. I will pick it up under the initials. L.J.K. 50. Signed, Verdier." Now they are at our mercy! (*she takes a blank envelope and copies the handwriting*) Now, I need a stamp... Ah, I have one!

(*La Grenouille and Galoubert do a little dance*)

CADET: What a joy!
AIMÉE: Silence. Lock up the kiosk.
CADET: Yes, Boss!
AIMÉE (to all): These wretches can't escape us now! By next week, they'll be in our hands!

(*She carefully drops the letter in the mail box*)

CURTAIN

## SCENE XII

Same as Scene XI.

AT RISE, Cadet is on the driver's seat of his cab parked before the kiosk. The window shades of the carriage are lowered. La Grenouille and Jodelet are in disguise on the sidewalk, Jodelet pretending to sell newspapers, La Grenouille, suspenders. Inside the Post Office, the employees are back at their desks.

JODELET: *Le Matin*! Ask for *Le Matin*! All the latest news!
LA GRENOUILLE: Suspenders with eight strings! With elastics and leather hooks!

(*Inside the Post Office, customers come and go. Outside, people drop letters in the mail slot*)

FIRST CUSTOMER: A first-class stamp, please
RINGARD: Give me the stamps, Bardoux.
BARDOUX: Here, Monsieur.
SECOND CUSTOMER: A Post Card, please.

JODELET: *Le Matin*! Ask for *Le Matin*! All the latest news!
CADET (*to La Grenouille*) I'm beginning to worry. It's nine o'clock and nothing yet.
LA GRENOUILLE: You are up there on your throne. We'd like to be in your place. Patience! The Boss will be here.

(*Simone appears and enters the Post Office, soon followed by Ludovic de Bressolles*)

THIRD CUSTOMER (*at the telegraph counter*): How many words that makes?
JULIEN: Eleven.
FOURTH CUSTOMER: I'll have three post cards.

(*the customers pay and leave*)

SIMONE: Monsieur de Bressolles!
LUDOVIC: Simone! Ah, my dear child, I'm glad to meet you! We got your letter. But you should have come to see us.
SIMONE: I didn't dare, so I wrote.
LUDOVIC: Come Sunday. Are you satisfied with your job?
SIMONE: Very happy!
BRESSOLLES: So much the better! I must go now, child. I have lots of errands to run. Until later.
SIMONE: All my respects to Mademoiselle Marie.
BRESSOLLES: And good luck to you!

(*Simone leaves. Outside, Ludovic hails Cadet's cab*)

LUDOVIC: Coachman!
CADET: Sorry, I'm taken
LUDOVIC: Taken with drink, you mean.

*(The curtain of the carriage window rolls up, revealing Commissioner Masse)*

MASSE: I'm sorry, but this carriage is taken, Monsieur.
LUDOVIC: Look here…
MASSE: In the service of the Sûreté.
LUDOVIC: Well then I'll go on foot.
LA GRENOUILLE: Suspenders with eight strings! With elastics and leather hooks!

*(Ludovic de Bressolles leaves; a lady enters and walks to the telegram counter)*

FIFTH CUSTOMER (DÉSIRÉE) (*dictating a telegram*): "I can't leave without you. RSVP."
JULIEN: Six words. One franc.
DÉSIRÉE: When will I get the reply?
JULIEN: Two o'clock.

*(She leaves)*

SIXTH CUSTOMER: Two first-class stamps, please.

*(Jodelet sees Aimée appear; she's wearing a veil over her face)*

JODELET: The Cat's Eye is here!
LA GRENOUILLE: Suspenders with eight strings! With elastics and leather hooks!
AIMÉE (*to La Grenouille*): Ah, Sophie! Where is Galoubert?

*(Galoubert appears from behind the kiosk; he is heavily disguised)*

GALOUBERT (*with a fake accent*): I'm here.
AIMÉE: Unrecognizable. Good. And Cadet?

LA GRENOUILLE: He's warming up his seat.
AIMÉE: Perfect.
CADET: Ah, Boss, I need to get down and stretch my legs!
AIMÉE: Patience!

(*she goes to the carriage and whispers instructions to the officers inside*)

AIMÉE: Sophie! Jodelet! You stay here, opposite the Post Office. Galoubert, keep your eyes and ear open behind the kiosk. When I give the signal, it means someone has come to pick up the reply from England. I will point that person out. The officers in the cab have already received their instructions.
GALOUBERT: Right, Boss.

(*Aimée enters the Post Office and walks the counter*)

AIMÉE: Is the Postmaster here?
BARDOUX: Certainly, Madame. The door at the back. (*opening the door*) Monsieur Mesnil, this lady desires to speak to you.

(*Meanwhile, Cadet is falling asleep on his seat; Aimée goes behind the counter*)

CADET: Hey, Sophie. Got a light?

MESNIL (*coming forward*): Madame.
AIMÉE (*presenting a letter*) Be so good as to read this warrant, Monsieur.
MESNIL: I see. I'm at your disposal, Madame. (*to Bardoux*) Bardoux, is there a letter coming from England to box L.J.K. 50?
BARDOUX (*checking*): Yes. Here's the letter you want, Monsieur.
AIMÉE: Ah!

MESNIL: Fine, hold on to it. You are going to place Madame near you in such a way that she cannot be seen by whoever comes to claim this letter. But she must be able to see that person. It is a Police matter.

BARDOUX: Certainly, Monsieur.

AIMÉE: A thousand thanks, Monsieur.

MESNIL: It is quite natural. Good luck, Madame.

(*Mesnil returns to his desk, Bardoux sits down, Aimée near him*)

JODELET: *Le Matin*! Ask for *Le Matin*! All the latest news!

LA GRENOUILLE: Suspenders with eight strings! With elastics and leather hooks!

(*Baron de Landelly enters as Maurice appears at the back*)

LANDELLY (*to La Grenouille*): Go to the devil with your suspenders!

MAURICE: Baron!

LANDELLY: Maurice!

MAURICE: What's going on with you? You are acting like a whore in church. What's wrong?

LANDELLY: I'm coming from city hall.

MAURICE: And?

LANDELLY: Idiots! Brutes! I lost my umbrella on the train somewhere. They showed me a room with ten thousand umbrellas.

MAURICE: You had trouble finding yours?

LANDELLY: Not at all! I recognized it right away!

MAURICE: But then, I don't see...

LANDELLY: They wouldn't let me have it! I told them who I am. But they wanted a proof that the umbrella was mine! They actually asked me for my birth certificate!

MAURICE (*laughing*): Ah, ah! I'm sure they were making fun of you.

LANDELLY: What a country! Cretins, all! But I got it in the

end! Where are you headed?
MAURICE: To the Post Office.
LANDELLY: I'll wait for you. Then we'll get a cab.

(*Landelly lights a cigar; Maurice heads toward the Post Office. Cadet, feigning sleep, has observed them*)

CADET (*aside*): Not mine, thank God!

MAURICE: First, a telegram to my mother. (*starts writing a dispatch*) I can't see her today.
AIMÉE: It's almost noon! Will they never come and pick up that letter!
BARDOUX: The time seems long to you, Madame?
AIMÉE: Yes, it does. Quite long.
BARDOUX: They might come as late as this evening, or even tomorrow. Am I to give this letter to whoever asks for it?
AIMÉE: Yes, immediately, in such a way as to not arouse any suspicions. Just let him come. He won't escape us.

LANDELLY: Perhaps I'll get a cab now... (*goes towards Cadet's carriage*) Why, it's my coachman—Cadet! Hey, Cadet!
CADET (*feigning waking up*): Huh? What? Ah, my monumental friend!
LANDELLY: What are you doing there?
CADET: I'm waiting for the new shift.
LANDELLY: But I was expecting you this morning.
CADET: Unable to come.
LANDELLY: What?
CADET: Hush!
LANDELLY: What?
CADET: Silence!
LANDELLY: I'm getting in.
CADET: Taken.
LANDELLY: Taken?
CADET: It's a trap.

LANDELLY: A trap?
CADET: They're going to nab him.
LANDELLY: Who?
CADET: Him! Listen!

(*Cadet and Landelly talk in whispers; Désirée returns*)

DÉSIRÉE: Has my reply come yet?
JULIEN: What name?
DÉSIRÉE: Désirée.
JULIEN: Yes. (*giving her a sealed telegram*) Here it is, Mademoiselle.

(*She takes it and leaves. She stops in the street, unseals it. Meanwhile Maurice goes to the counter*)

DÉSIRÉE: Ah, it's all over! He no longer loves me! Oh, but I'll get even with him.

(*She leaves*)

MAURICE (*pulls a document and presents it to Bardoux*): Monsieur, do you have a letter for box L.J.K. 50? This is my identification.

(*Aimée hearing Maurice's voice experiences a sudden, violent shock*)

AIMÉE (*aside in a strangled voice*) That voice! It's him!
BARDOUX (*after checking the document*): Yes, Monsieur. Here it is.

(*Maurice takes the letter and leaves*)

AIMÉE: Ah!

(*Bardoux looks at Aimée who has recoiled in the grip of a*

*terrible emotion. She takes a few steps and collapses*)

LANDELLY (*seeing Maurice*): Ah, Maurice!
MAURICE: Yes?
LANDELLY: It's monumental, old boy.
MAURICE: What is?
LANDELLY: The assassin of the Père Lachaise...
MAURICE: Yes. What about him?
LANDELLY: They're going to arrest him.
MAURICE (taking his arm): Well, so much the better!

(*They leave*)

CURTAIN

## SCENE XIII

An office. There is a door at the back, two side doors, a window on the right .At the rear, there are  two book cases. There is a table, a desk covered with books, an armchair by the fireplace. It is night.

AT RISE, the room is empty. A key can be heard in the door at the right, then it opens. Galoubert enters, a bunch of nightingales in hand.

GALOUBERT: There it is! Two doors to unlock. The one from the street, and that one here. I had some trouble. (*speaking to someone still outside*) Come in, Boss.

(*Aimée enters, followed by Cadet and La Grenouille*)

AIMÉE: Shut the door.

(*La Grenouille shuts the door; Galoubert lights a lamp on the table. Aimée casts a glance around her*)

AIMÉE: His office... (*aloud*) Pull the curtain so that no one outside can see the light in this pavilion.

(*Cadet and Galoubert pull the curtains*)

AIMÉE: Now we must search the papers here for anything relative to Pierre Lartigues or Verdier. Look in all the drawers, force the locks. I will inspect this room, you take the others.
GALOUBERT: Rest assured, Boss, that we won't neglect any corner.
CADET: Soon I'll be an upholsterer!

(*They all leave*)

AIMÉE (*alone*): I'm searching my son's place. No, he can't be guilty... While he's waiting for me to sign his marriage contract, I'm here searching his rooms. (*pause*) (*approaching the desk*) An open book... (*reading*) "Lord Byron... Man is never the master of his fate." In the margins, there's a note. "That's false. Man is always the master of his destiny." That's not the idea of a criminal. An unfinished letter. It's to me. (*reading*) "Dear adored mother, I love you and will always love you. This marriage will increase our happiness." And I dare suspect him? No, no, it's crazy. It's impossible! (*tearfully*) He cannot be a criminal. If he's become their instrument, it's without knowing it. (*inspecting the papers*) Letters, newspapers, articles he's written, articles he's working on... A list of names and addresses. ..Octavia... Why the name of that woman? She had many lovers, he could be one of them... (*unfolding a paper*)What's this? (*unable to repress a scream of shock*) It's a codebook, like the one I used to decode the letter Verdier sent to London. Doubt is no longer permissible. Maurice is an accomplice of his father! Lartigues has stolen my son from me! But how did he find him? What kind of monster have I unleashed upon the world? He left me just before Count Yvan came to bring me the turquoise cufflink... And within a few hours. Octavia was dead... My God, my God, take pity on me! No, no, I don't believe it yet. I need more than evidence!

(*Galoubert returns, followed by Cadet and La Grenouille*)

GALOUBERT: You said you needed more evidence, Boss? Here is some. (*presenting a sheath of papers*)
AIMÉE (*terrified*): More evidence?
CADET: A handful. We found it at the bottom of a suitcase.
AIMÉE: Let me see. (*looking at the papers breathlessly*) A will. Arnould d'Harville's... Marie de Bressolles... Simone... Michel Brémont... And these notes... All becomes clear now! To get the inheritance, Simone and Marie are to be killed. What a monstrous plan! And Maurice! Maurice!
CADET: Well, did we have a lucky hand or what?
GALOUBERT: Are these the proofs we were looking for?
AIMÉE (*darkly*): All that we could ever ask for.
LA GRENOUILLE: Whose place is this, anyway?
AIMÉE (*with an effort*): That of an accomplice of Lartigues and Verdier.
CADET (*who's been listening to noises outside*): Hush! Someone's coming! They're opening the front door...
AIMÉE: You are all armed?
ALL: Yes. (*they pull revolvers from their pockets*)
AIMÉE: Who can this be? Hide somewhere and put out the lights.

(*All disappear. We hear the sound of a key turning inside the lock. Verdier and Lartigues enter. Verdier locks the door behind them*)

LARTIGUES: What devilish locks! Put on a light!
VERDIER: Hold on.
LARTIGUES: I hate being in the dark. (*lighting a match*)
VERDIER (*blowing it out*): Imbecile! I need darkness to see what's happening at Madame Debief's. We must be sure Maurice has actually executed our orders.
LARTIGUES: He told you Simone died last night. All we

need to do now is to wait patiently for his return to learn what happened tonight at the De Bressolles' Mansion.

VERDIER: Yes.

LARTIGUES: Are you worried?

VERDIER: Not really. The Cat's Eye is there, with Maurice, to cosign his wedding contract. Ah, look!

LARTIGUES: I see two Magistrates... Paul de Gibray is one of them...

VERDIER: They've come to verify Simone's death... The death of his daughter!

LARTIGUES: He will find the birth certificate that Maurice left there.

VERDIER: That's all I wanted to know. You can light up now, if you like.

LARTIGUES (*lighting a candle*): We are nearing our goal, old boy. In an hour, the signatures on the marriage contract will be certified. Tomorrow, the marriage will be recorded at city hall, and then there'll be the church ceremony. By the end of the week, we'll have joined Brémont in London.

VERDIER: And we'll wait for your son to come and spend his honeymoon in London and receive, in the name of his wife, the millions we are going to share.

LARTIGUES: And then, it's on to America to enjoy the good life!

(*Aimée reveals herself*)

AIMÉE: You think so?

LARTIGUES: Aimée!

VERDIER: The Cat's Eye!

AIMÉE: Yes, it is I, who's come to ask you what you've done to her child.

LARTIGUES (*still in shock*): What?

AIMÉE: I've found you at last, Pierre, after having searched for you for so long. I know all your crimes, those you've committed, and those you are planning to commit. But I didn't expect fate would place my son in your hands, my son that

94

you've turned into your accomplice! Only yesterday did I get proof of it, and despite the evidence, I still cannot bring myself to believe it. It must be you, his father, who must tell me that this monstrous thing is real… That you have made him into a murderer like yourself. Your life, both your lives, depend on your response.

LARTIGUES: What can I tell you that you don't know already, Aimée? I've been on a criminal path for years. The Guillotine wants me, but so far, I've kept my head firmly attached on my shoulders. You were in my way, so I had to destroy you. Nothing personal. I destroyed you as I would have destroyed anyone else. Maurice, having my blood in his veins, must fatally resemble me. He took a knife and he killed.

AIMÉE: It's false! Maurice hasn't killed anyone!

LARTIGUES: Your son, our son, has killed more people in two weeks than I have in twenty years. Chance put him on the trail of our secrets. He followed the scent, and to possess the millions he saw shining before him, he used his knife.

AIMÉE: You lie, wretch!

LARTIGUES: Oh, you think so? Then, who killed Jenny, Verdier's servant, in Kouravieff's tomb to steal our correspondence? Who else but Maurice?

AIMÉE: Maurice!

LARTIGUES: And who stuck a knife in Gustave Perrier who'd been sent by Brémont from England? Maurice again!

AIMÉE: No, no! I don't believe you!

LARTIGUES: Who killed La Belle Octavia? Who killed Simone?

AIMÉE: Simone!

LARTIGUES: Maurice! Always, Maurice! Ha, ha!

AIMÉE (*crazed*): Simone is dead, and Marie de Bressolles' life is threatened, and Maurice did all that?

LARTIGUES: Yes! He's our boy, word of honor! Your son's made a promising beginning in file. Good blood always tells.

AIMÉE: Have I gone mad? Maurice, a murderer!

LARTIGUES: Yes, a multiple murderer. But you can save him, and us, too.

AIMÉE (*wildly*): Save you! You! Never!

LARTIGUES: If you don't, your son will go to the Guillotine with us.

AIMÉE: The Guillotine...

LARTIGUES: Yes, the Guillotine. (*A silence*) You'll see him cash in his last chips at La Roquette.[4]

AIMÉE: Ah, no, not that!

LARTIGUES: Then, I can leave France with him tonight and his life will be saved.

AIMÉE: Never! Never! Never! I've got you and I won't let you go!

VERDIER: In that case, dear lady, you won't leave here alive! (*he pulls a revolver from his pocket*)

AIMÉE (*fumbling in her pocket*): Ah! Wretch! (*she goes to fire, but Verdier is faster and fires first*)

(*Aimée screams and falls. Lartigues shoots her, too. They hear rapping at the back*)

LARTIGUES: The bitch! She's brought the Police with her! Get the keys to the garden! We'll go through the Dubief grounds.

VERDIER (*looking out through the window*) There's no one there.

LARTIGUES: We'll escape that way!

(*They rush out to the right*)

AIMÉE (*rising*): Are they actually going to escape me?

CADET (*outside*): Madame Joubert! Madame Joubert!

AIMÉE: Help me! Help me!

(*The door breaks down, Cadet, Galoubert and La Grenouille enter*)

---

[4] Prison where executions were conducted.

CADET (seeing Aimée): Ah!

LA GRENOUILLE The Boss! All that blood! She's wounded bad!

AIMÉE: Never mind me! Go after them!

GALOUBERT: Where?

AIMÉE: Through the Workshop next door. Go! Go!

LA GRENOUILLE: I'll go fetch a doctor!

CADET: Ah, damn it! Damn it!

(*They leave*)

AIMÉE: If they succeed in escaping I'll die without my revenge and Maurice will commit more crimes... No! It mustn't be! (*with growing energy*) Come on, woman, back on your feet! I must have strength... What one wants, one can do... On your feet, come on, on your feet! (*she manages to stand up*) He's at the De Bressolles' Mansion. That's where I'll find him. (*shivering*) Ah, come on, do your duty! (*she staggers, takes a few steps, and stops*) Ah, one can do nothing against death. I can't! I can't! (*she falls down, exhausted*)

(*After a while, the door at the left opens and Maurice, pale, overwrought, enters. He doesn't notice Aimée at first, but as he speaks, she seems to revive*)

MAURICE: What a scandal! Ten o'clock and my mother never showed up. I was forced to leave to see what might have delayed her. Everything was locked up at her place. Verdier and Théroux were supposed to wait for me here. Why aren't they? (*lighting a candle with his back still turned to Aimée, then he notices the disorder in his papers*) What's this? Drawers pulled open... This place has been searched. Who's stolen my papers? It cannot be Verdier or Théroux. Who can it be?

AIMÉE (*suddenly standing up before him*): It was me!

MAURICE (terrified) : You!

AIMÉE: Shot by Pierre Lartigues—your father.

MAURICE: Pierre Lartigues is my father?

AIMÉE: And by Verdier!

MAURICE: So you caught us!

AIMÉE: Yes. You are lost.

MAURICE: Then all I can do is flee.

AIMÉE: Flee! Do you believe that I would allow you to flee, to escape, to commit other crimes? So long as I have a breath left, never! I'm going to die here, but you will die like me!

MAURICE: Die!

AIMÉE: It's the only way for you to escape the shame of the guillotine! (*She gives him her revolver*)

MAURICE: Oh, no, no, no!

AIMÉE: Ah, monster! You were cowardly enough to kill, but you lack the courage to die!

MAURICE: Mother, I've got to flee!

AIMÉE: I said: Never!

MAURICE (*rushing towards her*) Let me pass!

AIMÉE: Shot me then! Dare to commit one last crime. Kill your mother! Finish me off =!

MAURICE (*recoiling*): Ah, my God! You offer me a gun! You, my mother! Can you have either mercy or forgiveness?

AIMÉE (furious): Toward a child like you, a mother can show no forgiveness!

MAURICE: Ah!

(*confused voices outside*)

AIMÉE: Listen! The Police are coming! You are lost. I don't want my son to be guillotined. End it now—or I'll do it for you!

MAURICE (*after a terrible struggle with himself, he takes the revolver*): You're right, Mother! I gambled and I lost. Now I have to pay up!

(*He blows his brains out. Aimée staggers, but hides the body*)

VOICES: This way! This way!

(*Commissioner Masse enters, followed by two policemen holding Lartigues and Verdier in handcuffs, followed by Magistrate Paul de Gibray, Cadet, Galoubert and La Grenouille, all excited*)

LA GRENOUILLE (*to Verdier*): I'm only a woman, but I've got a strong hand, my lad.
MASSE (*going to Aimée, who manages to stand up by a prodigious effort of will*): The Cat's Eye is wounded!
AIMÉE (*pulls a paper from her pocket and gives it to Paul*): Monsieur, read this. Read it at once. It's the will of Arnould d'Harville. It explains everything.

(*Paul takes the paper and reads*)

VERDIER: Rats!
LARTIGUES: Damn it!
CADET: Shut your gob!
LA GRENOUILLE: Or I'll twist your neck!
PAUL (*after having read it*): I understand now. It's for that inheritance that they killed Simone—my daughter!
AIMÉE: Your daughter!
PAUL: And it's for that same inheritance that one of them was going to marry Marie Bressolles. The infamy!

(*Count Yvan Samoiloff and Baron de Landelly enter*)

LANDELLY (*to Cadet*): Monumental! By my word! Monumental!
PAUL: The infamy!
AIMÉE: Monsieur  de Gibray, Commissioner, I promised to deliver Pierre Lartigues and Verdier to you...
YVAN: Pierre Lartigues!
AIMÉE: ...I have kept my word. There they are!
VERDIER: There are only two of us here, but there ought to be a third one. Ask Madame where that other is.
AIMÉE (*staggering, hiding the body of her son*): There is no

other…. (*she falls to her knees; the truth is revealed at last*)
ALL: Ah!
LARTIGUES: Maurice!
AIMÉE: Maurice, my son! Goodbye! (*she supports his head, embracing him, then she dies*)
PAUL: Poor mother!
GALOUBERT: Have kids!
LA GRENOUILLE: Like that one? Don't need 'em!

CURTAIN

Le Medecin des Folles, *here translated as* The Madwoman of
Melun, *was a play first performed at the Theater of the
Ambigu-Comique in Paris in 1891. It is based upon an epon-
ymous* feuilleton *collected and published in two volumes by E.
Dentu in 1879 (Volume 2 was entitled* L'Hôtel du Grand Cerf
[The Great Stag Hotel]).

# THE MADWOMAN OF MELUN
*by Xavier de Montépin & Jules Dornay.*

## CHARACTERS
*in order of appearance*

MADAME LORIOL, proprietor of the Great Stag Hotel
ROSE, a waitress at the Great Stag Hotel
ELISE, a second waitress
TOINETTE, a third waitress
ETIENNE, the sommelier
SORLIN, a customer
LAMBERT, another customer
MAURICE DELARIVIÈRE, a wealthy banker
JEANNE, Maurice's mistress
EDMÉE DELARIVIÈRE, their daughter
DOCTOR GEORGES VERNIER, a local MD
CLAUDE MARTEAU, a former sailor
SPIGOT, his sidekick, a stutterer
FABRICE LECLERC, Maurice's nephew
RENÉ JANCELYN, Fabrice's secretary
RAOUL DE LANGEAIS, a friend of Fabrice
GABRIEL D'AUTUN, another friend of Fabrice
ADÈLE DE CIVRAC, another friend of Fabrice
MATHILDE LONGJUMEAU, another friend of Fabrice
PAUL MOUGIN, another friend of Fabrice
PAULA BALTUS, Frédéric Baltus' sister

PIERRE, a vagrant convicted of the murder of Frédéric Baltus and about to be executed

THE WARDEN of the Melun Jail

THE PUBLIC PROSECUTOR of the Tribunal of Melun

FATHER VINCENT, a priest

THE PUBLIC EXECUTIONER

DOCTOR FRANZ RITTNER, an alienist and the proprietor of the Melun Asylum

DOCTOR HERMAN SCHULTZ, a doctor at the Asylum

MARCEL, the Chief Orderly at the Asylum

LOUISE, the Chief Nurse at the Asylum

JACQUES LEFEBVRE, an investor

PAULINE LEFEBVRE, his wife

M. LEHARDY, a boat builder

LITTLE PIERRE, a 13 year-old boy who assists him

MADAME MARIE TALLANDIER, his mother

MARIETTE, Doctor Vernier's maid

DOCTOR VULPIAN, a distinguished professor of medicine

CUSTOMERS OF THE HOTEL, GUARDS AT THE JAIL, A COURT CLERK, ORDERLIES AT THE ASYLUM, etc.

# *ACT I*
## *SCENE I*

The interior of the Great Stag Hotel located in Melun, just outside Paris. There is a bar on the left, restaurant tables in the middle, doors leading outside, to the kitchens, and to the reception, and a mezzanine accessible through a staircase. It all looks plush and comfortable.

AT RISE, the proprietor, Madame Loriol, is instructing her waitresses to attend the various customers sitting at the tables ort at the bar.

MADAME LORIOL: Rib steak to Number 1, rare. Fish to Number 2, with lots of onions. Ribs to Number 4... Come on, ladies! Look sharp!
ROSE: Going! Going!

(*she leaves to go to the kitchen*)

FIRST CUSTOMER (*at the bar*): A beer!
ELISE: Coming!
MADAME LORIOL: I don't know where to turn. I'm exhausted!
SORLIN (*at a table*): It's like complaining that the bride is too beautiful, Madame Loriol. Business is booming!
MADAME LORIOL: Yes, but what a lot of work!

(*Maurice Delarivière is visible on the balcony of the mezzanine; he seems impatient.*

(*Elise leaves to go to the reception.*

103

(*Rose returns from the kitchen with a plate, which she serves to Sorlin*)

ROSE: Here's the fish, Monsieur.

(*Etienne the sommelier serves him wine. Elise returns from the reception*)

ELISE: Madame, more people are coming asking if there are any windows free?
MADAME LORIOL: All our windows are taken.
ELISE: But they want them. They'll pay whatever price you demand.
MADAME LORIOL: I told you, girl, there aren't any more windows available. All are rented out.

(*Maurice disappears from the balcony*)

SORLIN: Hey, I understand! It's not everyday that one has an opportunity to see a public execution in Melun. Today, June 19, 1872 ,will go down in the annals of the city.
LAMBERT (*from another table*): The head of the condemned will fall tomorrow morning. I understand why they are fighting over your windows.
SORLIN: For sure!

(*René Jancelyn, sitting at yet another table, listens without saying a word. From time to time, he looks at his watch on the sly, and appears uneasy*)

FIRST CUSTOMER: Another beer!
SECOND CUSTOMER: A soda!
THIRD CUSTOMER: A pint!
MADAME LORIOL: Elise, Rose, Etienne! Serve, will you?
ELISE, ETIENNE, ROSE: Coming!

MADAME LORIOL: The loafers! And where is Toinette? I sent her to find Doctor Vernier. She's loafing too, for sure, instead of coming back.

SORLIN: You've got somebody sick here?

MADAME LORIOL: Yes, a lady traveling with her husband who took ill on the train, and couldn't go on to Paris.

(*Toinette enters, followed by Doctor Vernier*)

TOINETTE: Madame, here's Doctor Vernier.

VERNIER: Bonjour, Madame Loriol!

MADAME LORIOL: Bonjour, doctor.

VERNIER: Toinette told me it's about a lady?

MADAME LORIOL: Yes. She's very ill. Her husband seems quite worried.

VERNIER: What floor?

MADAME LORIOL: On the mezzanine. Toinette will show you.

FOURTH CUSTOMER: Where's my dessert?

SORLIN: Rose, my coffee!

ROSE: Coming!

(*Customers come and go. Claude Marteau, dressed as a sailor with a beret, and Spigot, enter*)

CLAUDE (*military bow*): Madame Loriol and everyone, hello

MADAME LORIOL: Ah, it's you Claude.

CLAUDE: Claude Marteau, for the ladies!

MADAME LORIOL: With your inseparable sidekick.

SPIGOT (*stuttering*): Sp-sp-spigot at your service!

CLAUDE: Yes, Spigot. His only fault is that he murders the language.

SPIGOT: It's not-not-not my-my…

CLAUDE: It's not your Daddy's fault! It's you!

SPIGOT: …fault!

CLAUDE: Do you need some fish, Boss-Lady?

MADAME LORIOL: Yes. I was waiting for you. What have you got?

CLAUDE: Lots. Good soles.

MADAME LORIOL: Well, take it all to the kitchen.

(They leave through the kitchen door.

(*A group of young men and women led by Fabrice Leclerc and Raoul de Langeais come in from the garden and everyone looks at them with curiosity; the party includes Gabriel d'Autun, Paul Mougin, Adèle de Civrac and Mathilde Longjumeau*)

MADAME LORIOL(*going to Fabrice*): Bonjour, Monsieur Leclerc. I received your telegram. I was expecting you.

FABRICE: Here I am, Madame Loriol. And as you can see, I'm not alone!

RAOUL: We're the Company of Fools!

MADAME LORIOL: Welcome all.

(*she arranges chairs at a round table so the women can sit*)

SORLIN: Flabbergasting!

LAMBERT: But sexy.

GABRIEL (*looking around*): Why, this is a nice place.

ADÈLE: It's filthy.

(*the women sit down*)

MADAME LORIOL: It's been a long while since we've seen you, Monsieur Fabrice. Forty-five days!

FABRICE: What a memory!

MADAME LORIOL: You stayed here the very same day they condemned the murderer or Monsieur Baltus.

FABRICE: My word, you're right.

106

MADAME LORIOL: And you can boast of having followed that trial everyday at the court house.

RENÉ (*aside*): That was the wrong verdict.

FABRICE: That trial interested me. That's why I've rented windows on the second floor. To be present at the end of that drama.

MADAME LORIOL: Those rooms have a great view.

FABRICE: Thank you, Madame Loriol.

ADÈLE: When will the execution will take place?

MADAME LORIOL: Tomorrow morning, at daybreak.

GABRIEL: So we can be present for this little party?

FABRICE: You'd do just as well to skip it.

ADÈLE (*drawling*): Why's that, darling?

MATHILDE: Haven't we the right to be curious?

FABRICE: When it's a matter of a bloody spectacle, curiosity is really cruelty.

GABRIEL: You are only a poseur, old boy. Why should women be forbidden what men allow themselves?

RAOUL: Because women are weak and sensitive things.

PAUL: While we are made of sterner stuff, my sweet.

RAOUL: And we have nerves of steel.

GABRIEL: Are you finished? If they said that you'd be the star of that party tomorrow, maybe I'd come to watch it. Just to see your nerves of steel.

RAOUL: I feel bad about it.

ADÈLE: Raoul's got no head.

GABRIEL: Only to tie his tie.

FABRICE: Anyway, the ladies are here now.

ADÈLE: It would have been stupid to miss such an opportunity.

SORLIN (*having finished his meal*): Ah, these women disgust me!

LAMBERT: Me, too.

GABRIEL: Say, is this all there is to drink? No aperitifs?
FABRICE: Waiter! Serve these ladies absinthes.
ADÈLE: Yes, I'll have an absinthe!
MADAME LORIOL: Etienne, serve the ladies!

(*Meanwhile, Fabrice glances around and notices René Jancelyn, who gestures, Fabrice approaches him*)

RENÉ: Hum! Hum!
FABRICE: Jancelyn.
RENÉ: I'm here.
FABRICE: Fine.

MADAME LORIOL (*to the company*): Are you ready to order?
ADÈLE (*to Fabrice*): How is the food here?
FABRICE: Excellent. Please serve us your specials, Madame Loriol.
MADAME LORIOL: I'll tell the chef.
ADÈLE: Before that, Madame, can you tell us exactly who is going to be executed tomorrow?
ALL: Ah yes! Please do.

(*Etienne serves the aperitifs*)

MADAME LORIOL: You really should ask Monsieur Fabrice. He knows the case much better than I.

(*she leaves to go to the kitchen; they all drink the absinthe as they speak*)

GABRIEL: So, Fabrice, we're waiting!
MATHILDE: Yes! Give us details about the condemned man!
ADÈLE His story, darling.
FABRICE (*moodily*): It's a tragic tale that I don't like to tell.
ADÈLE: But we want to hear it!
GABRIEL: Gives us a good fright!

RAOUL: You're going to laugh.

ALL: The story!

RAOUL (*to Fabrice*): You've got to give in, old boy.

FABRICE (*nervously*): OK! You asked for it! So on the banks of the Seine by the highway going from Melun to Seine-Port, there was the Villa Baltus, inhabited eight months a year by Frédéric Baltus and his sister Paula...

GABRIEL (sipping her absinth): Old folks?

FABRICE: No, quite young. Frédéric was rich, and a bit of a rake, always going to Paris to part. On December 3, the gardener found a body near the Villa, half buried in snow...

GABRIEL: His master's body?

FABRICE: Yes. He'd been shot three times.

ADÈLE: What was the motive for the crime?

FABRICE: Theft. His wallet was missing.

GABRIEL: And the murderer?

FABRICE: He was nowhere to be found, naturally. But two days later, a vagabond, a sort of beggar with a paralyzed right arm, was stupid enough to give a bartender a fifty-franc note pulled from a wallet pierced by a bullet and stained with blood.

GABRIEL: Now there's an idiot!

FABRICE: The man was arrested and searched. In his pocket, they found Frédéric Baltus' wallet.

ADÈLE: All that remained for him to do was confess.

FABRICE: That's what he didn't do. He has insisted up to this moment that he is innocent.

ADÈLE: How does he explain being in possession of that wallet?

(*Madame Loriol returns and listens*)

FABRICE: Rather stupidly. He claimed it was given to him by a stranger whom he'd met in the woods when he asked him for charity.

MADAME LORIOL: A gift of 15,000 francs! Because that's what Monsieur Baltus had in his wallet! That was proven.

*(Claude and Spigot come out of the kitchen and start listening too)*

FABRICE: They tried to make him understand that his explanation was absurd. Compromising him even. But that was a waste of time. He obstinately persisted with it. "It was charity," he said. "I am not guilty of any murder."
ADÈLE: And who was this wretch?
FABRICE: To all questions, he replied, "I am without family. My name is Pierre. I have no other name."
GABRIEL: Now there's a bull-headed man!
MATHILDE: And what's more, pretending to be innocent!
ADÈLE: But what if he isn't guilty?
CLAUDE *(a bit drunk)*: as far as I'm concerned, I'd swear he's not.

*(General reaction of surprise. René Jancelyn shivers and rises)*

ALL: Who are you?
CLAUDE: I'm Claude Marteau!
GABRIEL: Well, what's this you're telling us, Claude Marteau? According to you, the murderer whose head is to be chopped off tomorrow morning would be innocent?
CLAUDE: Yes!

*(René and Fabrice exchange a look)*

GABRIEL: How do you know?
CLAUDE: I don't, but I sincerely believe it.
GABRIEL: You must have some reasons to do so?
CLAUDE: Yes. Good ones, too.
GABRIEL: Well, then, tell them to us.
FABRICE: Come on! There's no need to weary these ladies with these absurd tales.
ADÈLE: Not at all! We want to hear these tales.

MATHILDE: Yes, yes!

GABRIEL: Tell us, Monsieur Marteau!

CLAUDE: First of all, I must tell you that my nose is often red enough…

SPIGOT: F-from white wine.

GABRIEL: Nothing wrong with that!

CLAUDE: Eight months ago, I was a sailor and watching the comings and goings of a character who owned property on the banks of the Seine. The night of the crime, I met some friends, Spigot here was one of them…

SPIGOT: T-that's…

GABRIEL: Hush! Don't interrupt him!

CLAUDE: The cold was getting to me, so I went back to my cabin, and wrapped myself in my hammock, I snored so loud that I could hear myself.

GABRIEL (*looking at Raoul*): I know someone who snores like that.

RAOUL: Shut up! Please continue, Monsieur!

CLAUDE: If I hadn't been snoring, I'm sure I'd have heard the shots.

ADÈLE: Well, if you saw nothing and heard nothing, why are you telling us this?

CLAUDE: Patience, will you, lady? When I woke up, I went to inspect my boat. I hadn't chained it up, just tied it up with a bit of rope.

GABRIEL: So?

CLAUDE: So, I noticed it wasn't tied the way I tie it.

ADÈLE: Hardly surprising since you were drunk from dawn to dusk.

CLAUDE: Yes, but no matter how drunk I am, my knot is always the same. I can tie it in my sleep.

FABRICE: What does that prove?

CLAUDE: That someone used my boat to cross the Seine while I slept.

FABRICE: A fisherman, no doubt.

CLAUDE: No, it wasn't a fisherman. It snowed that night and when I looked on the banks, there there were the imprints of

111

boots, such as that poor devil who's going to get his head chopped off tomorrow could never afford. Boots like yours. (*points at Fabrice's boots*)

FABRICE: And you conclude?

CLAUDE: I conclude that the real murderer was well-to-do man, and the poor devil whom they arrested and convicted was only his accomplice—his tool—at best. Tomorrow, perhaps, the former will come and see the latter being guillotined, to be quite sure he won't speak.

WOMEN: Brr!

FABRICE: That's all?

CLAUDE: No.

FABRICE: There's more?

CLAUDE: Yes. I found something.

FABRICE (*nervous*): What was it?

CLAUDE (*looking at him*): Something which might actually be evidence.

FABRICE (*nervous*): Evidence?

(*René comes closer*)

CLAUDE: But I've said enough.

FABRICE: Not at all! Speak, will you!

(*Claude remains silent*)

FABRICE: Meaning, you found nothing! You're lying! You started a story you don't know how to finish.

CLAUDE: If you say so.

FABRICE: If you'd discovered something, regardless of how important it was, you would have reported it to the police.

CLAUDE: Reported it? You must be joking! Am I a policeman? Is it my job to go and report my finds to the police? If they'd asked me, for sure, I'd have told them. But go to them on my own, no.

ADÈLE: What about the condemned man?

CLAUDE: So much the worse for him. It's his job to defend himself.

112

SPIGOT: As-as b-best he c-can.
CLAUDE: Till tomorrow, Madame Loriol. Good night everybody. Come on, Spigot!

(*They leave*)

RENÉ (*low, to Fabrice*): Now there's a dangerous man.
FABRICE (*low*): We'll see.
RENÉ (*to Rose*): A glass of gin, if you please, Mademoiselle?
ROSE: Coming!

(*René returns to his table and sits down*)

FABRICE (*to Madame Loriol*): Very original, that lad. Is he an old sailor?
MADAME LORIOL: He was convicted once, himself.
FABRICE: Really? Ah, the devil!
MADAME LORIOL: Oh, not for any big crime. Stealing a loaf of bread.
FABRICE: For a loaf of bread!
MADAME LORIOL: Yes. Maritime law is harsh. He was placed under police surveillance. But everybody loves him here despite his conviction.

(*Toinette enters from the kitchen*)

TOINETTE: The ladies and gentlemen are served—in the garden.
GABRIEL: That tale of murder made a pit in my stomach.
MATHILDE: Me, too.
ADÈLE: God! How common can you be!
GABRIEL (*to Adele*): Come on, poseur, let's go.

(*The party moves to the garden. Fabrice follows, but stops at the sight of a veiled woman, Paula Baltus, who enters without seeing him*)

MADAME LORIOL: Ah, Madame Baltus!

(*Fabrice and René shiver.*)

FABRICE: Madame Baltus!
PAULA: You've reserved a window for me, Madame?
MADAME LORIOL: Yes, Madame.
PAULA: Can you take me there?
MADAME LORIOL: Certainly, Madame. Please follow me.

(*Madame Loriol and Paula Baltus leave through the reception*)

FABRICE: What's she here for?
RENÉ (*to Fabrice*): That's Frédéric Baltus' sister!
FABRICE: Keep a cool head, René! We'll talk tonight.

(*Doctor Vernier returns from the mezzanine, accompanied by Maurice Delarivière*)

MAURICE: So, my dear Doctor, I have no need to worry about my lady friend's health?
VERNIER: Jeanne is very nervous, Monsieur. Fatigue is the sole cause of that malaise which scared you so much. Still, you were right to stop here. Traveling further would certainly have aggravated her condition.
MAURICE: The arrival of our daughter, who she hasn't seen in a long while, doesn't seem to you as it might be a problem?
VERNIER: Quite the contrary. Happiness is the best of all remedies!
MAURICE: She should be here any moment. You'll come back this evening, won't you, Doctor?
VERNIER: I shall. I might be a bit late, however. I've got a lot of house calls to make, but I promise you, I'll come.
MAURICE: Till this evening then, Doctor.

(*Doctor Vernier leaves; Maurice turns around to return to the mezzanine but suddenly notices Fabrice*)

MAURICE: Fabrice?
FABRICE: Uncle? You're here? I thought you were in New York.
MAURICE: No, I was on my way to Paris.
FABRICE: Why did you stop here?
MAURICE: Jeanne was taken ill on the train. Doctor Vernier just reassured me. You should go and see her.
FABRICE: Why, certainly.

(*A young girl, Edmée Delarivière, enters from the garden*)

MAURICE (*running to her*): My dear child!
EDMÉE: Papa! My dear Papa! Where's Mother?
MAURICE: In her room. You're going to go and kiss her. But first, say hello to your cousin, Fabrice.
EDMÉE (*offering him her hand*): Cousin Fabrice.
FABRICE: Dear Edmée.
EDMÉE: I'm happy to see you both. Papa, let's go and see Mummy.
MAURICE: Come with us, Fabrice.

(They leave)

MADAME LORIOL (*appearing on the mezzanine with Paula Baltus*): You will be staying of this floor.
PAULA: Perfect! From here, I'll see the head of my brother's murderer fall.

CURTAIN

## SCENE II

A suite at the hotel. There a window in that back that gives onto the square.

AT RISE, Jeanne Delarivière is seated on a sofa, Edmée is holding her in her arms. Maurice and Fabrice are seated facing her.


JEANNE: My dear child, I'll never kiss you enough!

EDMÉE: Me too, my dear Mummy!

MAURICE (*to Fabrice*): We haven't seen Edmée for more than two years. So, finally, we decided to come home, but we couldn't come straight away.

FABRICE: Why not?

MAURICE: The affairs of my bank called me to England, Portugal, and Spain.

FABRICE: And my aunt followed you everywhere?

MAURICE: Yes, but she overestimated her strength.

FABRICE: Luckily, you stopped here in time.

MAURICE: Yes, but it gave me a scare.

FABRICE: What are your plans now, Uncle?

MAURICE: As soon as Jeanne is completely recovered, we'll be returning to New York with Edmée.

EDMÉE: Wouldn't it be better for you to stay in France?

MAURICE: What about my bank?

EDMÉE: Sell it!

MAURICE: Easier said than done.

JEANNE: Maybe Edmée has a reason for wanting to stay in France?

FABRICE (*smiling*): That's easy to believe.

EDMÉE (*slightly embarrassed*): No, no, I assure you.

FABRICE: Will you not be going to Paris?

MAURICE: I don't think so. The only two people I needed to see in Paris are you and Jacques Lefebvre. You're here, and he lives nearby at Seine-Port. I don't need to go to Paris.

JEANNE: We've concocted a lot of plans, one of which concerns you.

FABRICE (*astonished*): Me?

JEANNE: Yes. You'll see. Because we think of you, even if you never think of us.

FABRICE: Oh, dear auntie, that; not true!

(*knocking on the door*)

MAURICE: Come in.

(*Doctor Vernier opens and enters*)

MAURICE: Welcome back, doctor.
EDMÉE (*with a cry of surprise*) Ah!
VERNIER (*moved*): Mademoiselle Edmée!
FABRICE: Uh-oh.
MAURICE (*astonished*): You know my daughter?
VERNIER: Indeed I do, but I didn't know her last name.
EDMÉE: I've seen the doctor at the College.
JEANNE: At the College?
VERNIER: The Director called me because one of the students was very sick. She'd suddenly come down with a dangerous fever. It was Mademoiselle Edmée.
EDMÉE (*blushing*): Er, yes.
JEANNE: You cared for my daughter—you saved her!
VERNIER (*uneasy*): Oh, Madame, I wouldn't say…
JEANNE: You have the right to all our gratitude.
FABRICE (*aside*): An idyll at the College. I suspected as much.
VERNIER: And how are *you* feeling, Madame?
JEANNE: Oh, doctor, I'm almost completely well.
VERNIER: You still need sleep. You should be in bed already.
MAURICE (*to Jeanne*): You see.
JEANNE: You're right. I'll go and lie down. We'll see you again tomorrow, won't we?
VERNIER: I'll call every day until you are completely recovered.
JEANNE: Thanks to you, that won't be long, I'm sure, and we'll be able to return to America with our Edmée.

VERNIER (*looking at Edmée who looks sad*): Ah. So you're planning to leave?
MAURICE: As soon as possible.
VERNIER (*repeating dully*): As soon as possible.
JEANNE (*noticing his concern*): Heavens! Until tomorrow, my dear doctor.

(*Doctor Vernier bows. Mother and daughter start to leave*)

JEANNE (*low to Edmée*): You love him, don't you?
EDMÉE: Yes, mother.

(*As they're about to leave, there is a rap on the door. Maurice opens and Claude Marteau appears with a telegram in hand*)

CLAUDE: Ah, sorry if I disturb you, but this is urgent. A telegram came in for Doctor Vernier. I was talking to the cook when it arrived, and Madame Loriol asked me if I wouldn't mind bringing it to you. Here it is. (*handing the telegram to the Doctor; then, noticing Fabrice, he scowls*)

FABRICE: Ah, our expert sailor knows our esteemed doctor.
VERNIER (*after reading*): Ah!
JEANNE: What's wrong, doctor?
MAURICE: Bad news?
VERNIER: Yes, my mother has been taken ill. I must go and see her at once. She lives in Saint-Maur.
JEANNE: Nothing serious, I hope?
VERNIER: I hope so, too, but I can't help feeling uneasy.
JEANNE: You must go.
VERNIER: I'm leaving immediately, but on my return, my first call will be to you.
MAURICE (*shaking his hand*): Go, doctor.
JEANNE: Till tomorrow.

(*Georges Vernier bows. Claude watches Fabrice suspiciously and leaves with the doctor.*)

118

EDMÉE: Poor Georges!
JEANNE: Come, my dear.

(*the women leave*)

MAURICE: Now that we're alone, I'm going to tell you about the plan your aunt alluded to just now. I couldn't do it in the presence of my daughter.
FABRICE: I'm all ears, uncle.
MAURICE: You know that Jeanne is not yet my wife, and that consequently Edmée is only our natural child.
FABRICE: You weren't free. You're married.
MAURICE: Now, I am free.
FABRICE: Really?
MAURICE: Yes! The wretched woman who left me twenty years ago just died. And the first use of my freedom will be to marry Jeanne.
FABRICE: Excellent!
MAURICE: So you approve?
FABRICE: Why wouldn't I?
MAURICE: You might think that the marriage would be prejudicial to you.
FABRICE: To me? But you don't owe me anything, my dear uncle.
MAURICE: I don't agree. You're my sister's only son, and you know that I've always loved you. I'm worth about twelve million dollars.
FABRICE (*shaking*): Twelve million dollars!
MAURICE (*playing with a pen*): I will divide my fortune into three shares. One will go for you. A million dollars. (*he drops the pen and picks it up*) It will soon be at your disposal if you accept the offer I'm going to make you.
FABRICE: Speak, dear uncle.
MAURICE: I would like to leave my bank in the hands of someone whose intelligence and aptitude I trust. Would you like to be that someone?

119

FABRICE: Such a gesture…

MAURICE: Will you come with us to New York? I'll set you up and bring you up to speed.

FABRICE: Yes, I would love to. You're the best of uncles!

MAURICE: Then you accept?

FABRICE: With enthusiasm!

MAURICE: You won't regret Paris and its pleasures?

FABRICE: I won't regret a thing!

MAURICE: Then, it's agreed. We all four will leave for New York... You cannot leave Melun tonight?

FABRICE: No, I came with a few friends desirous to watch the public execution tomorrow.

MAURICE: Ah, yes. I didn't mention it to Jeanne. I was afraid of upsetting her needlessly.

FABRICE: You did the right thing.

MAURICE: Then we'll talk again tomorrow.

FABRICE: I'm at your disposal, uncle.

MAURICE: Then until tomorrow morning, my dear child.

FABRICE: Till tomorrow. (*they shake hands*)

FABRICE (*as he goes, aside*): It's not one million I need, it's all twelve!

(*he leaves*)

CURTAIN

## SCENE III

Pierre's cell at the Melun Jail. Cot, table, chairs.

AT RISE, Pierre is stretched out on a cot, his mutilated arm on his breast. He is in a deep sleep. A Guard reads a book by the light of a lamp on the table.

FIRST GUARD (*looking up from his book at Pierre*): To be able to sleep so near to death!

(*The cell door opens and the Warden comes in, accompanied by the Public Prosecutor, his Clerk, Father Vincent, a Priest, and two more Guards. The Warden makes a sign. The First Guard goes to Pierre and touches him on the shoulder.*)

FIRST GUARD: Get up.

PIERRE (*getting up and seeing the newcomers, remaining very calm*): Ah, it's for this morning, right?

WARDEN: Your appeal has been rejected.

PIERRE: I refused to file one. My lawyer insisted.

WARDEN: The President didn't grant your request for mercy.

PIERRE: I asked for nothing, I hoped for nothing. Do what you must.

WARDEN: Be brave.

PIERRE: I've never shown weakness before.

PROSECUTOR: You have nothing more to reveal?

PIERRE: I've said everything I had to say. I'm innocent! They didn't believe me. It's my misfortune.

PROSECUTOR: You've never spoken frankly.

PIERRE: I've told you the truth, and nothing but.

PROSECUTOR: But I feel you have a secret that you plan to take to the grave with you.

PIERRE: No, I have no secret.

PROSECUTOR: The obstinacy with which you hid your identity doomed your cause.

PIERRE: As I aid, it's my misfortune.

PROSECUTOR: Why won't you tell us your name?

PIERRE: My name's Pierre, that's all you need to know.

WARDEN: Do you have any family?

PIERRE: No.

WARDEN: No dear one whose thought might fill your heart at this moment?

PIERRE: No one.

WARDEN: A wife? Children, perhaps?

PIERRE (*with an emotion he cannot completely control*): A wife! Children! No... No, I'm completely alone in the world. I won't leave it with either a regret or a memory, and no one will take the trouble to ask themselves if the man who's about to be executed was truly guilty, or innocent.

FATHER VINCENT: My son, at the moment of appearing before God, it would be a Christian act to enlighten Justice.

PIERRE: I have nothing to say to Justice, but I have a favor to ask.

FATHER VINCENT: What is it?

PIERRE: I'd like to talk to you for a moment—without witnesses.

*(Father Vincent gestures and they all leave)*

PIERRE: Father, is the secret of the Confessional absolute?

FATHER VINCENT: Yes, my son. No human power can authorize a priest to reveal the secrets of confession.

PIERRE: Then you will never repeat what I'm going to say to you? Never?

FATHER VINCENT: Never.

PIERRE: You swear it?

FATHER VINCENT: On the body of Christ!

PIERRE (*weeping*): Well, then, yes, I do have a wife, and a child—a dear little boy. I have a name. And if I didn't reveal it, it's because I don't want it to be covered with shame. Yet, I am innocent—truly. But it is impossible to prove it. All the evidence is against me. It's incredible, but it's true. I swear it on Christ. When the stranger who gave me the wallet had left, and I found the 15,000 francs in it, I thought of my wife and child. I put the bank notes in an envelope and mailed it to her, with a note saying that she would never see me again. She won't. Then, after I mailed my letter, I went to an inn to get food. I hadn't eaten in two days. Now you understand why I didn't reveal my name. They would have sought out my wife. She would have been forced to return the money, and I would still be right where I am, unable to prove my innocence. Ah, he was clever, giving me the product of his crime, and sending me to the scaffold in his stead! Father, do you believe me?

FATHER VINCENT (*with emotion*): Yes, I do believe you, my son. I believe you.

PIERRE: That's a consolation—really.

FATHER VINCENT: Tell me the name of your wife and son. I will find them and tell them everything.

PIERRE: Oh, no, no. Not that. I don't want for them to know how I died.

FATHER VINCENT: The secret of the confessional is inviolable. Let me bring your wife your final goodbye.

PIERRE: No, I refuse.

FATHER VINCENT: At least, let me tell them that you died an innocent man.

PIERRE: You know it. If you believe it, that's enough for me. Bless me, father.

FATHER VINCENT: My son, I absolve you and I bless you.

PIERRE (*rising*): I'm ready.

(*The Priest goes to the door and the others return, followed by the Executioner who enters last*)

PIERRE (*seeing the executioner*):   Ah, the last *toilette*, right? Let's go.

(*he leaves, escorted*)

CURTAIN

## *SCENE IV*

Same as Scene II, except that hammering noises can be heard outside. It's night.

AR RISE, Jeanne enters, opening her door.

JEANNE: What's all this noise? It's keeping me from getting any sleep. Why such hammering at this time of night? (*taking a few steps, listening*) What's going on outside? (*going to*

123

*window and pulling back the curtain. The noise of hammering increases*) A crowd in the square? Guards?
GUARD (*outside*) Company, halt!
JEANNE: Police. Carpenters erecting a… Ah, it's a scaffold!

(*Edmée enters and goes to her mother*)

EDMÉE: What's going on, mother? I heard noises.
JEANNE: They're erecting a scaffold on the square outside. Someone's going to be executed, I think.

(*The hammer blows stop. Dawn breaks. The executioner can be seen mounting the scaffold. The Guards form in ranks*)

JEANNE: Here comes the carriage. (*pause*) It's a man accompanied by a priest. I cannot see his features. (*upset*) I don't want to see any more. I don't want to look. But I cannot take my eyes off him.

(*Pierre, Father Vincent and the Executioner are on the platform*)

JEANNE: My God! My God! That face! (*she leans out the widow*)
PIERRE (*on the scaffold*): I am dying innocent!
JEANNE (*delirious*): That voice! It's him! (*she screams*)

(*The blade descends. Jeanne collapses. Edmée runs to her mother*)

CURTAIN

# ACT II

## SCENE V

A couple of days later. Doctor Franz Rittner's surgery at the Melun Asylum. He is seated behind his desk. Doctor Herman Schultz, Marcel, the Chief Orderly, and Louise, the Chief Nurse, stand before him.

RITTNER: What news this morning?

SCHULTZ: Number 8 passed away.

RITTNER (*writing*): Noted. How about the madwoman in number 2?

SCHULTZ: She has no more than two or three days to live.

RITTNER (*writing*): Noted. Is that all?

SCHULTZ: That's all on my watch.

RITTNER (*to First Orderly*): What about you, Monsieur Marcel?

MARCEL: The madwoman in number 22 broke the stool in her cell.

RITTNER: Put her in a straight jacket.

MARCEL: also, the repairs to the isolation ward have been completed.

RITTNER: I'll go inspect them. Is that all?

MARCEL: Yes.

LOUISE: Doctor, number 19 demands an increased amount of food. She says she's starving. She makes a hellish amount of noise.

RITTNER: Doctor Schultz, you will place the recalcitrant patient on a diet. If she continues to scream, the straight jacket. If the straight jacket has no effect, cold showers. Perhaps that will calm her down. Is that all, Nurse Louise?

LOUISE: Yes.

(*An Orderly enters holding a package*)

ORDERLY: Doctor, there's a package for you. (*handing it*)
RITTNER: I know what this is. (he places the package on his desk) Fine. I'll do an inspection at 4 o'clock.

(*all leave, except Doctor Schultz*)

RITTNER: Ah, Schultz…
SCHULTZ: Doctor?
RITTNER: Two words with you, if you please. I've decided to sell this Asylum.
SCHULTZ: Really? You'd be giving away a fortune.
RITTNER: I'm bored here. (*pointing to the package*) I've had a prospectus printed up. The place should sell easily. Don't worry about your position. My successor will keep you on.
SCHULTZ: Thank you, Doctor.
RITTNER: You may go now.

(*Schultz leaves*)

RITTNER (*taking a pen and calculating as he writes*): Number 8 died leaving his nephew a million, for which I'll receive 15% for the good care I've taken of the deceased. In three or four days, Number 2 will pass away too, generating a smaller amount, but nonetheless substantial. What I can get for the sale of this place will be, let's see, one million, one hundred ninety thousand francs, and my business partners, Fabrice Leclerc and René Jancelyn, won't be able to take their cut out of it because they won't know of its existence. Despite all my advice, they're just dumb. They'll end by compromising me more than I am already.

(*the electric bell rings; an Orderly enters*)

ORDERLY: Monsieur René Jancelyn is here to see you, Doctor.
RITTNER: Show him in.

(*René Jancelyn enters*)

RENÉ: Good afternoon, my friend. I was afraid I might not find you here.

RITTNER: I was expecting you.

RENÉ: I barely had time to change clothes.

RITTNER: So what happened yesterday? Do we have anything to fear?

RENÉ: No. The Guillotine did its work.

RITTNER: Did he say anything before dying?

RENÉ (*laughing*): He said: "I am innocent!"

RITTNER: What about his name?

RENÉ: Still unknown.

RITTNER: I'll breathe easier. Fabrice saved us from the galleys by risking the scaffold. So be it. But it was a great gamble. Are we beyond suspicion?

RENÉ: No, not yet.

RITTNER: What? Are there complications?

RITTNER: Yes. An old sailor who lives near Melun claims to have more evidence about the murder of Frédéric Baltus.

RITTNER: What has he found?

RENÉ: We don't know exactly. Clues.

RITTNER: What clues?

RENÉ: Fabrice supposes that it's a handkerchief bearing his coat of arms and monogram that fell from his pocket after he'd used it to wipe off the handle of the gun which he clumsily left near the body.

RITTNER: Ah.

RENÉ: There were no prints on the revolver. That was established in court.

RITTNER: And that sailor hasn't informed the police of his discovery?

RENÉ: No, he's afraid of the police.

RITTNER: Then does it really matter? A man was convicted and executed for that crime. It's over.

RENÉ: Perhaps.

RITTNER: What? Is there more?

RENÉ: Fabrice met his uncle last night.

RITTNER: So?

RENE: He told me that his uncle's lady-friend went mad seeing the presumed assassin just before he was guillotined.

RITTNER: She went mad from seeing a man being executed... It could be a normal reaction for a woman...

RENÉ: No. Fabrice thinks there's some connection between her and the deceased.

RITTNER: Hm. That might explain why he obstinately refused to reveal his name. It could lead to a new inquest—which might in turn lead to that old sailor you mentioned. It might be wise to stop her from recovering her faculties.

RENÉ: That's possible, right?

RITTNER: That would be easy if I had her here. In my hospital, I can do anything I want.

RENÉ: Good, because she'll be here shortly.

RITTNER: Are you speaking seriously?

RENÉ: Yes. Fabrice convinced his uncle of the need to send his friend to a sanatorium, and naturally, he chose yours.

RITTNER: I see! Our Fabrice intends to kill two birds with one stone!

(*knocking at the door*)

RENÉ: That might be them, in fact.

RITTNER (*pointing to a side door*): Leave through that door, so that no one will recognize you.

(*René leaves. More knocking. The Orderly enters*)

ORDERLY: Doctor, there are two gentlemen, accompanying a lady and a young woman, who're asking to speak to you.

RITTNER: Show them in.

(*The Order leaves. Jeanne enters, supported by Edmée. Maurice Delarivière, very somber, and Fabrice follow*)

128

FABRICE (*low to Rittner*): You've been briefed?

RITTNER: Yes. One hundred thousand francs.

FABRICE: You'll have them tomorrow.

RITTNER (*to Maurice*): To what do I owe the honor of this visit, Monsieur?

MAURICE: A very sad reason, Doctor.

FABRICE: We've been cruelly struck. (*pointing to Jeanne, silent, haggard*) See.

EDMÉE: My poor mother appears to have suffered from a great shock. But surely you can make her better, can't you, doctor?

RITTNER: I'll do all I can, Mademoiselle.

FABRICE: The excellent reputation of your sanitarium convinced my uncle to come to you. We've come to ask you to care for someone who is very dear to us.

MAURICE: Yes, very dear.

EDMÉE: Cure my mother, Doctor, and I will bless you.

RITTNER: Do you have all the necessary papers?

MAURICE (*presenting papers*): A declaration signed by two doctors in Melun.

RITTNER (*perusing the papers with satisfaction*): It's all in order. (*placing them on the desk*)

EDMÉE (*to Jeanne*): Mother! Mother! Don't you recognize us? Say something!

(*Jeanne stares and remains motionless*)

RITTNER (*to Edmée*): Excuse me, Mademoiselle... I need you to step away.

(*Edmée obeys, weeping. Doctor Rittner places his hand on Jeanne's head. Jeanne looks at him but says nothing*)

RITTNER (*to Maurice*): How long has she been like this?

MAURICE: For the last week more or less.

RITTNER: Before that, were there any symptoms?

MAURICE: None.

RITTNER: Was there something that might have foreshadowed this sudden onset of manic depression?

MAURICE: No, Doctor.

RITTNER: Are you certain? Nothing happened in her life to disturb her sanity?

FABRICE: Well, yesterday, she found herself the unwilling witness of a public execution.

RITTNER: I see. That could indeed have produced such results…

(*Jeanne suddenly screams and becomes agitated; everyone looks at her in horror*)

RITTNER: We must proceed with caution.

JEANNE (*wildly*): Listen, listen…. What's that noise?

MAURICE: Doctor, do something!

RITTNER: Silence!

JEANNE (*wildly*): What is that hammering? What are those lights? It's a guillotine! They're building a guillotine!

EDMÉE (*begging*): Mother!

RITTNER: Silence!

JEANNE: Look! Listen! A carriage is coming... The man is getting out... He's mounting the scaffold... My God! My God! If it were him! If it were him!

RITTNER (*imperious*); Silence!

JEANNE: If it were him! If it were him!

RITTNER: Silence, all! Let her speak! I must insist!

JEANNE (*forcefully*): He's innocent. Don't kill him. Ah, the Executioner. I'll snatch you away from him! (*rushing to Edmée*)

EDMÉE: Mother!

JEANNE (*grabbing Edmée by the throat*): You won't escape me!

EDMÉE: Ah!

MAURICE: Edmée!

RITTNER (*seizing Jeanne's arm and forcing her down*): I have her. Let me handle her.

EDMÉE: My God! My God!

(*Jeanne, now under Rittner's physical control, collapses on a couch*)

RITTNER: I'm going to take her to the room she'll occupy. Wait for me here, please.

EDMÉE: She's my mother! I want to stay with her!

MAURICE: In a sanitarium? Is it wise?

FABRICE: Doctor, my uncle and I are obliged to leave in a few days for America. We would be happy to have you board my cousin during our absence so that she can can remain close to her mother—if you agree, of course? (*low to Ritter*) Say, yes.

EDMÉE: Please, Doctor, I beg you!

RITTNER: Well, what you are asking me to do is totally contrary to our policies, but I'll make an exception in your case on the condition that you obey all my instructions without questions.

EDMÉE: Thank you, Doctor! I promise absolute obedience! (*goes to her mother*)

RITTNER: I'm going to have a room prepared for you in the same ward that your mother will occupy.

MAURICE (sadly): We must go now. (*goes to Jeanne and hugs her*)

FABRICE (*to Rittner*): On my return, I don't want to find either mother or daughter.

RITTNER: You won't.

C U R T A I N

## SCENE VI

The Gardens of the Villa Lefebvre.

AT RISE, Monsieur Lefebvre is sitting comfortably in a lounge chair reading a newspaper. There is a table and several chairs. His wife, Pauline, sits nearby.

LEFEBVRE (*reading*): Another notary has absconded with his client's funds. Decidedly, I prefer a banker to a notary.

(*The bell rings at the gate, he turns*)

PAULINE: It's Monsieur Delarivière.

(*Maurice Delarivière enters, with Edmée and Fabrice*)

LEFEBVRE: Maurice, my old friend! What a surprise! I am happy to see you again!
MAURICE: My dear Jacques!
PAULINE: And this is Mademoiselle Edmée, I suppose?
MAURICE: Indeed! My daughter!
LEFEBVRE: She is adorable! And here's Fabrice. Bonjour, Fabrice.
FABRICE: Bonjour, Monsieur Lefebvre.
LEFEBVRE: But where is your lovely companion? How is she? Did you leave her in New York?
MAURICE: Er, yes. She was a little ill.
LEFEBVRE: Nothing serious, I hope?
MAURICE: Would have I left if it were?
LEFEBVRE: That's true. (*looking at Edmée*) Why, is this the same young Mademoiselle who used to run around in this very garden only five years ago? And now, you're at an age to be married.
FABRICE: Always the tireless matchmaker, Monsieur Lefebvre!
LEFEBVRE: Watch out, Fabrice. I'll get you, too!
PAULINE: Sit down, will you? Edmée, get rid of your hat. You've come to spend the day with us. (*she does*) That's nice.
MAURICE: Ah, but…

LEFEBVRE: No buts, my friend! We would be crushed if you didn't stay. And Fabrice, I have just the girl for you!
PAULINE: He's mad!
LEFEBVRE: I'm not! You'll meet her this evening.
FABRICE: This evening? You pique my curiosity, Monsieur. No doubt she's a country girl.
LEFEBVRE: A country girl who lives ten miles from Paris. It's a perfect match.
FABRICE: We'll see.
MAURICE: Fabrice is right. We'll see—but on my return.
PAULINE: What? You're leaving already?
MAURICE: In three days, but I'll be back soon. I intend to stay in Paris for good.
PAULINE: Ah, good news!
MAURICE: I've ordered Fabrice to find me some property, giving him carte blanche, and I'd like to open a credit line with your investment house, Jacques.
LEFEBVRE: Of course. Of what amount?
MAURICE: Unlimited.

(*Paula Baltus appears in a smart black dress*)

LEFEBVRE My dear Fabrice, here's my country girl.
PAULINE: Mademoiselle Paula Baltus.
FABRICE (*with a shiver*): Ah.
PAULA: My dear friends… (noticing Fabrice) Ah, Monsieur Leclerc.
FABRICE (*with controlled emotion*): Mademoiselle Baltus
LEFEBVRE (*surprised*): What! You know each other?
FABRICE: Why, certainly.
LEFEBVRE: In that case, let's go and take a walk. My plan appears to have misfired.
PAULA: What plan?
LEFEBVRE: I was counting on you to dazzle him when I introduced you. Now I'm the one who's mystified.

FABRICE: No need to be. I had the honor to be introduced to Mademoiselle Baltus at a gala given by Baroness Brégnac. I've met her several times since.

PAULA: Five times.

FABRICE: Ah, you remember.

PAULA: Yes.

LEFEBVRE: Well, then, so much the better. Now we're cooking!

PAULA: What?

LEFEBVRE: Just an idea I have. Meanwhile, allow me to introduce to you Fabrice's uncle, Monsieur Maurice Delarivière, a banker from New York…

PAULA: I've often heard your name mentioned, Monsieur.

PAULINE: And I have the pleasure to introduce our friend's daughter and Fabrice's cousin, our sweet little Edmée.

LEFEBVRE: Who would make a ravishing maid-of-honor.

PAULA (*uncomfortable, looking at Fabrice*): Monsieur Lefebvre!

LEFEBVRE: I've told you before, I'll take care of finding you a husband.

PAULA: Hum. (*to Maurice*) So you are coming to live in Paris, Monsieur?

MAURICE: Not right away, Mademoiselle. First, I'm obliged to return to New York and dispose of my bank.

PAULA: But you plan to return soon?

MAURICE: As soon as I can.

FABRICE: I will be pressing my uncle, be sure of it.

PAULA: You're going with him?

FABRICE: Yes. I'll be taking over the business.

LEFEBVRE (aside): Excellent!

PAULA: Ah. (*suddenly sad*) Please, excuse me. (*putting her handkerchief to her eyes, embarrassed*) I'm sorry.
(*Silence*)

LEFEBVRE: My dear child, what wouldn't I give to wipe out your sad memories.

PAULA: I'm so sorry. I don't want my sorrow to raise a barrier between the world and me. (*getting a grip on herself*) But don't ask me to forget; that I will never do!

FABRICE: The memory of a beloved mustn't prevent you from thinking about the future.

PAULA: The future. God gives us the future to avenge those taken from us.

LEFEBVRE: But you have been avenged. The murderer paid for his crime with his life.

PAULA: Did he really? Are you so sure?

FABRICE (*worried*): What do you mean?

PAULA: Yes, a man was executed. But what proves that that man was the only person involved?

LEFEBVRE: Why, absolutely everything! The judgment of the court…

PAULA: …Was insufficient. Innocent or guilty, more than one person was involved, and the accomplice is still alive and free.

FABRICE: The crime was very simple and not premeditated.

PAULA: I disagree.

FABRICE: But they took his wallet.

PAULA: Not for the money it contained.

LEFEBVRE: In that case, what became of the 15,000 francs that I gave to your brother only a few hours before he was murdered? The wallet found in the hands of the murderer had only a small sum in it.

PAULA: The Police have sought repeatedly to discover the truth, but in vain! Well, I'm going to find out.

LEFEBVRE: Before I gave your brother that cash, I had also given him a check a few days earlier, which my cashier later paid to a stranger. Someone had forged his signature and falsified the amount. When I showed him to Frédéric later, he claimed to recognize the handwriting, but didn't say whose it was.

PAULA: If we identify the counterfeiter, we will know who the true murderer is.

FABRICE: But you have no evidence.

PAULA: I'll get some.

(*The bell rings again; it is Claude Marteau and Spigot*)

CLAUDE (*from outside*): Pardon me, Madame Lefebvre, but we'd like to know if you need any fish today?
PAULINE: Come in, come in, Monsieur Claude!

(*Claude and Spigot join the group*)

CLAUDE: Excuse us, everybody. (*noticing Fabrice, he scowls*)
PAULINE (*to Spigot*): Take your fish to the kitchen.
CLAUDE: Do what the lady says, Spigot.

(*Spigot takes the catch of the day to the kitchen*)

FABRICE: I wonder if... (*to Claude*) Are you available?
CLAUDE: What?
FABRICE: We'd like you to work for us.
CLAUDE: In what way?
FABRICE: I'm about to purchase a large estate for my uncle and we need someone to supervise his yacht,
CLAUDE Where is it?
FABRICE: Near Neuilly.
CLAUDE Ah, that's too far away. It's impossible. I can't.
FABRICE: What if we offer you two hundred francs a month, plus free lodging and meals, of course.
LEFEBVRE: While you discuss this, we'll take a tour of the garden.
PAULINE: You should accept Fabrice's offer, Claude. You will do well.
CLAUDE: I'm not saying otherwise, Madame, no, but…

(*all leave except Fabrice and Claude*)

FABRICE: So you don't want to live near Neuilly?

CLAUDE: Well, yes, Monsieur.

FABRICE: You don't say why… I bet I know why.

CLAUDE: You do?

FABRICE: Yes. It's because you've been assigned to residence by the police.

CLAUDE (*troubled*): Well, er…

FABRICE: You must stay in this Department, am I right?

CLAUDE: For the love of God, Monsieur, don't mention it!

FABRICE: Don't worry, my good man, no one can hear us, and I'll keep your secret.

CLAUDE: Who told you?

FABRICE: It's no big deal. You were convicted of theft five years ago. But in two days, I will obtain permission for you to move and live near Neuilly. I will answer for you.

CLAUDE: Knowing what you know, you'd help me all the same?

FABRICE: Of course I would.

CLAUDE: I am not a dishonest man, Monsieur.

FABRICE: I believe you. My offer proves it.

CLAUDE: Then I accept and I thank you from the bottom of my heart. Ah, you're a real gentleman!

FABRICE (*giving him a card*): You know how to read?

CLAUDE: Yes, Monsieur.

FABRICE: As soon as you've received your papers from the Police, present yourself at this address in Neuilly. Monsieur René Jancelyn, my secretary, will set you up and give you my instructions.

CLAUDE: Yes, Monsieur. What about the yacht?

FABRICE: I'll trust you to buy one, of course.

CLAUDE: I will need an assistant.

FABRICE: Hire one.

CLAUDE: Can I hire whomever I wish?

FABRICE: That's your concern.

(*Spigot returns*)

CLAUDE: Stop right there. I'm quitting my current job and I'm going to introduce you to the nephew of my new master.
SPIGOT: T-the n-nephew…
CLAUDE: And you'll be my new assistant.
SPIGOT: W-where…?
CLAUDE: Neuilly.
SPIGOT: To d-do w-what?
CLAUDE: Sail a yacht, my lad.
SPIGOT (delighted): Hu-hurray!

(*the others return*)

PAULINE: Well, are you in agreement?
CLAUDE: Yes, Madame! And my word of honor, I'll be a good servant.
FABRICE: Until I return from America. Monsieur Jancelyn will be your supervisor.

CURTAIN

## *SCENE VII*

A hangar by the Seine where river boats are constructed. Half of the stage is the interior of the hangar, with a tool shed and a backdoor; the other half is the launching pad outside giving onto the river Seine.

AT RISE, Lehardy, a worker, is in the hangar, finishing driving screws into the hull of a new boat under construction.

LEHARDY: Almost done! I just have to add that weathercock. The nutcases will be pleased. (*screws a copper weathercock on the boat, then calls out*) Little Pierre! Little Pierre!

(*A boy of thirteen in shirtsleeves emerges from behind the tool shed*)

LEHARDY: The nutcases are going to be here soon to chris-
ten their new boat. Sweep up a bit, willya?
LITTLE PIERRE: Ah, yes, the nutcases. All the same, they're
okay, boss.
LEHARDY: You think so?
LITTLE PIERRE: I find them funny. And not just the ladies.
LEHARDY: What so funny about the ladies?
LITTLE PIERRE: They're not quite as uppity as they could
be, but not slutty at all.

(*Madame Tallandier, a basket of food on her arm, comes in
from outside*)

MADAME TALLANDIER: "Slutty?" I should wash your
mouth with soap, your man!
LITTLE PIERRE: Oh, Mama!
MADAME TALLANDIER: You're going to make me seri-
ously angry. I've forbidden you to use words like that, words I
don't like in the mouth of a child. I haven't brought up to talk
like that.
LITTLE PIERRE: I'm sorry, Ma! I won't do it anymore!
LEHARDY: Your mother's right.
MADAME TALLANDIER: OK. He promised not to do it
anymore.
LEHARDY: You've come to bring us lunch, Madame
Tallandier?
MADAME TALLANDIER: Yes, Monsieur Lehardy. I'm go-
ing to warm it up.

(*She leaves through the back. Raoul appears from outside*)

LEHARDY : Ah, Monsieur de Langeais!
RAOUL: Bonjour, Monsieur Lehardy. (*they shake hands*) Is
she ready as you promised?
LEHARDY: Yes! Here she is. (*showing the boat*) Have a
look.
RAOUL: Very nice. (*tapping the hull*) Is it solid?

LEHARDY: Best wood. She'll will move like a fish.

RAOUL: No change in the program. We'll christen her at 10:30. Then we'll have lunch. And at noon, we'll launch her into the Seine. Have you got three bigger boats to rent for the day? I've got some guests.

LEHARDY: Sure. Little Pierre, prepare the *Zanzibar*, the *Hummingbird* and the *Sparrowhawk* to go.

LITTLE PIERRE: Yes, boss.

RAOUL: Now let's settle our accounts.

(*they all go into the shed. Claude and Spigot appear from outside*)

SPIGOT: T-this is the p-place.

CLAUDE (*looking around*): Nice work they do here. A real American style yacht. I think Monsieur Fabrice will be pleased when he returns.

(*Little Pierre returns*)

LITTLE PIERRE: You want something?

CLAUDE: No. We're just looking over that boat. (*pointing to the yacht*)

LITTLE PIERRE: Look all you like. (*looking outside*) Boss, the rest of the nutcases are here.

(*Gabriel, Adèle, Mathilde and Paul enter from outside, talking*)

GABRIEL: It's a long walk.

ADÈLE: It makes you thirsty.

MATHILDE: You're always thirsty, you boozer.

LITTLE PIERRE (*aside*): "Boozer!" That must be slang!

GABRIEL (*noticing Claude*): Why, that's the fisherman from Melun!

MATHILDE: The story-teller.

PAUL: Who frightened us all!.

ADÈLE: Not me!

CLAUDE: It's plain to see that Fabrice isn't here.

GABRIEL: No. He left us to go to America, to live like a millionaire with his uncle.

ADÈLE: When is he coming back?

GABRIEL: Around Easter.

MATHILDE: He'll be back to see his aunt and his cousin.

MATHILDE: They didn't go with him?

ADÈLE: No. His aunt was taken ill. I've heard she's gone mad. One of his friends told me the two women are in a sanatorium near Melun.

MATHILDE: Ah, the poor woman.

(*Claude listens to all this with great interest*)

SPIGOT: What's she s-saying?

CLAUDE: Shut up!

(Raoul returns)

RAOUL: Ah, you're all here! Let's get ready for the christening.

ALL: To the dock! To the boathouse!

(*They all go outside, and leave*)

CLAUDE: What's this all about? What does it mean?

SPIGOT: W-what?

CLAUDE: Shut up! You don't understand!

(*Lehardy returns*)

LEHARDY (*coming up to Claude*): You want something, sailor?

CLAUDE: Yes. It's about this yacht. But we'll talk about it later.
LEHARDY: As you wish.
CLAUDE: When we're rid of all these fair-weather sailors.
LEHARDY: I get you, buddy!

(*Outside; Raoul is now holding a bouquet*)

RAOUL: Take your places for the ceremony!

(*They all return dressed in outlandish costumes. Paul is disguised as a Maharajah, wearing a turban; Gabriel is dressed as a Harlequin, and holds a drum; Mathilde is dressed as a sexy water sprite and Adèle as a Marquise with a powdered wig*)

PAUL: Drum roll, please!
(*Gabriel gives a drum call*)
PAUL: Who is the Godfather?
(*another drum roll*)
RAOUL: I am!
PAUL: Do you entertain loose women?
MATHILDE: That's all he does.
PAUL: Who is the Godmother?
(*another drum roll*)
ADÈLE: That's me!
PAUL: What's your position?
RAOUL: Vertical!
PAUL: No, your position in society?
RAOUL: Ah. *Bon vivant*!
PAUL: Do you have all your teeth?
RAOUL: All but my wisdoms.
PAUL: Godmother, come forth.
(*another drum roll*)
ADÈLE (*stepping forward*): Present!
PAUL: Have you ever fished?
ADÈLE: Me? Never!

PAUL: Do you consent to care for the child we are baptizing?
ADÈLE: I do!
RAOUL: Seriously?
ADÈLE: At last until it grows teeth.
SPIGOT (*watching from inside*): I-I'd like to be that child.
PAUL: Drum roll!
(*roll of drums*)
PAIL: In the name of Great Bashi-Boozook....
GABRIEL (*to Adèle*): I think he sells candy in Montmartre.
PAUL: Silence! I said, In the name of Great Bashi-Boozook...
ALL: Hail the Great Bashi-Boozook!
PAUL: ...Who would have been an idiot if he wasn't that smart...
GABRIEL (*to Mathilde*): The very opposite of him.
MATHILDE: Leave it alone, will you, Gabri?
PAUL: In the name of Great Bashi-Boozook
ALL: Hail the Great Bashi-Boozook!
PAUL: ...God of fezzes, turbans, and Turkish delights, what name would you give to this boat?
GABRIEL: *The Trafalgar*!
RAOUL: Shut your trap!
MATHILDE: *The Joséphine*.
ADÈLE: *The Zephyr*.
RAOUL: No! No!
GABRIEL: Damn it, call it what you like.
CLAUDE: Stop!
RAOUL: What do you want?
CLAUDE: I have a better idea.
ALL: Let's hear it!
CLAUDE: Call your boat *The Nutcase*.
ALL: *The Nutcase*! Yes! Yes!
MATHILDE: *The Nutcase*, it is. Well, then, you are her God-father. I kiss you. (*she kisses him*)
ALL: Let's all go to lunch!

(*They all go out merrily*)

143

LEHARDY (*to Claude*): Now, we can talk.

CLAUDE: Yes.

LEHARDY: You wanted to buy that yacht, didn't you? Have you looked it over?

CLAUDE: Yes. Let's talk plainly. I'm here to buy her. What's your price?

LEHARDY: Fifteen thousand.

CLAUDE: I'll give you ten thousand francs, not a *sou* more.

LEHARDY: Ten thousand one hundred?

CLAUDE: No!

LEHARDY: The hundred will go to the kid here.

LITTLE PIERRE: Not for me, for my mother.

CLAUDE: OK then. Ten thousand one hundred. (*to Lehardy*) Shake on it?

LEHARDY: Shake on it! (*they shake hands*)

CLAUDE: I also need a smart kid about twelve to help us. I'd like him to know the sea and have a taste for it. I'll teach him the ropes. Can you recommend someone?

LEHARDY: I've got just the boy for you.

CLAUDE: Really?

LEHARDY: A kid who's not stupid. The son of a fine woman.

LEHARDY: Is it this kid by chance?

LITTLE PIERRE: Me? A cabin boy—go to sea, go fishing? I'd love it—if Mama permits it.

CLAUDE: Where's she hiding?

LITTLE PIERRE: She's in the kitchen.

LEHARDY (*calling*): Madame Tallandier!

(*Madame Tallandier returns*)

MADAME TALLANDIER: You need me, Monsieur Lehardy?

CLAUDE: I'd like to hire your son as a cabin boy on a yacht.

MADAME TALLANDIER: On a yacht!

CLAUDE: I'll take him in hand and make an able seaman of him.

MADAME TALLANDIER: But he'll be away from me.

LITTLE PIERRE: Ma!

CLAUDE: We won't take him very far. My employers live in Neuilly. When the kid can't come to see you, you can go to see him.

MADAME TALLANDIER: What would he be doing in Neuilly? He will get paid?

CLAUDE: Dressed, lodged and fed, plus 30 francs a month to begin with.

LITTLE PIERRE (*doing the math*): That's 360 francs a year, Ma.

LEHARDY: It's a good offer, Madame Tallandier.

MADAME TALLANDIER: Yes, but I'd have to be away from him, and I don't feel I have the courage. He's all I have left on Earth.

LITTLE PIERRE: Neuilly isn't far, Ma. Let me go.

LEHARDY: Be reasonable.

MADAME TALLANDIER (*hugging Little Pierre*): Well then, I accept.

CLAUDE: You won't regret it. I'll have an employment contract ready for you tomorrow Madame. Monsieur, here is 1000 francs on account, and one hundred for Madame.

MADAME TALLANDIER: Oh, thank you, thank you!

LITTLE PIERRE: I want 40 *sous* to have the priest ay a Mass for my father.

CLAUDE: Your husband is dead, Madame?

MADAME TALLANDIER: He disappeared.

CLAUDE: And you've never had news of him?

MADAME TALLANDIER (*tearfully*): Yes, one time. A letter saying he would never see me or our son again.

CLAUDE: How long ago was that?

MADAME TALLANDIER: Eight or nine months ago.

CLAUDE: And that's all?

LEHARDY: The letter contained money.

MADAME TALLANDIER: Fifteen thousand francs.

CLAUDE: A large sum.

(*Silence*)

MADAME TALLANDIER: I don't know how he could get so much money. He was unable to work because he'd injured his arm. (*she cries*)

LITTLE PIERRE: Aw, don't cry, ma.

MADAME TALLANDIER: I think we need a little lunch. Take care of Little Pierre, Monsieur. Love him as if he was yours.

CLAUDE: I shall! I swear it. (*aside*) If I'd had the courage to speak, I might have saved this kid's father. But I didn't have that courage. (*hugs the boy*) Yes, son, I'll love you. You'll never know how much.

CURTAIN

# ACT III
## SCENE VIII

Doctor Georges Vernier's office.

AT RISE, the Doctor is sitting behind his desk. There is a knock on the door.

MARIETTE (*announcing*): Doctor Vulpian is here, Doctor.
VERNIER: Show him in.

(Doctor Vulpian enters)

VERNIER (*happily*): Ah, my dear master!
VULPIAN: Your old professor is happy, indeed very happy, to shake the hand of his best student.
VERNIER: But why are you in Melun?
VULPIAN: For a consultation. And I didn't want to leave without seeing you.
VERNIER: How about dinner?
VULPIAN: I'd be delighted.

(*Mariette returns and presents a card*)

VERNIER: Paula Baltus?
VULPIAN: A patient?
VERNIER: No. She's the sister of Frédéric Baltus, who was murdered a couple of months ago.
VULPIAN: Ah yes! I followed the reports of the trial in the papers.
VERNIER: A strange case, wasn't it?
VULPIAN: Quite.
VERNIER (*to Mariette*): Please show Mademoiselle Baltus in.

147

(*Mariette introduces Paula then leaves*)

VERNIER: Mademoiselle.

PAULA: Pardon me, doctor, for– (*seeing Vulpian, she stops, speechless*)

VERNIER: Doctor Vulpian is my mentor.

VULPIAN: And a close friend, Mademoiselle.

PAULA: I'm happy to meet you here, Doctor. If I may, I'd like to ask you some questions.

VERNIER: By all means. Please sit down.

PAULA (*sitting down*): Doctor, is it possible to cure madness caused by terror?

VULPIAN: By terror?

PAULA: Yes. From witnessing an execution?

VERNIER: A death on the scaffold?

PAULA: Yes. (*pause*) Well…

VULPIAN: Well, if the condemned was a relative, or a close friend…

PAULA: So a woman seeing the head of a member of her family fall beneath the guillotine might go mad?

VULPIAN: That's certainly possible.

PAULA: And could she be cured?

VERNIER: Yes, I believe so.

PAULA: Are you certain? Both of you?

VULPIAN: By a similar terror.

PAULA: A similar terror… (*to Vernier*) If I were to ask you to attempt this cure, would you consent?

VERNIER: With all my heart.

PAULA (*offering her hand*): Thank you, Doctor.

VERNIER: Now it's my turn to ask you a question.

PAULA: Yes. What is it?

VERNIER: How old is this woman.

PAULA: She's still young, that's all I know.

VERNIER: You don't know her personally?

PAULA: No. This may seem strange to you, right?

VERNIER: More than you can imagine.

PAULA: Why?

VERNIER: Because I've heard of a similar case.

PAULA: A woman gone mad witnessing an execution?

VERNIER: Yes.

PAULA: Where?

VERNIER: Here, in Melun. The day…

PAULA (*interrupting*): The day when the supposed murderer of my brother was executed, right?

VERNIER: Yes.

PAULA: So we're talking about the same woman, no doubt about it. You must know where she is.

VERNIER: That, I don't know.

PAULA: She was staying at the Grand Stag Hotel with a man who might have been her husband.

VERNIER: Yes, I remember. I was called to see her because she was taken ill. That was just before the execution.

VULPIAN: Then you must know who she is?

VERNIER: That, I do.

PAULA: What's her name?

VERNIER: Jeanne Delarivière

PAULA: The wife of the banker from New York?

VERNIER: The same.

PAULA: Why, that's impossible. Monsieur Delarivière had left his wife in New York. He told me so himself, and Edmée, his daughter, confirmed it.

VERNIER: You know them?

PAULA: Yes. This is all very strange.

VULPIAN: No doubt they sought to to conceal the condition of the unhappy lady.

PAULA: She must be in a sanatorium somewhere nearby. We must find her. And you will cure her.

VULPIAN: But there are lots of sanatoriums...

PAULA: So?

VULPIAN: You see, it's the duty of the doctors to protect the confidentiality of their patients' identities… They will tell you nothing.

PAULA: I have an idea. I'll write to Monsieur Delarivière. He will tell me where she is.

VERNIER: If he's hiding her, and his pain, do we have the right to intervene?

PAULA: If Monsieur Delarivière won't tell me, Fabrice will.

VERNIER: Fabrice Leclerc? His nephew?

PAULA: My fiancé. We became engaged before he left for New York. He promised me to avenge my brother. To do that, Madame Delarivière must be cured.

VERNIER: Why?

PAULA: The man who killed my brother did not act alone. I am sure he had at least one accomplice. I need to know the name of the man who was executed in order to find the name of the accomplice. Madame Delarivière knows who the condemned man was, I'm sure of it. And it's clear that knowing it drove her mad. So you think that a similar terror might cure her?

VULPIAN: Yes.

PAULA: We must cure her so she can tell us that was Pierre's real name. He had a family, and that is proved by his obstinate silence. (*to Doctor Vernier*) You are my ally, aren't you? Can I count on you? (*she offers her hand*)

VERNIER: Certainly.

VULPIAN: You can also count on me, Mademoiselle.

PAULA: I'm going to write to both Fabrice and Monsieur Delarivière. As soon as I learn where she is, we'll go and get her.

VULPIAN: That may be impossible.

PAULA: Why?

VULPIAN: I see. You don't know the law…

VERNIER: Private individuals are forbidden to keep lunatics in their home.

PAULA: I've got money, gentlemen. Lots of it. We'll buy a sanatorium. That's simple.

VULPIAN: There are several for sale.

PAULA: My fortune is at your disposal. Purchase one of these establishments. The price doesn't matter.

VULPIAN (*to Vernier*): You should accept, Georges.

VERNIER: I will do as you request, Mademoiselle.

PAULA: Thank you, Doctors.

(*she wipes her eyes and leaves*)

VERNIER: Now, we can go to dinner.
VULPIAN: We certainly have plenty to discuss.

CURTAIN

## SCENE IX

Same set as Scene V.

AT RISE, Doctor Rittner is seated at his desk dressed in a traveling outfit. He looks at several bottles before him and discards them after emptying them. Doctor Schultz comes in.

SCHULTZ: Doctor Vernier is here.

(*Georges Vernier and Paula enter*)

RITTNER: Madame. Doctor.
VERNIER: This lady is the party who acquired your sanatorium, Doctor.
RITTNER: A wise purchase, Mademoiselle. (*to Georges*) My dear successor, I've been waiting for you impatiently.
VERNIER: My dear colleague, I've come to take possession. I've inspected everything. How many patients do you have at this moment?
RITTNER: Forty-eight. Rather than ask me questions, take a look at the registry. It provides a complete explanation. Here are the keys as well.
VERNIER (*taking the keys*): Thanks, we'll go over everything this evening.
RITTNER: I'm afraid it might be impossible.
VERNIER: Why?

RITTNER: As I told you, pressing family affairs made me decide to sell my establishment. This morning, I received a telegram which forces me to leave this very evening.

VERNIER: This abrupt departure puts me in a bit of a fix. At least leave me someone capable of helping me.

RITTNER (pointing to Doctor Schultz): Of course! I'm leaving you my right arm, Doctor Schultz. I recommend him to you very warmly. He will stay with you if you retain his services.

VERNIER: Certainly, I'll be happy to.

SCHULTZ: You can count on me, Doctor. (they shake hands)

VERNIER: We'll inspect the patients together, Doctor Schultz. You'll bring me up to date on their condition.

SCHULTZ: Of course, doctor. But before leaving, Doctor Rittner himself will bring you up to date on one patient about whom he's especially concerned.

RITTNER: Ah, yes, you're right, Doctor Schultz. She was strongly recommended to me. To keep her under closer observation, I've placed her in a ward near this office.

VERNIER: What's the cause of her affliction?

RITTNER: Terrors.

PAULA (reacting): Terrors!

VERNIER (ditto): Terrors, you say? I certainly would like to have a look at her.

PAULA (to Vernier): Should I stay?

RITTNER: That would not be advisable, I think, Mademoiselle.

PAULA: But if she sees me…

SCHULTZ: You wouldn't be in any danger.

(Doctor Rittner opens a curtain revealing an adjacent room behind a glass partition. Jeanne can be seen in there. Doctor Schultz goes in through a side door and brings her in)

JEANNE (seeing Paula): Ah! There you are! I was expecting you.

SCHULTZ: She thinks you're her daughter.

PAULA: Her daughter...
VERNIER: How long has she been under your care?
RITTNER: Six weeks.
VERNIER: Is she likely to recover?
RITTNER: I don't think so.

(*Doctor Vernier goes to Jeanne and examines her*)

JEANNE: Ah, I recognize you! It's you, Maurice. (*to Paula*) Get out of here, you're not my daughter! (*screaming*) Get out!
PAULA: Ah, it's horrible!
VERNIER: But it is she! It's Jeanne Delarivière!
PAULA: That can't b!
VERNIER: I recognize her. (*to Rittner*) That woman's name is Madame Delarivière, isn't it?
RITTNER (*uneasily*): er, yes. Why? You know her?
VERNIER (*explosively*): Yes, I do know her. And if my faith in medical science isn't in vain, I will cure her!
PAULA: And we'll learn the name of the real murderer of my brother.
RITTNER: The murderer of your brother?
PAULA: Frédéric Baltus.
RITTNER: You're Paula Baltus?
PAULA (*going to Jeanne*): Jeanne! Jeanne!

(*An Orderly enters*)

ORDERLY: Doctor Rittner, your carriage is here.
RITTNER: I'm obliged to leave you.
VERNIER: Goodbye, Doctor. I'm sure Doctor Schultz will be quite able to assist me.
RITTNER: Goodbye then, Doctor.

(*Doctor Rittner leaves with the Orderly*)

VERNIER (*to Schultz*): So what treatment was this patient receiving?

SCHULTZ (*presenting a file*): See for yourself, Doctor.

VERNIER (*looking at the file*): Why, this doesn't make any sense! Looking at all these prescriptions, I'm tempted to believe that Doctor Rittner was trying to kill her.

PAULA: Kill her?

VERNIER (*to Schultz*): You will prepare a mixture of belladonna that can be administered in a beverage that the patient will drink of her own free will. While you are doing that, I will work with the patient. I need to establish a more precise diagnosis.

PAULA: Doctor Schultz told me just now that Jeanne mistook me for her daughter.

SCHULTZ: Yes, Mademoiselle.

VERNIER: Then, let's bring her in. We need to find Mademoiselle Edmée.

SCHULTZ: She's here.

PAULA & GEORGES (*surprised*): Here?

SCHULTZ: Yes. I'll go and fetch her at once.

(*Schultz goes out and returns with Edmée who is pale and ill*)

SCHULTZ: Here she is.

PAULA & GEORGES: Edmée!

EDMÉE (*uttering a cry of joy*) Ah, Georges! Georges! (*she rushes into Georges' arms.*)

PAULA: My dear Edmée!

EDMÉE: My friend! How did you find us? Who told you our secret? Doctor Rittner?

VERNIER: No. Doctor Rittner is no longer here. This sanatorium belongs to us now.

EDMÉE: To you. Then you will never leave us?

VERNIER: Never.

EDMÉE: And you'll cure my mother?

VERNIER: I will.

(*Edmée leads Georges to her mother. Paula follows him*)

EDMÉE: Mother! Mother! It's Georges. Georges, whom I love. (*tearfully*) He'll cure you.
JEANNE (*holding them*) Yes, yes… I love my children. (*falls back*)

(*The Orderly returns*)

ORDERLY: Doctor, there's someone here to see you.
VERNIER (*to Schultz*): Close this curtain and deal with it. I'll stay here.

(*Schultz closes the curtain and goes to sit behind the desk. The Orderly introduces Fabrice who enters dressed in travel attire. There is a black band of mourning on his hat. The Orderly then leaves, closing the door behind him*)

SCHULTZ: Monsieur Leclerc.
FABRICE: Doctor Schultz… where is Doctor Rittner?
SCHULTZ: Gone, I'm afraid. He sold the sanatorium.
FABRICE (*shocked*): Sold the sanatorium?
SCHULTZ: Yes. A week ago. His successor took possession today.
FABRICE: What about my aunt and cousin?
SCHULTZ: They are still here, Monsieur.
FABRICE: And who is the new director?

(*Georges Vernier and Paula come out from behind the curtain*)

VERNIER: I am, Monsieur.
FABRICE: Doctor Vernier!
PAULA: Fabrice.
FABRICE: Paula.

(*Doctor Schultz discreetly leaves*)

PAULA: My dear Fabrice, you've arrived just in time to be present at our triumph.

FABRICE: What triumph? I'm happy to see you, my dear Paula, but I am dumbfounded by your presence here.

VERNIER: Indeed, you must be surprised.

PAULA: Did you not receive my letter in New York?

FABRICE: Yes, but as I was returning to France, I thought I'd get here as soon as my reply. (*to Georges*) Doctor, how is my aunt?

VERNIER: Quite weak.

FABRICE: And my cousin?

VERNIER: Rather sick, as well.

PAULA: What about your uncle? In my excitement, I forgot to ask you about him. Why isn't he with you?

FABRICE (*pointing to the mourning band on his hat*): Alas!

PAULA & GEORGES: He passed away! What happened?

FABRICE: He fell… He was carried away by the sea in a storm during our return crossing.

PAULA: Poor Edmée!

VERNIER: Ah, don't let her know about that new misfortune.

(*Doctor Schultz returns with a carafe*)

SCHULTZ: Doctor Vernier, here's the preparation you requested.

VERNIER: The dosage?

SCHULTZ (*presenting a paper*): Here.

GEORGE (*inspecting it*): Very well. Place this carafe on the patient's table. Renew this preparation night and day.

SCHULTZ: Yes, Doctor.

(*Doctor Schultz heads toward the room behind the curtain. Edmée appears*)

EDMÉE: My mother's sleeping, doctor.

SCHULTZ: I won't wake her, Mademoiselle.

PAULA (*to Edmée, pointing to Fabrice*): Edmée, Fabrice is here.

VERNIER (*to Fabrice*): Not a word.

EDMÉE: Ah, Fabrice! (*she runs to him*)

FABRICE: My little Edmée!

EDMÉE: They didn't tell me you were here.

FABRICE: I just arrived.

EDMÉE: Where's father?

FABRICE (*hesitant*): Er, he stayed in New York.

VERNIER: His business kept him.

EDMÉE: No. You're lying to me. I can tell!

FABRICE: I assure you…

EDMÉE: I can always tell when you're lying!

FABRICE: Edmée, calm down.

EDMÉE (*noticing the crepe in Fabrice's hat*): Ah! That band! My father is dead! My father is dead! (*she faints in Georges' arms*)

PAULA: My God!

VERNIER: Ah, the emotion I feared! (*to Paula*) Help me, Mademoiselle! (*they carry her to the couch*) Monsieur Leclerc, will you hand me that flask of ether… yes, from that cabinet…

PAULA: Edmée! Edmée, dear child!

FABRICE (*opening the cabinet and reading the labels*): Ah! I have it!

VERNIER: Bring it to me! Quickly!

(*Fabrice takes a flask which he brings to George. As the Doctor and Paula tend to Edmée, he cuts the bell line, then pockets another flask from the cabinet*)

EDMÉE (*coming to*): Father! My poor Father!

FABRICE (*to himself*): Jeanne won't talk. I'll make sure of it!

C U R T A I N

## ACT IV

### SCENE X

A dock near a pavilion.

AT RISE, Claude Marteau is working on finishing building a beautiful panoply, helped by Little Pierre.

LITTLE PIERRE: Here comes Monsieur Jancelyn.
CLAUDE: Who cares? Get me some nails.

(*Little Pierre leaves in search of nails; René Jancelyn enters*)

RENÉ (*holding a telegraph in his hands*): So, my good Claude, how are we coming with it?
CLAUDE: Here's one that's ready. (pointing to another panoply standing at the back) I'm finishing the other one.
RENÉ: Good. We need two in the vestibule.
CLAUDE: The day's not over yet.
RENÉ: True. But I'd like the pavilion to be completely ready for the arrival of Monsieur Leclerc.
CLAUDE: Is he coming?
RENÉ: I've just received this telegram from him.
CLAUDE: So he's back in France?
RENÉ: He must be in Paris by now, and perhaps en route to Neuilly.
CLAUDE: That's news that pleases me. And is Monsieur Delarivière back with him?
RENÉ: I haven't been told.
CLAUDE: Ah. And what about Madame Delarivière and Miss Mademoiselle Edmée?
RENÉ: You're quite curious today!
CLAUDE: I'm going to hang this panoply in the vestibule.
RENÉ: No, let me do it. I'll hang it there myself.

158

(*René takes the panoply and goes into the pavilion, where he starts hanging it.*

(*Meanwhile, Madame Tallandier appears at the gate*)

MADAME TALLANDIER (*looking around*): This must be it. (*seeing Claude*) Bonjour, Monsieur Marteau!
CLAUDE: Ah, Madame Tallandrier! What a nice surprise.
MADAME TALLANDIER: I had to come to Neuilly to run an errand for Monsieur Lehardy so I thought I'd come to say hello to you while I was at it. Are you still pleased with Little Pierre?
CLAUDE: Very much so. He works hard and well.
MADAME TALLANDIER: Does he study?
CLAUDE: His teachers are pleased with him.

(*Having finished hanging the first panoply, René comes out of the pavilion*)

RENÉ: Madame?
CLAUDE: This is Little Pierre's mother. She came to see her son.
RENÉ: Very well. But hurry up.
CLAUDE: Don't worry. Everything will be ready in time. I need more nails and I sent Little Pierre to get them.

(*René nods and leaves*)

MADAME TALLANDIER: Who is that gentleman?
CLAUDE: A friend of Monsieur Leclerc
MADAME TALLANDIER: Your boss, right?
CLAUDE: Sort of. The one with the money is his uncle, Monsieur Delarivière.
MADAME TALLANDIER (*recollecting*): Delarivière...
CLAUDE: You know him?

MADAME TALLANDIER: I know that name... What does he do?

CLAUDE: Nothing. I mean, he's a banker.

MADAME TALLANDIER: Doesn't he live in New York?

CLAUDE: Yes. But what of it?

MADAME TALLANDIER: And he's married, isn't he?

CLAUDE: Yes, and he has a daughter.

MADAME TALLANDIER: Do you know his wife's name?

CLAUDE: It's Jeanne.

MADAME TALLANDIER: Monsieur Marteau, my Little Pierre cannot stay another moment under this roof. I'll wait and take him back with me.

CLAUDE: Take him back with you? What do you mean? You must be joking!

MADAME TALLANDIER: I'm not joking. He'll be leaving with me.

CLAUDE: But why?

MADAME TALLANDIER: Don't ask!

CLAUDE: On the contrary, I must ask. You entrusted your child to me, and to take him away without an explanation is an insult.

MADAME TALLANDIER: You cannot think that, Claude.

CLAUDE: I do think that, since I say so. Look, speak!

MADAME TALLANDIER: Your Madame Delarivière is not his wife. His legitimate wife.

CLAUDE: What?

MADAME TALLANDIER: She's his mistress. Her name is Jeanne Tallandier. She's my husband's sister.

CLAUDE: His sister?

MADAME TALLANDIER: Yes. My husband never wanted to see her again. That's why I can't allow my little boy to stay in this house.

CLAUDE: But...

MADAME TALLANDIER: Surely, you must understand!

CLAUDE (*feverishly*): I understand... I understand that you are exaggerating the situation. So your sister-in-law is not Monsieur Delarivière's legitimate wife. So what? That's

160

common today. How does that affect your boy? Little Pierre should stay. You'd be ruining his future if you take him away.

MADAME TALLANDIER: His future!

CLAUDE: You trust me, don't you, Madame Tallandier?

MADAME TALLANDIER: Well, yes.

CLAUDE: You believe that I love your son?

MADAME TALLANDIER: Like his own father!

CLAUDE: Then let him stay with me. He'll be with me—not with them!

MADAME TALLANDIER: Ah, Monsieur Claude, you make me do anything you wish.

(*Little Pierre returns with a toolbox*)

CLAUDE: Here he comes. Not a word.

LITTLE PIERRE (*seeing his mother*): Ma!

MADAME TALLANDIER: My dear child. (*they hug*)

LITTLE PIERRE: It's nice of you to have come.

MADAME TALLANDIER: Do you like it here?

LITTLE PIERRE: Oh, yes! The work is fun. And Monsieur Claude is really good to me.

CLAUDE: Yeah, I love him like my own. But give me that tool box so I can finish my work. (*he takes the toolbox*)

MADAME TALLANDIER: As for me, I should leave now.

LITTLE PIERRE: Already?

MADAME TALLANDIER: I have to.

CLAUDE: Go with your mother.

MADAME TALLANDIER: Thank you. I trust you.

(*She takes Little Pierre's hand and they leave.*

(*Claude, muttering to himself, works on the second panoply. He reaches into the toolbox*)

CLAUDE What's that? A revolver! (*taking it out*)What is it doing there? (*looking at it more closely*) It's a fancy piece. There's a silver escutcheon. (*examining the butt*) What's this?

161

Initials… "F.L." It resembles the one I once found by the river… (*fumbles in his pocket, pulls out a wallet and removes a small silver escutcheon which he compares*) Yes. Like two drops of water... Ah! If only I'd had the courage to take this to the Police, telling them what I knew, I might have saved that poor bastard's life... But I was afraid of the Police... But now that I know who is really guilty, my duty is clear. Justice will be done. Meanwhile, I must hide this revolver... I have an idea! (*he nails it on the panoply*) That way, I'll know where to find it when I need it.

(*Spigot arrives*)

SPIGOT: The boats are ready.
CLAUDE: Good. (*giving him the panoply*) Go and hang this in the vestibule, will you?

(*Spigot takes the panoply, goes into the pavilion and hangs the panoply*)

CLAUDE (*aside*): Now, Fabrice Leclerc, I understand why you hired me. You're paying me 200 francs a month for my silence, and you intend to hold me.

(*Spigot returns and starts helping Claude.*)

(*Fabrice and René arrive; they enter the pavilion. Fabrice notices the revolver on the second panoply, takes it and slips it into his pocket.*)

(*Outside, Little Pierre returns*)

LITTLE PIERRE: I'm back, Monsieur Claude!
CLAUDE: Good kid!

(*Fabrice and René come out; they all give a pseudo-military salute, after removing their hats*)

FABRICE (*shaking Claude's hand*): Bonjour, Claude.

CLAUDE (*hesitating, but shaking Fabrice's hand*): Monsieur Leclerc.

FABRICE: I'm very pleased with you. And Monsieur Jancelyn tells me you've executed all my instructions very intelligently.

CLAUDE: I've done my best. Are you well, Monsieur?

FABRICE: Better than ever.

CLAUDE: What about your uncle?

FABRICE: Ah! Your question revives a cruel sorrow in me.

CLAUDE: A cruel sorrow?

FABRICE: My uncle is dead.

CLAUDE: Dead! A man who was in such good health!

FABRICE: He was swept overboard in a storm during the return voyage.

CLAUDE: Then you are going to leave us.

FABRICE: Why should I?

CLAUDE: Because of the mourning, I suppose?

FABRICE: You supposed wrong. My aunt and my cousin will be here in a few days. Nothing will be changed. (*pointing to Spigot and Little Pierre*) This is your crew?

CLAUDE: Yes, Monsieur.

FABRICE: This child will make an excellent cabin boy. He's the son of a Madame Tallandier, Monsieur Jancelyn tells me?

CLAUDE: Yes, Monsieur.

FABRICE (*to Little Pierre*): What does your family do?

LITTLE PIERRE (*looking at Claude*): Huh?

CLAUDE: His mother works as a cook at the dockyards.

FABRICE: And your father?

LITTLE PIERRE: My Papa is dead.

FABRICE: Did he have any family?

LITTLE PIERRE: I don't know, Monsieur.

CLAUDE: I think his mother would have told me if he did.

FABRICE: Well, I thank you for having put these panoplies together. Those weapons are prized and expensive. I'm quite attached to them.

163

CLAUDE: I don't know much about weapons.

FABRICE (*giving him two gold coins*): Here's a tip for you and your crew.

CLAUDE: We'll spend them wisely. We'll go to dinner in town and then to the theater.

LITTLE PIERRE (*excited*): To the theater!

CLAUDE: Let's go! (*singing*) To the theater we go, heigh ho! Heigh ho!

(*they leave*)

FABRICE (*to René*): Rittner has compromised everything by selling out and fleeing. Give me the keys to the sanatorium.

RENÉ: Be careful!

FABRICE: I cut the electric bell. I have nothing to fear.

RENÉ: Here. (*giving Fabrice a set of keys*)

FABRICE: I'll be back in two hours. Wait for me.

(*René leaves. Fabrice starts to leave, then stops. Claude reappears, trailing Fabrice, with Spigot and Little Pierre at his heels. Fabrice fumbles in his pocket*)

CLAUDE: Now what's he doing?

(*Fabrice throws an object in the water, then leaves*)

CLAUDE: He just threw something in the water. I bet that's the evolver... The murder weapon! (*to Spigot*) Spigot, my lad, you must follow that man so I know where he's going. Don't lose him, but don't let yourself be spotted.

SPIGOT: D-Don't worry.

(*Spigot follows Fabrice out discreetly.*

(*Claude grabs a fish net from the dock*)

CLAUDE: My turn, now.

LITTLE PIERRE: You're going to cast the net?

CLAUDE: Yes, kiddo, I saw a carp jump.

LITTLE PIERRE: Where'd you see it? I saw nothing.

CLAUDE: Over there.

LITTLE PIERRE: What? Another carp?

CLAUDE: Don't move. You know fish are frettish. (*he casts the net and pulls it in slowly*) I've got it!

LITTLE PIERRE: That's no carp. It's a gun!

CLAUDE (*extricating the gun*) Yes, little one, a revolver, which, without firing a shot, can kill all the same.

CURTAIN

## SCENE XI

Same set as Scene X. Night.

AT RISE, René is reading a newspaper inside the pavilion. The stage is empty. Fabrice appears and closes the door behind him.

FABRICE: Tonight will be my third visit to that sanatorium. It will also be my last. (*mopping his face*) It's suffocating in here tonight.

(*he heads toward the pavilion where René is sitting. Claude appears*)

CLAUDE: There he goes. Spigot can't be far behind him.

(*René gets up and exchanges a few words that cannot be heard with Fabrice. Then he takes a lamp and leaves with Fabrice*)

CLAUDE (*to Little Pierre*): Don't move, kid! (*opening door*) Get in here quick!

165

(*Spigot appears*)

CLAUDE: Well?
SPIGOT: I-I followed him everywhere.
CLAUDE: Where did he go?
SPIGOT: T-to that s-sanatorium.
CLAUDE: How did he get in?
SPIGOT: B-by the s-side entrance. He had a k-key
CLAUDE: He uses the side door for his nocturnal visits. What can he be doing there?
SPIGOT: T-That's the q-question.
CLAUDE: I'm going to find out. Be ready to go out again tonight.
SPIGOT: What a job!

(*He goes with Little Pierre into the pavilion*)

CLAUDE (*alone*): For sure, Mademoiselle Edmée and her mother are there. He goes to see them every day. But that proves nothing. But at night… it's another matter. Now to my watching post! (*he climbs a tree*)

FABRICE (*going to the balcony*): The heat is suffocating.
RENÉ: You're going out again tonight?
FABRICE: Yes.
RENÉ: Jeanne?
FABRICE: She won't be alive tomorrow. As for Edmée…
RENÉ: We don't need to worry about her for the moment. It's Claude Marteau who worries me. That man knows too much.
FABRICE: And you haven't yet found a way of getting rid of him?
RENÉ: None. What should we do?
FABRICE: Listen to me…

CLAUDE (*aside*): I will—most attentively!

FABRICE: Act boldly. Claude must disappear tonight.

166

CLAUDE (*aside*): Thanks a lot!

FABRICE: It must look like an accident. I leave the details to you.
RENÉ: OK. I'll take care of it.
FABRICE: Arm yourself. He's strong. The man has no family. His death will pass unnoticed. (*he fills a small flask from a larger flask, then puts the large flask away inside a cabinet, after putting the small flask back in his pocket*) Time to leave now.
RENÉ: Good luck.

(*René and Fabrice leave after extinguishing the lamp*)

CLAUDE: Spigot!
SPIGOT (*appearing*): I'm here!
CLAUDE: He's leaving again. Follow him. Follow him everywhere.
SPIGOT: Have no fear.

(*He leaves discreetly following Fabrice.*

(*Claude climbs on to the balcony and goes inside. He lights a small lamp and looks for the small flask from the cabinet; writes down a name on a piece of paper, and climbs down after extinguishing the lamp*)

LITTLE PIERRE: What did you find?
CLAUDE: "*Datura Stramonium.*"[5] What is it?

---

[5] *Datura stramonium*, known by the common names thorn apple, jimson weed or devil's snare, is a species of flowering plant in the nightshade family. *D. stramonium* has frequently been employed in traditional medicine to treat a variety of ailments. It has also been used as a hallucinogen. It is unlikely ever to become a major drug of abuse owing to effects upon

LITTLE PIERRE: Search me.

CLAUDE: How could I find out?

LITTLE PIERRE: Maybe in my dictionary? (*pull a small book out of his pocket*)

CLAUDE: What does it all mean?

LITTLE PIERRE: *Data, Datura, Datura Stramonium.* Substantive masculine.

CLAUDE: Screw the substantive.

LITTLE PIERRE: A type of plant from which poison is extracted.

CLAUDE: Now I understand the whole thing. Thanks, Little Pierre.

LITTLE PIERRE: You're welcome, Monsieur Claude!

CLAUDE (*giving him the revolver*): Take this weapon.

LITTLE PIERRE: Who do I have to shoot?

CLAUDE: Jancelyn, if he tries to come out. You must stop him.

LITTLE PIERRE: OK.

CLAUDE: If he comes at you, shoot him.

LITTLE PIERRE: I will.

CLAUDE (*holding the boy*): Hug me. It will bring me luck. Now, to your post. I'm going to the sanatorium.

(*Claude leaves. After a moment René appears*)

LITTLE PIERRE: No one can pass, Monsieur Jancelyn.

RENÉ: Huh? Who's there?

LITTLE PIERRE: It's me, Little Pierre. You can't leave.

RENÉ: What kind of joke is this?

LITTLE PIERRE: No joke. If you go any further, I'll have to shoot you.

---

both mind and body frequently perceived subjectively as highly unpleasant, giving rise to a state of profound and long-lasting disorientation with a potentially fatal outcome. It contains tropane alkaloids which are responsible for the deliriant effects, and may be severely toxic.

RENÉ (*laughing*): I'm going to strangle you, you little brat! (*He comes toward Little Pierre, his hands open, preparing to strangle him. Little Pierre shoots him. René falls*)

LITTLE PIERRE: I told you.

CURTAIN

## *ACT V*

### *SCENE XII*

Same set as Scene V. Night.

AT RISE, all are grouped around Jeanne's bed.

EDMÉE (*tearfully*): Mama, my dear Mama!

JEANNE: I'm suffocating... I'm suffocating…

PAULA: She's going to die!

EDMÉE: Doctor Vernier, please save her. I don't want her to die.

VERNIER: I beg you. Don't take my strength and courage away with your tears.

PAULA: Edmée, calm down.

EDMÉE: Calm down? When my mother is dying? Doctor, you must do something!

VERNIER: I believed in all my medical science. What a fool I was!

EDMÉE: Georges! You can't abandon my mother!

(*noise outside*)

VERNIER: The one man who can save her has arrived!

(*Schultz enters with Doctor Vulpian*)

VERNIER: Master! Master! Have you got here in time?

EDMÉE: My mother is dying!

(*Doctor Vulpian rushes to Jeanne and examines her*)

VULPIAN: Let me see her.

JEANNE: Help me! Help me!

VULPIAN (*recoiling*): Gentlemen! What have you done? What have you done?

VERNIER (*wildly*): What? What did we do?

VULPIAN: You committed a mistake that would be a crime if it were not involuntary.

ALL: A crime!

VULPIAN: This poor woman has been poisoned!

ALL: Poisoned!

VERNIER: By me?

VULPIAN: Yes, by you. The dose you gave her was too strong, and must inevitably lead to death.

VERNIER: No! I have made no mistake! Neither am I guilty of carelessness. The medication was prepared by Doctor Schultz under my supervision. It could not possibly have poisoned her.

SCHULTZ: I can attest to that on my honor!

VULPIAN: But the evidence is here—irrefutable and undeniable.

VERNIER: Master, allow me to contradict you. She cannot have been poisoned by a weak dose of Belladonna.

VULPIAN: Who said anything about Belladonna? She's dying from one of the worst poisons known to man: *Datura Stramonium.*

VERNIER & SCHULTZ: *Datura Stramonium*!

VULPIAN: It alone can cause these muscular contractions, this dull look, these vitreous eyes... Have you become so blind as not to see it?

VERNIER (*crushed*): How...? Who then gave her the poison?

VULPIAN: That's what I'm asking you!

JEANNE (*moaning*): Ah, ah...

EDMÉE (*to Vulpian*) If you know the cause, you must know the remedy. Save her!

PAULA: Yes, save her!

VULPIAN (*to Schultz*): Prepare a mixture of tannin right away!

SCHULTZ: Immediately, Doctor!

(*Schultz rushes out*)

VERNIER: My God! My God!

PAULA (*low*): Courage!

VULPIAN (*to George*): Listen, and answer me. This is important.

VERNIER: Go ahead.

VULPIAN: Did you mix the Belladonna potion for the patient yourself?

VERNIER: Doctor Schultz took care of that. The carafe was kept full, morning and night. Jeanne drank at her whim.

VULPIAN: Are you sure of Doctor Schultz?

VERNIER: I take him to be a fine doctor and an honest man.

VULPIAN: Is the patient's door kept locked?

VERNIER: No.

VULPIAN: Who has the right to visit her?

VERNIER: Edmée, Mademoiselle Baltus, Doctor Schultz, myself, and the Orderly on duty. But why all these questions?

VULPIAN: Because I'm certain that a crime is being committed in your sanatorium.

EDMÉE: That's horrible!

VERNIER: Who do you suspect?

PAULA: A crime necessarily has its motive. People murder for hate, vengeance, or greed.

EDMÉE: My mother never hurt anyone. Who would hate her?

VERNIER: And what could they steal from her? Master, you must be mistaken; I don't believe there's any crime here.

EDMÉE: My God!

(*Schultz returns with a bowl*)

SCHULTZ: Here's what you've asked for, Doctor.

VERNIER: Give it to me.

VULPIAN: No. As of this moment, I and I alone will care for this patient. A spoonful, please.

SCHULTZ: Here, Doctor.

VULPIAN: We must pull her teeth apart gently. Help me, both of you.

(*George Vernier and Schultz help Doctor Vulpian administer the potion, slowly. Paula and Edmée wait, tensely*)

EDMÉE (*tearfully*): Have mercy, dear God.
PAULA (*going to her, tactfully*): Edm.ee, my poor child. I will always be here to watch over you.
EDMÉE: My poor mother!

(*Doctor Vulpian finishes his work*)

VERNIER: What do you think?
VULPIAN: We'll know in an hour. She'll either be dead or recovered.
EDMÉE: Ah!
VULPIAN: You can only pray, my child!

(*a knock; George goes to open the door*)

VERNIER: What is it?
ORDERLY: A sailor is asking to see you urgently, Doctor.
ALL: A sailor?

(*Claude pushes his way in*)

CLAUDE: Yes, it's I, Claude Marteau. (*seeing Paula and George*) Mademoiselle Baltus, Doctor Vernier!
VERNIER: Claude, we're in the middle of a crisis…
CLAUDE: More than you know. Which one of you is Doctor Rittner?
VERNIER: Doctor Rittner is no longer here. I purchased this institution from him.
CLAUDE: Then you're in charge?
VERNIER: Yes, but…

CLAUDE: And Madame Delarivière is here, with Monsieur Leclerc's cousin, Mademoiselle Edmée?

VERNIER: Yes. (*pointing to Edmée*)

CLAUDE: Ah. Right. I didn't recognize her.

VERNIER: But what's this about?

CLAUDE: I've come to warn you that a scoundrel is coming here to murder one of your patients—Madame Delarivière or her daughter, probably both.

VULPIAN: Ah! You see!

EDMÉE: My mother! My mother!

PAULA: This is terrifying.

VERNIER: But no one can get in here.

CLAUDE: What about the side door on Boulevard Montmorency?

SCHULTZ: That's not possible. If the murderer came that way, Doctor Vernier would be warned immediately.

VERNIER: How?

SCHULTZ: There's an electric alarm bell. The side door cannot be opened without setting it off.

VULPIAN: Let's see…

(*He follows the wire and discovers it's been cut*)

VULPIAN: See! The wire's been cut!

ALL: Ah!

VERNIER: By whom?

CLAUDE: By a man who comes here during the day without causing suspicion, but returns at night to commit foul deeds.

VULPIAN: Who returns at night?

CLAUDE: He'll be back soon.

PAULA: But who is that wretch?

VULPIAN: Yes! Do you know him?

CLAUDE: I should say so. And so do you, Doctor. Vernier.

PAULA: His name! Tell s his name!

CLAUDE (*hesitating*): Perhaps, it would be best if…

VERNIER: No! Speak!

CLAUDE: Fabrice Leclerc!

PAULA (*laughing*): That's ridiculous!

EDMÉE: Fabrice—the murderer of my mother?

CLAUDE (*presenting a flask to Doctor Vulpian*): Is this the poison he's been using?

VULPIAN: *Datura Stramonium!*

PAULA (*forcefully*): Fabrice—a poisoner! You're lying. You're all lying! Why would he want to kill his aunt. Why?

CLAUDE: I'm going to tell you, Mademoiselle...

(*At this moment the side door opens. All stop, stupefied*)

ALL: Ah!

CLAUDE: Hush! He's coming.

PAULA (*recoiling, shocked*): Oh!

VULPIAN: Whoever he is, he's coming to finish his victim.

VERNIER: Silence! Not a word! He'll be surprised *in flagrante delicto*! (*to Schultz*) Cut off his retreat!

(*Schultz leaves*)

PAULA (*falling in a chair*): I'm terrified!

(*George puts out the lamp. Then he pulls the curtain. Only a single light burns near Jeanne's bed. Everyone hides in the shadows. There is a long silence.*

(*Fabrice enters furtively looking around him. He takes a flask from his pocket, uncorks it, then goes to the table near Jeanne, takes the carafe and pours some liquid in it, then recorks the flask. Paula and Edmée show great anxiety during this mute scene.*

(*Doctor Vulpian turns on the lights*)

VULPIAN: Why don't you pour it all, Monsieur Leclerc?

FABRICE (*dropping the flask*): Ah!

175

(*Fabrice turns to flee but comes face to face with Claude*)

CLAUDE: You're nabbed, my lad!
FABRICE (*in a rage*): Ah! Trapped like a rat!

(Jeanne sits bolt upright)

JEANNE: Ah! Ah!
EDMÉE: Mother!
VULPIAN: Hush! (*to Paula*) Do you require further proof or do you find the evidence sufficient?
PAULA: Oh, My God! My God!
FABRICE (*babbling*): Yes, I tried to kill her. I don't know why. I was mad. But, since Jeanne is living, grant me mercy. I repent! Forgive me!
CLAUDE: Don't listen to him, Mademoiselle.
FABRICE: Claude!
CLAUDE: This is not his first murder!
FABRICE: That is a lie!
CLAUDE: You killed Frédéric Baltus. (*to Paula*) This is the real murderer of your brother!
FABRICE: It's a lie!
CLAUDE: No! I have proof! (*showing the revolver*) Aren't these your initials?
PAULA (*in despair*): And I have loved this murderer of my brother? Jeanne's murderer! Ah! (*coldly*) Deliver him to the police. I was looking for the murderer of my brother. I didn't have far to look. And now we've found him, that's all I want.
CLAUDE (*to Fabrice who is looking around like a trapped animal*): Don't bother trying to escape.
EDMÉE (*to Paula*): Your brother will be avenged, but what about my mother?
VULPIAN: I've saved her life; I will restore her reason.

(*Jeanne rises and looks vaguely around her*)

CURTAIN

## SCENE XIII

Same set as Scene IV. Everything is placed in exactly the same position as when Jeanne went mad.

AT RISE, Doctor Vernier, Doctor Vulpian and Doctor Schultz are talking.

VERNIER: As the moment approaches, I'm getting very worried.
VULPIAN: What are you afraid of?
VERNIER: Failure.
VULPIAN: Calm down, my dear George. We need strength, courage. (*to Schultz*) You've prepared the potion?
SCHULTZ: Here it is, Doctor.
VULPIAN: Fine.

(*Claude Marteau enters followed by Spigot*)

CLAUDE: Doctors.
VERNIER: Ah, it's you, Claude?
CLAUDE: To the hour and the moment.
VERNIER: You've brought the persons you were asked to bring?
CLAUDE: Yes, Doctor.
VERNIER: They will want to know the results of what we are going to attempt here.
CLAUDE: Yes, Doctor.
VULPIAN: Who are these persons?
CLAUDE: It's a secret, Doctor.
VULPIAN: A secret I need to know.
CLAUDE: Not yet. I am bringing someone who's come a long way.
VULPIAN: Who?
CLAUDE: Mademoiselle Edmée's father.

177

(*He goes to open the door; Maurice Delarivière enters*)

CLAUDE: Come in, friend
MAURICE: George, my friend!
VERNIER: You! But you were…
MAURICE: Yes. Pushed overboard by my nephew.
CLAUDE: I suspected as much.
MAURICE: Thrown into the sea. Saved by the grace of a floating spar, and picked up by a marauding Portuguese vessel. I was stuck in Lisbon for several months.
VERNIER: You know everything?
MAURICE: Yes. Claude brought me up to speed. You are now going to attempt the impossible. May God help you!

(*Noise of voices outside*)

VULPIAN: Hark! Listen!
VERNIER: The time has come.

(*The noise increases. George opens Jeanne's door and looks inside*)

VULPIAN: What is she doing?
VERNIER: She appears to be asleep.
VULPIAN: Leave the door open, so that the noise from outside reaches her. We don't want her to sleep through this.
MAURICE: Jeanne! Jeanne!
VULPIAN: Get back, get back, gentlemen!

(*Paula enters*)

PAULA: Doctor, Jeanne's awake. She's getting up.
VERNIER: Now, we'll see.

(*He puts out the lights. Silence, except for the sounds of hammering outside. Jeanne comes to listen in the doorway*)

178

VULPIAN: It's evoking memories.

(*The hammering gets louder.*

(*Jeanne staggers is, leaning against the doorway*)

JEANNE: Those blows. They're resonating in my head. Where are they coming from?

(*She moves forward slowly. Edmée appears behind her, terribly nervous. Jeanne points to the window*)

JEANNE: They're coming from that direction.
VERNIER: She's remembering!

(*Jeanne slowly pulls back the curtain and sees the same things we saw in Scene IV*)

JEANNE (*leaning out*): The crowd! Torches!
EDMÉE (*tearfully*): My God! My God! Make a miracle!
JEANNE: Soldiers! Ah, a scaffold. A scaffold!
VERNIER: I'm actually shaking.
VULPIAN: Courage!
JEANNE: An execution. A carriage. A man's getting out. A priest is with him...

(*Fabrice can be seen mounting the scaffold, accompanied by a priest*)

JEANNE: I see him! I see him! I see his face.... It's not Pierre... It's... It's... (*she utters a terrible scream and faints into George's arms*)

(*Doctor Schultz closes the curtain*)

PAULA: Ah!
EDMÉE: Mother!

VERNIER: Silence! Wait!

(*George take's Jeanne's hand and examines her*)

PAULA: My brother is avenged. But what about Jeanne?
VULPIAN: She will live.

(*Jeanne wakes as if from a long dream. She looks about and sees George*)

JEANNE: Ah, it's you, Doctor. But what's wrong with you? You should be content with your patient this morning.
VERNIER (*stunned*): Yes, yes, of course, Madame.

(*Schultz tenders the potion*)

VULPIAN: Drink this!
JEANNE: Yes. Yes. (*she drinks*)
VERNIER: Ah, dear master!
JEANNE: Where's Edmée?
EDMÉE: I'm right here, Mother.
JEANNE: Ah, my darling daughter. I'm cured. We will soon leave Melun. But where's your father?
MAURICE: I'm here, Jeanne!
PAULA: Monsieur Delarivière!
EDMÉE: My father—alive!
JEANNE: Well, of course, he's alive! But... I remember... I... (*runs to curtains*) There, on the square. There was a crowd, soldiers, a scaffold, and a man going up the steps...
VERNIER: You knew that man?
JEANNE (*weeping*): It was my brother!

(*Claude goes out and returns with Little Pierre and Madame Tallandier*)

CLAUDE: And here is his son.

(*Jeanne pulls the child into her arms*)

CLAUDE(*pointing to Madame Tallandier*): And here's his widow!
JEANNE: Marie! My sister-in-law!
MADAME TALLANDIER: Jeanne!
JEANNE: But your husband, my brother, was guillotined.
LITTLE PIERRE (*tearfully*): And Papa was innocent.
MADAME TALLANDIER: He died a martyr!
JEANNE: But who committed the crime then?
MAURICE: Fabrice Leclerc.
CLAUDE: Who has just now paid his debt to society.
JEANNE: I thought I recognized him.

CURTAIN

*"Jules Mary" was the nom-de-plume of Jules Martinie, born in 1851, a French journalist, popular novelist, and a school friend of poet Arthur Rimbaud. After fighting in the Franco-Prussian War of 1870 as a sniper, Martinie became a full-time writer, penning numerous war stories, before being promoted to Editor-in-chief of* L'Indépendant *at age 23. He then worked at* Le Petit Parisien *and* Le Petit Journal *before becoming an editor at* Le Petit Moniteur, *while still writing popular feuilletons. His* Docteur Madelor *(1878) was so successful that it considerably increased the circulation of* Le Petit Moniteur. *In a few years, the talented and prolific Martinie was known as the "modern Alexandre Dumas." His novels were often about miscarriages of justice. Many were adapted to the theater, and later as films. His best-known work is* Roger la Honte *[Roger the Shame] (1886), which was filmed five times.* Zizi-la-gueuse *[Zizi the Beggarwoman] was collected and published by Tallandier in 1914, before being adapted into a play. Martinie passed away in Paris in 1922.*

# ZIZI

## by Jules Mary.

## CHARACTERS

*in order of appearance*

COUNT HENRI DE LA ROCHE-AIGLON, a retired Judge
SONIA, his wife
STANISLAS LAVROYER, the Count's henchman
BAPTISTIN ROUSCOUBON, another henchman
GEORGES DE LA ROCHE-AIGLON, Henri's youngest son
LUDOVIC DE LA ROCHE-AIGLON, Henri's oldest son
DIRKO, owner of Dirko's Circus
JARRY, a clown
OUDJA, a belly dancer

WALTER HOLMCROFT, an American millionaire
ZIZI, a beautiful tiger-tamer
DOCTOR RIVES, a MD
LEWIS MORLAND, Holmcroft's attorney
ALBERTO SPOLETTO, a farmer in Brittany
RITA, Alberto's lady-friend
TINA, a nine years-old child
ÉMILE, her brother, slightly older (can be played by a girl)
MATHURINE COLET, an old Breton fisherwoman
PAPA KERMADOC, an old Breton fisherman
MARIE-ANNE KERMADOC, his wife
JAOUEN TUSSERIC, another fisherman, but younger
M. RENAULT, an Investigating Magistrate
THOMAS, a policeman
MAÎTRE ERNEST PATELOT, a Notary

# *ACT I*

## *SCENE I*

A living room in the Chateau of the Count de la Roche-Aiglon. At the back, there is a door giving onto a park. There are doors right and left, a sofa, chairs and armchairs.

AT RISE, the Count de la Roche-Aiglon opens one of the doors at the back, letting the light of the setting sun flood the room.

ROCHE-AIGLON (*calling*): Come in, my dear Sonia.

(*Sonia enters*)

SONIA: After such along stay abroad, I cannot tell you what emotion I'm feeling returning to the Chateau.
ROCHE-AIGLON: Which witnessed our honeymoon and our children at play.
SONIA: My children, Henri. When you left for Brazil, you took them away from me and you never told me why. Or why you exhibit such an icy countenance toward me.
ROCHE-AIGLON: I intend to be the sole master of their education. But stop your needless complaints. You're going to see them again.
SONIA: Oh, that's wonderful! Bless you!
ROCHE-AIGLON: Today is July 23$^{rd}$, Sonia. Does that remind you of something?
SONIA: No. What?
ROCHE-AIGLON: It was 25 years ago today that we were married. And I promised to bring you back here to celebrate our silver wedding anniversary. Wander through that room which is filled with mementos. I'll come and get you soon.

(*Sonia looks at him suspiciously but steps inside*)

ROCHE-AIGLON (calling): Lavroyer! I know you got here ahead of us. I saw you on the terrace. Come here!

(*Stanislas Lavroyer appears; he's a fat man, carrying several suitcases*)

LAVROYER: Here I am, Your honor.
ROCHE-AIGLON: I'm no longer a Judge, Monsieur Lavroyer, and there no longer worthy of the title. Where's Ludovic?
LAVROYER: In the green room.
ROCHE-AIGLON: Fine. First of all, you may recall a conversation that I had with you ten years ago, and with Baptistin Rouscoubon, another devoted servant.

(*Baptistin Rouscoubon enters; he's thin, wiry and very louche-looking*)

ROUSCOUBON: Bonjour, Lavroyer. It's been a long time since I last saw you. You are indeed the most remarkable swine I've ever known.
LAVROYER: You're trying to flatter me.
ROUSCOUBON: No. I know you very well. Remember: I was your comrade and accomplice for a long time. (to the Count) You could easily have had us up both on charges. But you didn't do your duty that day.
ROCHE-AIGLON (*sitting on the sofa*): I entered a dismissal in your favor. After that, I resigned.
ROUSCOUBON: And you entrusted Georges, your youngest son, to me.
LAVROYER: And Ludovic, your oldest one to me. And told us to make criminals of them, without faith nor law.
ROCHE-AIGLON: Yes. I asked you to raise them in your image.
LAVROYER: I asked myself then, why you would do that?

ROCHE-AIGLON: But you never asked me.

LAVROYER: I think I guessed.

ROCHE-AIGLON: I forbid you to make suppositions. Did you succeed?

LAVROYER: Beyond your hopes. I, Stanislas Lavroyer, disbarred attorney, employed all my skills to destroying the morals of the boy you entrusted to me. I must confess the terrain was fertile. I don't know of a man better prepared than your Ludovic for a life of fraud and crime. Ah, you can thank me.

ROCHE-AIGLON (*coldly*): Here's your reward. (*he gives him a check*)

LAVROYER: Fifty thousand. Thank you, Count. In return for this gift, I'll give you some advice. After you've released him, lock everything up as you would lock up sheep when famished wolves are on the prowl. Ludovic is no longer a man, he's a starving predator.

ROCHE-AIGLON: I am thrilled. Tonight you'll dine with your pupil in the right wing of the Chateau.

LAVROYER: As you wish.

ROCHE-AIGLON: Go, rejoin your worthy student.


(*Lavroyer leaves*)


ROUSCOUBON (*rather embarrassed*): Hum! Hum!

ROCHE-AIGLON: What?

ROUSCOUBON: I gave Georges the most execrable advice as befits a former professor of Theology like myself. I employed all my skills to the high mission of destroying his moral compass...

ROCHE-AIGLON: Get to the point.

ROUSCOUBON: At first, things didn't go too badly. But the bad news is that, despite my best efforts, your son, Georges, remains an honest man. (*reaction by Roche-Aiglon*) That's not all. He himself converted me, and you see before you a man a little ashamed by this metamorphosis. He revolted against me and, in the end, he conquered me. As for you, Count, I understand your dissatisfaction. Condolences.

ROCHE-AIGLON: I thought I knew men. I was mistaken. Still, here's your money. (*he gives him a check*)

ROUSCOUBON: Fifty thousand. But my mission was to make Georges a criminal. I failed. I haven't earned this. Keep your money. (*he tears up the check*) Say what you will, being a honest man costs dearly.

ROCHE-AIGLON: Send Georges to me, and tell Lavroyer to send Ludovic to me.

ROUSCOUBON (*apologetic*) : My most sincere regrets.

(*he leaves*)

ROCHE-AIGLON: I dreamed of a more complete vengeance.

(*Georges enters*)

GEORGES: Father.

(*The Count offers his hand to avoid a hug*)

GEORGES: You recognize me, don't you? A child turned into a man.

ROCHE-AIGLON: I recognize you perfectly, Georges.

GEORGE: Why you don't hug me?

ROCHE-AIGLON: Because you're a man now. Let's not waste time on such sentimental effusions. Have you seen your brother?

GEORGES: No, but Monsieur Rouscoubon said he was coming.

ROCHE-AIGLON: Here he is!

(*Ludovic enters*)

GEORGES: Ludovic!

LUDOVIC: Georges!

GEORGE (*hugging his brother*): At least, you don't refuse to hug me.

LUDOVIC (*to Roche-Aiglon*): You wanted to see me, Monsieur? After such a long separation, I won't dare to call you "father" until after you've called me "son." (*silence by Roche-Aiglon*) I wanted to tell you that I don't have any rancor toward you for my long exile. You've taken care of all my needs, and you've given me a precious advisor in Monsieur Lavroyer. Thanks to him, I'm armed to the teeth for the struggles of life. I must thank you.

GEORGES: And our mother... Where is my poor, dear mother?

ROCHE-AIGLON: She's here. (*reaction by Georges, none by Ludovic*) Stay here with your brother, Georges. In a few minutes, you'll be able to see her.

(*He leaves*)

LUDOVIC: No doubt you've understood our father's attitude?

GEORGES: No, but I've suffered terribly.

LUDOVIC: Isn't it clear? He doesn't believe we're his children.

GEORGES: Don't insult our mother. You'll feel remorseful for that.

LUDOVIC: Remorseful, I? I don't know the feeling. Anyway, I've no intention of insulting her. I'm only explaining to you what's going on in our father's head. My father wanted to make me what I am. What is it? I don't know yet. But I'm ready to play with the lives of others. What about you?

GEORGES: I paid no attention to Rouscoubon's teachings. I only thought of what Mother taught us.

LUDOVIC: If you are sincere, I pity you. You've lost before the battle even begins.

GEORGES: Are you sure of that?

LUDOVIC: One has to eat or be eaten. Fortunately, I have a good appetite. I want a fortune and I know where to find it.

GEORGES: And you fear no obstacle in your path?

LUDOVIC: Best not put yourself between me and my dreams.

GEORGES: I'm stronger than you think. I believe in honor, justice, and all that is beautiful.

LUDOVIC: I'll bet you believe in love, too?

GEORGES: Don't you?

LUDOVIC: I love women, but not the way you do. You'll be their slave, I'll be their master. Here, look at this. (*pulls out a picture*)

GEORGES (*concealing his surprise*): Zizi!

LUDOVIC: She tames tigers.

GEORGES: She's very beautiful. And you love her?

LUDOVIC: I want her.

GEORGES: Is she your mistress?

LUDOVIC: Not yet. Let me have it back. (*takes back the picture*)

(*The Count de la Roche-Aiglon returns with Sonia*)

ROCHE-AIGLON (*to Sonia*): Here are your sons.

GEORGES (*running to her*): Mother! (*kissing her tenderly*)

SONIA: My George. And you, Ludovic. (*she embraces her eldest son*) Finally, I've got you back. (*to Roche-Aiglon*) Forever, right?

ROCHE-AIGLON: Don't worry, they'll never leave you again. Only death will separate you. But I have important things to tell you. I want to dine alone with you, as we did 25 years ago. (*to the two young men*) Leave us now.

LUDOVIC: Your wishes are orders, Monsieur.

GEORGES : Till later, Mama. (*he kisses her again*)

(*The two young men go out*)

SONIA: It seems like yesterday that we left this love nest.

ROCHE-AIGLON: Everything has remained just as we left it. Those were my orders.

SONIA: I was so happy here. I've always wanted to die here.

ROCHE-AIGLON: May your wish be fulfilled.

(*Sonia looks at him. A silence*)

SONIA: I've never stopped loving you.

ROCHE-AIGLON (*with an ironic smile*): Let's eat. I have the appetite of an ogre. (*serves Sonia and starts eating*) I'm devouring this as if I were eating for the last time. You aren't eating, Sonia. Drink at least to our love. To forgetting the past. (*filling the glasses*)

SONIA (*after drinking*): I've never taken my heart back, and I'm waiting for you to tell me at last why you took back yours.

ROCHE-AIGLON: You'll learn everything. I must tell you, first of all, that this chateau no longer belongs to me. The sale was signed yesterday; the money received and paid in equal shares to Georges and Ludovic. When I married you, you were poor. Your children had nothing to expect from you.

SONIA: Are we ruined?

ROCHE-AIGLON: Completely ruined.

SONIA: How will we live?

ROCHE-AIGLON: Is it really necessary to live?

SONIA: What do you mean? I've been a martyr to your silences for far too long. I demand to know the truth.

ROCHE-AIGLON: Sonia, I loved you madly. How did you respond? By the most infamous treachery.

SONIA: Me?

ROCHE-AIGLON: Yes! It was here, in this very room, when you thought I was away, that I found you in the arms of your lover. Why didn't I kill you both? I still wonder… listened. I learned that you'd been seeing him in secret. Later, I found his portrait, which bore a striking resemblance to your two sons.

SONIA: Yes, it's true.

ROCHE-AIGLON: You confess at last! Your children are not mine. They are his. And I wanted to exercise over them a terrible vengeance. But one resisted.

SONIA: Georges, right?

ROCHE-AIGLON: No matter. The other, at least, will be a criminal.

SONIA: But you're the one who committed a crime, for I am innocent.

ROCHE-AIGLON (*sneering*): Innocent!

SONIA: That man wasn't my lover, he was my brother!

ROCHE-AIGLON: Your brother?

SONIA: Yes, and those kisses were goodbye kisses. He went into exile, and I never saw him again.

ROCHE-AIGLON: That's a lie! You had only one brother, and I know he died a long time ago.

SONIA: No. He lived, I tell you. He was involved in some shameful things...

ROCHE-AIGLON: Speak!

SONIA: Yes, my brother Karl... The truth of it is that he was an anarchist. He'd killed the Chief of Police in Saint Petersburg. Then he fled to France, and from France, he went to America. (*she cries in bitter sorrow*)

ROCHE-AIGLON: Tell me you are lying.

SONIA: No. Karl was my brother. You are sick!

ROCHE-AIGLON: So be it then. I poisoned the wine. I wanted to die with you, here.

SONIA: My misfortune. It was my silence that killed me. (*she falls*)

ROCHE-AIGLON: Ah, this is too terrible! Have mercy, Sonia. Please, forgive me! (*staggering and falling*) I don't want you to die.

(*Using all his remaining strength, he opens the door*)
ROCHE-AIGLON: Help!

(*Georges and Rouscoubon appear*)

ROCHE-AIGLON Help her! Save her! (*he falls*)

GEORGES (*running to his mother*): Mother! She's still breathing. Answer me, Mama!

ROCHE-AIGLON: Forgive me, my son! (*he dies*)

ROUSCOUBON (*leaning over Roche-Aiglon*): He's dead.

GEORGES: She's opening her eyes!

SONIA: Is it you, George? Your father and I wanted to die. Swear to me to watch over your brother and save him from a life of crime at any cost.

GEORGES: I swear it. But I want you to live!

(*Lavroyer and Ludovic appear; Ludovic starts to go toward his mother*)

LAVROYER (*holding him back*): I taught you never to cry. Come, let's get out of here.

(*They leave*)

ROUSCOUBON: The scoundrels are leaving

GEORGES (*leaning over his mother*): Mama! Mama!

CURTAIN

# *ACT II*

## *SCENE II*

The Circus Dirko. Circus posters on the wall. Zizi's dressing room to the right.

AT RISE, Dirko, the Circus' owner, is conferring with Jarry, one of the clowns.

JARRY: Boss, the house is full and we've had to turn away at least fifty customers.

DIRKO: That was expected, Jarry. With all the publicity I put out... Huge posters all over town... Articles in all the papers.... And once Zizi does her number with her tigers...

(*Rouscoubon enters*)

ROUSCOUBON: Mademoiselle Zizi, if you please?.

JARRY: Monsieur?

DIRKO: I am the manager of Dirko's Circus. What do you want, Monsieur?

ROUSCOUBON: I'd like to talk to Mademoiselle Zizi.

DIRKO: Ah, it's impossible, Monsieur. Her act is extremely dangerous and she cannot be disturbed before her performance. Also, I've decided that, after tonight's performance, she won't see any more journalists.

ROUSCOUBON: Do I look like a journalist? I am Baptistin Rouscoubon!

DIRKO: That doesn't mean much to me.

ROUSCOUBON: That maybe, but Mademoiselle Zizi knows me.

DIRKO: I don't want anyone to see my star before the show. I must respectfully ask you to leave, Monsieur Rousconbon. Good-bye.

(*Dirko leaves*)

ROUSCOUBON: Not Rous*conbon*, Rous*coubon*, Monsieur Ditko!
JARRY: Not Ditko, Dirko.
ROUSCOUBON: Right. Sorry.
JARRY: You have a ticket?
ROUSCOUBON: Yes, it cost me a tenner, and I'm seated between two fat ladies.
JARRY: I tell you what, come back later and I'll see what I can do.
ROUSCOUBON: Thank you, buddy. Till later.
OUDJA'S VOICE: M'sieur Jarry, they're calling you!
JARRY: Coming!

(*As Rouscoubon starts to leave, he bumps into Holmcroft, an American*)

ROUSCOUBON: Excuse me, Monsieur.
JARRY (*noticing the new arrival*): Monsieur Holmcroft!
HOLMCROFT: Yes?
JARRY: You're back in Paris!
HOLMCROFT: Yes.
JARRY: And you're thinking about Mademoiselle Zizi?
HOLMCROFT: Not quite. I'm merely leaving my card here for Mr. Dirko and returning to my seat.

(*He goes to sit at a table and writes on the back of his calling card.*

(*Oudja enters; she's a beautiful woman dressed in a belly dancing outfit.*

(*Meanwhile, Rouscoubon stopped when he heard Holmcroft's name, and returns*)

195

OUDJA: Jarry! We're waiting for you to begin!

JARRY: Yeas, yes, I'm coming!

ROUSCOUBON: Are you Mr. Holmcroft? I've read a lot about you in the papers.

HOLMCROFT (*still seated*): It's probably the truth. They can't lie all the time.

ROUSCOUBON: Allow me to introduce myself. I'm Baptistin Rouscoubon.

HOLMCROFT: Pleased to meet you. You see, I bet a million dollars with a friend, Tom Lewis. It's a question of whether Mademoiselle Zizi will be killed by her tigers. Tom bet she wouldn't; I bet that she would.

ROUSCOUBON: That's a stupid bet.

HOLMCROFT: Almost all the bets we make in America are stupid bets. That's why I follow Mademoiselle Zizi everywhere.

ROUSCOUBON: Does she know why?

HOLMCROFT: Yes, and she laughs about it. I'm beginning to think I may lose.

ROUSCOUBON: Lose what?

HOLMCROFT: My bet. Because Mademoiselle Zizi has a gift, you see. She is truly astonishing. With tigers, she doesn't need a whip or special commands. They leap on her; she just looks at them, and they lie down. Then she puts her arm around their neck...

ROUSCOUBON: And you bet that... You're a monster!

HOLMCROFT: No, not all. I'm really a very nice man. But tell me, Mr. Rouscou... Rouscou...

ROUSCOUBON: Rouscoubon

HOLMCROFT: Yes. Rouscoubon. Do you know Mademoiselle Zizi?

ROUSCOUBON: I knew her as a child.

HOLMCROFT: Ah?

ROUSCOUBON: It's a touching story.

HOLMCROFT: I'd love to hear it.

ROUSCOUBON: I lived in Le Havre, with my student, Georges, then fifteen. Across our courtyard, there was a poor old woman with her granddaughter, barely twelve at the time. Her real name was Zinz. She turned it into Zizi later. She was quite a looker!

HOLMCROFT: And had she the gift already?

ROUSCOUBON: Georges and Zizi met often. They loved each other innocently, without being aware of it. What we didn't grasp was that Zizi and her grandmother were in a terrible financial situation. One winter night, when it was particularly cold, Zizi brought something home that she shouldn't have—a big lump of coke. But you know what can happen if you burn a lump of coke in a closed room…?

HOLMCROFT: Yes, I do.

ROUSCOUBON: The next morning, Georges knocked on their door. No response. He broke a window. The old lady was lying on the floor, dead already. Zizi was on the bed. Fortunately, he was in time. A doctor was able to revive her.

HOLMCROFT: That's nice. What happened then?

ROUSCOUBON: Then the two kids never saw each other again because of that Moneyman.

HOLMCROFT: What Monkeyman?

ROUSCOUBON: Dirko. A circus director who lived in a neighboring hotel. He heard about the accident. He saw Zizi and was struck by her beauty.

HOLMCROFT: He recognized she had the gift?

ROUSCOUBON: Yes. He trained her to tame tigers. You know the rest.

HOLMCROFT: And your pupil?

ROUSCOUBON: He's a man now. They keep in touch. She writes to him from time to time. He asked me to bring her his latest reply. The death of his parents keeps him from coming himself. I plan to give it to her after her performance.

HOLMCROFT: Yes. Afterwards. Zizi has always been a good girl. Lots of men have laid their fortune at her feet. When they toured the States, a young millionaire blew his brains out because she rejected him.

(*Dirko returns*)

197

DIRKO: What! You're still here!
ROUSCOUBON: I was talking to this heartless man. I'll leave now.

(*he leaves*)

DIRKO: Ah! Mr. Holmcroft.
HOLMCROFT: Weren't you expecting me?
DIRKO: You haven't renounced your bet yet?
HOLMCROFT: You'd be the loser if I did. It's made you a lot of money.

(*Zizi enters*)

ZIZI: Why, it's Mr. Holmcroft! I'd have been very disappointed if you hadn't crossed the ocean to follow me.
HOLMCROFT: I'm deeply touched when you blow me a kiss when you enter the cage.
ZIZI: And I like it when you get up, bow, and take off your hat.
HOLMCROFT: Sincerely, I really want to lose my bet. (*kisses her hand*) The French way. Now the American. Shake. (*shakes her hand*) I'm going to my seat.

(*He leaves; Oudja returns*)

DIRKO: Feeling good tonight, Zizi?
ZIZI: Very good, my dear Dirko.
DIRKO (*to Oudja*): Well, Oudja, how did the belly dance go?
OUDJA: Nit so good. I don't think they even looked at me. They're all waiting for Zizi. But I love her too much to be jealous of her!
DIRKO: Make sure her hair is right, and that she puts on some lipstick. (*to Zizi*) You really aren't enough of a coquette.
OUDJA: She's beautiful enough to not need it.

(*She and Zizi go into the latter's dressing room; Jarry returns*)

JARRY: Boss, there are eight journalists who want to speak to you.
DIRKO: Right. I'll go.

(*They go out. Lavroyer and Ludovic enter*)

LAVROYER: Well, here we are. We got in easily enough with that fake Police ID. I always carry it with me. But let me tell you, you are wrong to neglect that other business for a mere woman.
LUDOVIC: No useless moralizing, Lavroyer. You know I want her. Besides, I don't want my brother to take her from me. Let him take care of the funeral of our parents instead.
LAVROYER: Still, to fall for a circus performer!
LUDOVIC: They say she's virtuous.
LAVROYER: They all say that.
LUDOVIC: Enough. While my brother's weeping in a grave-yard, I have time to act.

(*Oudja emerges from Zizi's dressing room; Ludovic approaches her*)

LUDOVIC: Mademoiselle Zizi?
OUDJA: She's going to appear with her tigers in five minutes. Right now, she can't see anyone.
LUDOVIC: I understand. All I ask is that you tell her my name: Monsieur de la Roche-Aiglon.
OUDJA: Should it mean something to her?
LUDOVIC: I hope so. It's the name of a friend. Tell her that I'm here.

(*Oudja goes back into the dressing room*)

LUDOVIC: We'll see if she remembers my brother's name.

(*Zizi emerges from her dressing room, beaming; she is with Oudja*)

ZIZI: Georges! It is you! How happy I… (*realizing she's not talking to Georges*) Excuse me, Monsieur. I thought you were Georges de la Roche-Aiglon.
LUDOVIC: I'm his older brother, Ludovic, Mademoiselle.
ZIZI: Ah, yes. He told me he had a, older brother. You were traveling in America, weren't you?
LUDOVIC: Yes. And that's where I first saw you, about two months ago. I didn't know you knew my brother.
ZIZI: Then why did you tell Oudja to use the name of De la Roche-Aiglon?
LUDOVIC: Because from the day I saw you. I felt I loved you.
ZIZI: But I don't love you, Monsieur. Excuse me, my tigers are waiting.
LUDOVIC: Forgive me for this confession that escaped me.
ZIZI: Gladly, if you give me news of your brother.
LUDOVIC: He's detained a long way from here. In Provence.
LAVROYER: Yes. On important family business.
LUDOVIC: He's getting married.
ZIZI (*in a strangled voice*): He's getting married? (*she grabs Oudja's arm and hides her emotion*)
LUDOVIC: But that won't prevent him from seeing his little friend again.
ZIZI (*in a blank voice, still under control*): I really hope so.
SHOUTING VOICE: On stage for the tigers! (*tigers can be heard roaring*)
LUDOVIC: We're going to applaud you, now. (*to Lavroyer*) She took it rather well.
LAVROYER: You think so?

(*They leave; Dirko returns*)

ZIZI (*to Oudja*): Oh, Oudja, I want to cry!
OUDJA: What's the matter?

ZIZI: Nothing. It's nothing... Just a little pain.

DIRKO: Now isn't the moment to think of pain, girl. You know that the least distraction could spell trouble.

ZIZI (*taking his hand*): Don't worry, Monsieur.

DIRKO: But your hand is trembling.

ZIZI: As soon as I set foot on the ring, all will be forgotten. Come.

(*She leaves with Dirko. We hear roars of applause as she enters the cage*)

OUDJA: How pale she was. What did those men say to her? Is it my fault? (*looking*) No. She's greeting the American who's bowing to her. (*Tigers roar*) They are all leaping on her. She's not defending herself... (*screams*)

SHOUTS: Help! Help! She's dead!

(*After a few moments, Rouscoubon enters carrying Zizi who is unconscious, covered with blood. He's aided by Dirko, Jarry, and other circus employees*)

DIRKO: A doctor! A doctor! (*to Rouscoubon who's injured and covered with blood*) I thank you for your courage, Monsieur.

ROUSCOUBON: Ah! I fear I was too late!

(*Doctor Rives comes in, followed by Holmcroft, then by Lavroyer and Ludovic*)

RIVES: I'm a doctor. Let me look at her!

HOLMCROFT (*aghast*): Tell me she isn't dead!

ROUSCOUBON (*to Oudja*): What happened? Do you know? It's like she wanted to die. Why?

OUDJA: I don't know. She was upset after talking to those two men (*pointing to Lavroyer and Ludovic*)

HOLMCROFT: Mercy! Tell me...

ROUSCOUBON: You, you are an imbecile! (*to Lavroyer and Ludovic*) And as for you, I think you are both murderers!

CURTAIN

# ACT III
## SCENE III

A luxurious room that also serves as Dirko's office. Doors to the middle, right and left.

AT RISE, Dirko is talking to Oudja.

DIRKO: I thank you again for the good news you are giving me.

OUDJA: The wounds are apparently not too serious, but the fever hasn't left her.

DIRKO: Yes, her hands were still on fire yesterday.

OUDJA: Last night her fever went down. She was able to get up this morning and I made her lunch. The Doctor is still with her.

DIRKO: Has she seen anyone since the accident?

OUDJA: No one.

DIRKO: It might be prudent to keep visitors away for a few more days.

(*ringing*)

DIRKO: Don't let anyone in. Tell them that the doctor is with her and get rid of them.

(*he goes out; Oudja goes out a different door and returns with Ludovic*)

OUDJA: Monsieur, I already told you, Mademoiselle Zizi cannot see anyone.

LUDOVIC: I've come almost every day to get news of her condition. I've learned from the concierge she's finally better. I absolutely must see her.

(*A door is heard opening and closing. Lavroyer appears*)

OUDJA (*aside*): There's the other one.

LUDOVIC: Lavroyer!

LAVROYER: My dear Ludovic. I arrived in Paris today. Where could you be if not prowling around here?

OUDJA (*to Lavroyer*): I was telling this gentleman that Mademoiselle Zizi cannot receive anyone.

LUDOVIC: Tell her my name.

OUDJA: Oh, I haven't forgotten that! What was it that you said to her before?

LAVROYER: You've got some nerve, for a belly dancer.

LUDOVIC (*gesturing to appease Lavroyer*): I merely told her that I love her.

OUDJA: I doubt it. That wouldn't upset her to the degree it did. You must have said something else.

LUDOVIC: This interrogation has lasted long enough. Help me with her. You won't be sorry. (*offers her some money*)

OUDJA: If she loves you, you don't need me. If she doesn't, I can't help you. You see, your money is useless. (*she returns the money*)

LUDOVIC: So be it. I will wait here.

OUDJA: The doctor is still with her.

LAVROYER: Excellent. I hope he'll give us hope that her recovery is complete. Please take my hat.

(*Oudja gives him a look of hate and defiance, but takes his hate and coat and goes out*)

LAVROYER: Now we can chat. Make sure no one can hear us.

LUDOVIC (*looking at the door to the right*): Hmm… There's a small staircase here...

(*He opens it and steps out*)

LAVROYER: It must give onto a side street. I noticed a door as I came in. Hey, where did you go?

(*Ludovic returns and shuts the door*)

LUDOVIC: The lock's a bit rusty. (*hiding the door key in his pocket*)

LAVROYER : Sit down and listen. While you were moping over Zizi, I took action. Your fortune is made. Once you are a millionaire – after deducting my commission, of course! – you can have all the women you want.

LUDOVIC: You did right, Lavroyer. I'll need money. Love hasn't made me forget that.

LAVROYER: Let's consider your uncle's will. He left all his money to his brother, the one that the Tsar – very wisely in my opinion – exiled to Siberia.

LUDOVIC: If there are no other other heirs, that fortune reverts to me and my brother, right?

LAVROYER: Actually, only to you, because I told him your brother was dead. The problem is to rid ourselves of the other heirs without creating a scandal. Since you left me, I acted with the help of a loyal accomplice. I went to Siberia. I'm back and your uncle's brother is dead.

LUDOVIC: You killed him?

LAVROYER: No. I never act myself. As I said, he'd been deported to Siberia. I offered to help him escape and hired a boat for him to take. Then, I informed the Tsarist Police of his plans and he was shot while trying to escape. I entrusted his two children to Spoletto. They're now in a secure place—a farm in Brittany.

LUDOVIC: These children must also be disposed of.

LAVROYER: Yes, but carefully. I won't act without you. It's only fair that you share the risk.

LUDOVIC: Tomorrow or the day after, I promise to go with you.

LAVROYER: Then you expect to conquer your beloved in two days?

LUDOVIC: Perhaps.
LAVROYER: Hark! Someone's coming.

(*They rise. Dirko comes in escorting Doctor Rives out*)

DIRKO: Thank you, Doctor. I will see you tomorrow. (*to Lavroyer & Ludovic*): Will you two at last leave?
LUDOVIC: I beg your pardon?
DIRKO: Gentlemen, I suspect you of being the cause, unknowingly perhaps, of that terrible accident that almost ruined me. Maybe it was a small thing, but it almost cost Zizi her life. I love her like a father. Your place is not here. (*pointing to the door*)
LUDOVIC: You are insolent, Monsieur. You cannot think I will abase myself by arguing with a mountebank.
DIRKO: It would be wise of you not to.
LUDOVIC: You'll hear from me.

(*Lavroyer follows Ludovic to the door; Rouscoubon returns holding a coat and hat*)

ROUSCOUBON (*to Lavroyer*): Here's your hat and coat, old buddy.

(*Lavroyer and Ludovic leave*)

DIRKO: Ah, Monsieur Rouscoubon, I haven't forgotten your name, and I greatly regret having prevented you from seeing Zizi that fatal night.
ROUSCOUBON: Yes, I think the misfortune might have been avoided.
DIRKO: Don't hold it against me. Without you, she would be dead.
ROUSCOUBON: How is she today?
DIRKO: Almost completely recovered. I'm going to tell our friends from the circus that she'll be back in a couple of weeks.

(*He leaves*)

ROUSCOUBON: I should tell Georges.

(*He leaves also; after a while Zizi enters with Oudja*)

ZIZI: I think I'm well enough now to receive visitors.
OUDJA: Mr. Holmcroft and his friend have been waiting for hours.
ZIZI: Show them in.

(*Oudja goes out and returns with Holmcroft and his attorney, Lewis Morland, esq.*)

ZIZI: As you can see, sirs, the tigers didn't entirely devour me.
HOLMCROFT: In America, the arbitrators debated for a month and they agreed you were sufficiently devoured.
ZIZI: What do you mean?
MORLAND: According to the terms of the bet, Miss, you are theoretically dead. Had it been otherwise, my client would have lost a million dollars. But now, he's won.
ZIZI: I still don't get it.
MORLAND: In other words, Miss, my client feels very remorseful for having made such an unconscionable bet and is offering his winnings to you.
ZIZI: But, Mr. Holmcroft, you had nothing to do with the accident.
HOLMCROFT: Oh, thank you for saying that! Nevertheless, I feel greatly ashamed. Please accept this token of my gratitude. It's my contribution to your future well-being.
ZIZI: Are you serious?
MORLAND: Nothing could be more serious, Miss.
ZIZI: A fortune like that, without conditions!
HOLMCROFT: None whatsoever.
MORLAND: Do you accept, Miss?

HOLMCROFT: So I can sleep again.

(*Zizi gets up and offers him her hand*)

ZIZI: Yes! And thank you!
HOLMCROFT: Oh, it's I who must thank you.

(*He kisses her hand, and leaves with Morland.*

(*After a moment, Rouscoubon pops his head in*)

ROUSCOUBON: Business's over?
OUDJA: Mr. Rouscoubon!
ZIZI: They told me you risked your life for me.
ROUSCOUBON: Let's not talk about that. Let me tell you how happy I am that you have recovered. I've brought some-one who absolutely insists on seeing you.

(he goes out)

ZIZI: What's he talking about?
OUDJA: I don't know.

(*He returns with Georges*)

ZIZI: Georges! (*she still thinks he's married so her expression grows cold*)
GEORGES: Zizi! I felt terrible about this frightful accident. (*he takes her hand which she tries to pull away*) What's wrong with you? Where's my little friend? You seem to want to get away from me?
ZIZI (*controlling herself*): Georges!
GEORGES: Ah, you've forgotten me! You still haven't writ-ten back to me.

(*Zizi collapses in tears on the couch*)

GEORGES: Why these tears? Say something! Tell me what's wrong!

ZIZI: It's… your marriage.

GEORGES: My marriage? What marriage?

ZIZI: I learned about it just before I was going to perform, and, well, it upset me greatly.

GEORGES: I don't understand. I'm not married. Who told you such a lie? Who?

ZIZI: So it's not true? Ah, I wanted to die! Now, I want to live!

GEORGES: Tell me who did this? Tell me his name!

ZIZI: Later, much later. But tell me, why are you so sad?

GEORGES (*calming down*): My sorrows don't come from a lie, but from a reality. My dying mother made me swear to watch over my brother, whose bad instincts shocked the poor, saintly woman. Wherever he goes, I have to follow him. In a word, I am his shadow. Because of this, we may not be able to see each other for a while.

ZIZI: But you do love me?

GEORGES: Of course, I love you!

ZIZI: Then don't despair. We know we love each other, and we'll find a way to endure being apart.

GEORGES: My darling! Till tomorrow.

ZIZI: Till tomorrow.

(*Georges and Rouscoubon leave*)

OUDJA: You are worn out.

ZIZI: No. I'm exhausted from the happiness of seeing Georges again. You don't need to watch over me now. You can leave me alone. I'm going to take a nap.

OUDJA: I'll sleep here on the couch all the same.

(*Zizi goes to her bedroom.*

(*Oudja begins putting out the lights; suddenly, a bell rings*)

OUDJA (*going to the door*): You again!

(*It is Lavroyer*)

LAVROYER: Excuse me for coming back at this late hour, but I think I took a hat that isn't mine.
OUDJA: I think it must belong to that lawyer. Yours must still be in the other room.
LAVROYER: Thank you.

(*He leaves after inspecting the place.*

(*Oudja continues putting out the lights, then curls up on the divan. As she's about to fall asleep, there's a noise at the side door*)

OUDJA: I thought I heard some noise…

(*She listens. Nothing. She then falls asleep.*

(*Slowly, furtively, Ludovic enters on tip-toe, but bumps into a footstool waking Oudja*)

OUDJA (*standing up*) You!

(*Ludovic grabs her and presses a rag with chloroform over her face. Oudja struggles but collapses*)

LUDOVIC: And now, Zizi shall be mine!

(*He goes to Zizi's room*)

CURTAIN

## SCENE IV

Same set.

AT RISE, Zizi and Oudja are sitting on the couch, talking.

ZIZI: You'll say nothing, won't you, Oudja?
OUDJA: I've sworn it.
ZIZI: If Georges knew what his brother did, he'd kill him. I don't want that blood on his hands. (*with a gesture of disgust*) The little Zizi he knew no longer exists. He must stop loving me. I'm no longer worthy of him.
OUDJA: But Zizi...
ZIZI: Oh, I know, he'll pity me. But he'll want to know all about what happened last night. And I'd rather die! And that's not all. It seems that love is dead in me. Yes, dead. I don't even have tears to cry. In its place, all there is is hate.
OUDJA: Monsieur Georges will never believe that you stopped loving him.
ZIZI: He must, Oudja! It's for his own good!
OUDJA: But he loves you!
ZIZI (*standing*): He must stop loving me. He'll suffer less than if he learns what his brother did to me.
OUDJA: And you'll forget Georges?
ZIZI (*after a silence*): No. I won't forget him. You're right. But what difference does it make? I'll love him secretly, all my life. That will be my strength. But he must forget me, scorn me even. Do what I say – or leave me.
OUDJA: I'll never leave you.

(*Ringing. She goes out to see who it is and returns immediately ly*

OUDJA: It's Monsieur Georges.
ZIZI (*standing*): Show him in. When Mr. Holmcroft comes, do what I told you.

211

(*Oudja introduces Georges and withdraws*)

GEORGES: I'm leaving today, Zizi. I'm saying good-bye now, but later…
ZIZI: …Later, we'll be together? No, it's too late, Georges.
GEORGES (*stunned*): Too late? Why? You are acting strangely.
ZIZI: Yesterday, I lied. Today, I want to be sincere.
GEORGES: What do you mean? You don't still doubt me?
ZIZI: No, you love me. Of that, I'm convinced. But they are right those who say that love is blind. Look around. See where I'm living. Look at these jewels. Do you think I could have paid for all this from my wages at Circus Dirko?
GEORGES: You wrote me that you hadn't forgotten me.
ZIZI: That was a year ago. A long time ago.
GEORGES: Yesterday, you said you almost died on account of me.
ZIZI: That only proves that I love you. It doesn't prove I'm worthy of your love. I must you the truth.
GEORGES: You're lying. I don't believe you! (*tries to grab her*)
ZIZI: Do you want to take me by force? Oh, maybe I would like that, but I would be betraying my benefactor…
GEORGES : …Your lover!
ZIZI: Yes, my lover.

(*Holmcroft enters from the back, then Rouscoubon*)

ROUSCOUBON (*to Zizi*): Excuse me. (*to Georges*) They're leaving by car tonight for Mayenne. We will follow them.
GEORGES: Never mind that!
ZIZI: Monsieur Rouscoubon, you are going to despise me, too.
ROUSCOUBON: Despise you? Why on Earth should I?
GEORGES (*taking Zizi's arm*): That man who stole you from me… Is it my brother?

212

ZIZI: Your brother? He's not rich enough for me.

GEORGES: I want to know who he is.

ZIZI (*who's seen Holmcroft*): So be it, if you swear not to seek a quarrel with him.

GEORGES: I swear it!

ZIZI (*to Oudja*): Oudja?

OUDJA: Madame, Monsieur is here.

GEORGE & ROUSCOUBON: Monsieur?

ZIZI (*to Oudja*): Don't make him wait. (*to Holmcroft*) How late you are, my friend!

(*She runs to Holmcroft and embraces him tenderly. George reacts*)

HOLMCROFT (*stupefied*): What is all this?

ZIZI (*low*): Hush! I'll explain everything later. (*tenderly*) Sit down. I was talking with these gentlemen.

HOLMCROFT: Ah! Monsieur Rouscoubon. I know him. A very brave man.

ROUSCOUBON: Don't disturb yourself.

ZIZI: And this is Georges de la Roche-Aiglon, a childhood friend.

HOLMCROFT: Enchanted, Monsieur.

GEORGES: Ah! I see! Good-bye, Zizi, good-bye! Come, Rouscoubon.

(*He leaves*)

ROUSCOUBON (*shrugging*): Lovers are imbeciles.

HOLMCROFT: My dear Zizi, I've come to say my good-byes.

ZIZI (*seeing Rouscoubon is still there*): Your good-byes, dear heart? But you mustn't go, or if you go, I'll go with you.

ROUSCOUBON: My compliments, Mister Holmcroft. A tale worthy of Philemon and Juliet.[6]

HOLMCROFT (*confused*): What?

OUDJA: Monsieur Ludovic is asking if you will see him?

ZIZI (*in a strangled voice*): I shall. You know very well that he's my lover. (*she goes to the right, sits down and conceals her tears in her handkerchief*)

ROUSCOUBON (*to Holmcroft*): Well, you heard her?

HOLMCROFT: Er, yes, but I'm – how do you say it?...

ROUSCOUBON: Furious?

HOLMCROFT: No, not furious. Sad. (*looks at Zizi*)

ZIZI: Gentlemen, I would be obliged if you would leave me alone with Monsieur Ludovic de la Roche-Aiglon. (*low to Holmcroft*) Come back later, I'll tell you everything.

ROUSCOUBON (*to Holmcroft*): Come on, friend, because, you see, you are no more Zizi's lover than I am.

(*They leave. Zizi rings. After a silence, Ludovic appears*)

ZIZI: You said you loved me and you were cruel enough to take me by force. But that's not enough impudence. You dare to appear before me.

LUDOVIC: Pardon! Pardon!

(*Zizi is lost in her thoughts and barely listens*)

LUDOVIC: Don't berate me. You cannot despise me as much as I despise myself. My only excuse is that I do love you. I saw you in America, and your portrait has never left me. It was always here. (*points to his heart*) And then—

ZIZI: You were jealous of your brother.

---

[6] Rouscoubon is likely mixing metaphors, or rather stories, combining *Romeo and Juliet* with *Philemon and Baucis*, a mythological tale written by Ovid and adapted in 1860 as a three-act opera by Charles Gounod.

LUDOVIC: Yes. And I lied to you about him getting married, and that lie almost cost you your life.

ZIZI: Today, I would prefer to be dead!

LUDOVIC: Ah! I will die if you demand it; but I want you to live. Listen, I am capable of all sorts of tricks, all sorts of cheats...

ZIZI (*calmly*): All sorts of crimes.

LUDOVIC: Yes, that's true, but what is even more true is that I adore you, and even more ardently, since I've held you in my arms.

ZIZI (*with a repulsive shiver*): Ah! Shut up!

LUDOVIC: If you won't ever forgive me, why then did you consent to see me?

ZIZI (*after a silence*): With your fierce jealousy, you wanted to break me up with Georges. You've succeeded. He doesn't know about your odious lies. He'll never know what you did to me last night. I'll never see him again. That should make you happy, right? When you had the effrontery to appear before me today, I should have kicked you out. But I agreed to see you. That's because I'm a different woman now. I've decided to remake my soul in the image of yours. (*a short silence*) Perhaps, I'll forget Georges. (*reaction by Ludovic*)

LUDOVIC: I will do everything. I am ready for everything. And as you know, I don't utter idle words.

ZIZI: Everything? That's quite abstract.

LUDOVIC: Tell me your dreams, your ambitions.

ZIZI: I shan't be your mistress, but will you accept an accomplice? Listen to me. I'm already rich. Today, a honest man gave me more money than I could dream of, asking for nothing in exchange. But that's not enough. I have only one passion now: money! I want money, immense amounts of it. I want to buy everything that is for sale—even honors and the conscience of others. I want to be able to throw millions around and humiliate others in my turn.

LUDOVIC: Those who made you suffer.

ZIZI: Yes. Before you knew me, a man...

LUDOVIC: Do you want me to get rid of him? There are two ways. I could challenge him to a duel. Then he'd be a dead man. Or, and that will show you to what degree I now belong to you, I could murder him.

ZIZI: No. He wouldn't suffer enough. I bet you didn't suspect that your little Zizi could hate so much.

LUDOVIC: I like you more for it.

ZIZI: It's money I want first of all.

LUDOVIC: I'll have some for you in a few days.

ZIZI: You are rich to such a degree?

LUDOVIC: I'm almost poor.

ZIZI: Are you expecting an inheritance?

LUDOVIC: You don't know how right you are. A hundred million.

ZIZI: Soon?

LUDOVIC: Next month.

ZIZI: That's singular. You plan on receiving an inheritance on a fixed date? You expect someone to die?

LUDOVIC: The testator is already dead. It's a question of waiting for the reading of the will. I will explain it all to you. Don't ask me if blood must be shed, but be confident.

ZIZI: I am.

LUDOVIC: And what is the name of the man you hate so much?

ZIZI: I will tell you after I have your fortune. Be confident, too. But I have a feeling you'll have to risk many perils in order to receive that inheritance.

LUDOVIC: For you, I'll brave all obstacles.

ZIZI: You've got me a little worried. You spoke of shedding blood just now... Has blood already been shed? (*a silence*) You don't reply. Did you do it alone?

LUDOVIC: The inheritance will be mine alone. Leave that to me.

ZIZI: I'm proud of you.

LUDOVIC (*going to her*): Am I then good enough for you to pardon me?

ZIZI (*pushing him back, concealing her hate*): No. Later, after I've got that promised fortune. After I am avenged…

CURTAIN

# ACT IV
## SCENE V

The courtyard of an old farmhouse. The house has only one floor and a single door, located at the edge of the stage. Near it is a tree in front of which is a table and several rustic chairs.

AT RISE, two children are seated at the table and barely eating milk and bread. The farmer's companion, Rita, is with them.

RITA: Well, children. You're not hungry this morning?
TINA: No, m'am! (*a silence*) No one wants to talk to us about our father Last night I dreamed he was dead.
ÉMILE: For sure, he's dead. If he weren't, he'd have come back from Siberia to see us. He wouldn't have left us with that fat guy.
TINA: And with your husband who has a nasty look too.
RITA: They don't mean you any harm, children. Come on, drink your milk.
TINA: Tell us the truth, Rita. You're nice. Are they always going to keep us here?
RITA: Really, I don't know.
ÉMILE: Why are we locked up like rabbits?
RITA: But I brought you to play outside this morning.

(*A silence. The children eat and cry*)

RITA: Come on, don't cry!
TINA: Do you have kids?
RITA (*blushing*): Me? No.

(*We hear the sound of an automobile approaching; the farmer, Alberto Spoletto, comes out of the house*)

SPOLETTO: Hey, Rita, a car is coming from the direction of Mayenne. It must be them. Did you prepare their lunch?

RITA: Yes.

SPOLETTO: Why did you let the kids out?

RITA: They need some fresh air.

SPOLETTO (*low to Rita*) They might run off. (*to the children*) Come on, kids, back inside!

RITA (*guilty*): Come.

ÉMILE (*to Tina*): He's got eyes that scare me.

(The children go into the house)

SPOLETTO: Be sure to lock the door. Then go get some ice to keep the wine cool. Ah, here they come!

(*Lavroyer and Ludovic enter, wearing goggles and dressed in white driving attire*)

LAVROYER: What a road!

SPOLETTO: I warned you in my letter, Monsieur Lavroyer.

LAVROYER (*to Ludovic*): My dear Ludovic, this is Alberto Spoletto. He accompanied me all the way to Siberia. You can have complete confidence in him.

LUDOVIC: The children are here?

SPOLETTO: Yes, in good health.

LAVROYER (*pointing to Rita*): Who's that woman?

SPOLETTO: My lady-friend. I brought her along so the kids wouldn't be afraid of me. I'm going to put your car in the shed. Rita has prepared your lunch.\

(*He goes out. They sit at the table. Lavroyer gets up and looks around*)

LUDOVIC: What's wrong? You seem uneasy.

LAVROYER: I wonder if we were being followed...

LUDOVIC: Who would want to follow us?

LAVROYER: I thought I noticed a car.

LUDOVIC: Yes, I saw it, too. But it continued on its way after we turned onto this road.

LAVROYER: You're right. I must be imagining things.

LUDOVIC: Come and drink. I'm dying of thirst.

(*Rita brings some drinks and glasses*)

LAVROYER: I must congratulate you. You didn't speak of Zizi once on this trip.

LUDOVIC: And I won't. I'm in a hurry to finish our business here.

LAVROYER: Good. We'll leave with the kids in half an hour.

LUDOVIC: You don't want to, er, finish it here?

LAVROYER: No. Besides, that woman might make a dangerous witness.

LUDOVIC: I trust in your prudence.

(*Rouscoubon appears in the distance and looks over the farm without being seen.*

(*Spoletto returns*)

SPOLETTO: I refilled you car. I also checked it out; it's ready. You can leave whenever you like.

LAVROYER: Thank you.

LUDOVIC: We haven't seen the two young heirs yet.

LAVROYER: You want to see them?

SPOLETTO: Let the kids out, Rita.

(*She does; the two children come out*)

ÉMILE: Uh-ho. Fatso's back. The one with the big rings.

LAVROYER: Why are you afraid of me? Have I done you any harm?

ÉMILE: No.

220

LAVROYER: This is one of my friends who takes an interest in you. (*to Ludovic*) These are Valentina and Emile de Saint-Claude.

LUDOVIC (*to the kids*): We've come to take you home.

ÉMILE: We're going home?

TINA: Are you taking us to Madame Sonia's? Father often spoke about her in his letters. She is the sister of his friend Karl.

LAVROYER: What did Karl do?

TINA: I don't know.

ÉMILE: I do. He was sentenced to death.

LAVROYER: Really?

ÉMILE: But he escaped.

TINA: I have a portrait of Madame Sonia. (*She shows Lavroyer a medallion over which Ludovic casts an impassive glance*)

LAVROYER: Well, I promise you, you are going to Madame Sonia's. (*getting up*)

ÉMILE (*aside to Tina*): Do you trust him?

TINA: No.

LAVROYER (*to Rita*): Our conversation can only bore these little ones. Take them back inside and fix dinner for them. (*to the children*) Till later.

(*Rita takes the children back into the house and locks the door behind her*)

LAVROYER (*to Spoletto*): I'm afraid we won't need your services any longer.

SPOLETTO: I'm sorry to hear it,

LAVROYER: But you'll be well paid for them. In gold.

SPOLETTO: I like the sound of that.

(*They all go into the house. The stage remains empty. The door opens quietly; it is Émile*)

ÉMILE: Tina, Rita forgot to lock the door. Come on, we're going to get out of here!
TINA: But they'll catch us.
ÉMILE: Not if we run very fast. There's no one.

(*They run off. Spoletto, followed by Rita, appears*)

SPOLETTO: I'll get another bottle of wine... (*seeing the children*) Ah, the little scoundrels! (*grabs a rifle and aims at the children*) Stop! Stop or I'll shoot!
RITA (*getting in front of him*): No, no! They'll go back in.
TINA: Yes. We don't want him to hurt you.

(*The children go back in. Spoletto carefully locks the door and pockets the key. Rouscoubon reappears and hides behind the tree*)

ROUSCOUBON (*aside*): He's got the key.
SPOLETTO: You left the door open, you stupid woman! (*slaps Rita violently*)
RITA: Stop! You're hurting me!

(*Spoletto pushes Rita inside, then goes toward a well to get the wine that had been left to cool.*

(*Rouscoubon emerges from behind the tree and knocks him out. He takes the key and then calmly throws Spoletto down the well. A splash can be heard*)

ROUSCOUBON: Nice deep well. He'll sleep with the fishes. Now, I've got to fix their car...

(*Rouscoubon goes into the shed; Rita comes out*)

RITA (*calling*): Alberto! Where are you? They want their wine. (*Seeing the bottles near the well, she takes them and goes back inside*)

(*Rouscoubon emerges from the shed*)

ROUSCOUBON: That wasn't difficult.

(*He hides again as Lavroyer and Rota come out*)

LAVROYER: Where's Spoletto?
RITA: I don't know what's become of him.
LAVROYER: I was going to tell him to warm up our car, but we can do that ourselves. Come Ludovic.

(*Ludovic comes out; the two men go into the shed*)

RITA: I'm beginning to think the Devil has taken Alberto...
ROUSCOUBON (*aside*): We've got to risk it. It's now or never!

(*He signals to Georges, who appears dressed in driving attire*)

ROUSCOUBON: The children are there. (*pointing to the house*) You'll take care of the girl, I'll take care of the boy. We'll run off with them. As for their car, I've already disabled it. Stay here.

(*He goes to the house and slowly opens the door*)

ROUSCOUBON (*to the children*): Hush! Follow us. We've come to save you.

(*Émile and Tina come out, look at Rouscoubon and Georges without fright*)

GEORGES (*to Tina*): Don't be afraid!
ROUSCOUBON: Hurry!

*(As Georges starts to leave with Tina, Ludovic and Lavroyer come out of the shed)*

LAVROYER: Sonofabitch! Nothing works.
LUDOVIC: And that Italian brute has disappeared! (*looking around*) Spoletto! (*noticing Georges*) My brother!
GEORGES: I order you to let me pass!
LUDOVIC: Never!
LAVROYER: Strike him down, or all is lost!
ROUSCOUBON: You wouldn't dare!

*(Ludovic stabs Georges, Rouscoubon rushes at him)*

LAVROYER (*hitting Rouscoubon with a tire iron*): Here's yours, old chum!

*(Tina and Mile scream)*

LAVROYER (*to Ludovic*): My compliments. You have no family inhibitions. We'll take their vehicle. Let's go!

*(Ludovic grabs Tina and Lavroyer Émile. The children scream but vanish with their captors. The nose of a vehicle starting and leaving can be heard)*

ROUSCOUBON (*regaining consciousness*): Ah! The wretches! (*crawling to go and check on Georges*) The poor boy! He's not breathing. Is he dead?

*(Rita comes out to help him)*

ROUSCOUBON: Ah! It's you! Can you help me get up? (*she does*) Georges! Stabbed by his own brother! He's killed him.

*(we hear another car)*

ROUSCOUBON: Help! Help!

(*The car is heard stopping. Zizi and Oudja appear dressed in driving attires*)

ROUSCOUBON: Mademoiselle Zizi!
ZIZI: Monsieur Rouscoubon!

(*Oudja goes to George and makes him breathe salts*)

OUDJA: Too late! He's dead!
ROUSCOUBON: No! He can't be! (*kneeling by George*) He's breathing! I think he'll be all right.
ZIZI: Ah! He'll live! He'll live!
ROUSCOUBON: I know you still love him. But we'd better get him to a hospital. Meanwhile, those poor kids...
ZIZI: It's for them that I came.
ROUSCOUBON: Then go after them. Follow them. I know they're heading toward Saint-Malo.

(*Zizi kisses Georges who remains unconscious*)

ROUSCOUBON: I'll take care of Georges.
ZIZI: And I'll save the children.

C U R T A I N

## SCENE VI

A shack on the beach near the port of Saint-Malo. The shabby house is built into the rocks. Inside, there is a straw mattress, table chairs, etc.

AT RISE, Old Mathurine stands on a rock and looks into the sea, then the shack. Papa Kermadoc comes out.

KERMADOC: What are you doing here, Mathurine?
MATHURINE: I'm not doing any harm, Papa Kermadoc.

KERMADOC: I don't like you prowling around here.

MATHURINE: Don't get angry. I thought I heard kids' voices.

KERMADOC: Children? Here? You're moonstruck for sure. My wife and I are too old to make them, and too poor to raise them. Be about your business, Mathurine, and don't come back. (*he goes towards her shaking his fist*)

MATHURINE: You're an old brute, but too drunk to catch me.

(*She leaves*)

KERMADOC: The bitch. (*staggering and falling on the stones*) That's funny. I only had a half liter of brandy this morning. (*he falls asleep and snores*)

(*Inside the shack, Marie-Anne, his wife, rises from the mattress*)

MARIE-ANNE: I'm thirsty. (*she looks for a bottle and starts drinking*) How are the children? (*going to the children's bed*) They're asleep. But they wouldn't eat. Better not wake them. They cried all night. We don't need more of that.

(*Outside, Lavroyer, followed by Ludovic, enters and wakes up Kermadoc*)

LAVROYER: Well, well, Papa Kermadoc. Is it all over?

KERMADOC: Er, no.

LUDOVIC: It was agreed you would finish the work last night.

KERMADOC: The Moon was too high and the sky was too clear. But the wind's changing to the West.

LUDOVIC: What nonsense is this! Then, tonight at the very latest. When it's done, you'll receive your ten thousand francs. And let me remind you that you've already got a down payment.

226

KERMADOC: Just a second, my fine gentlemen. There are risks here. What proves to me you will come back?

LAVROYER (*to Ludovic*): Give him another five hundreds. (*To Kermadoc*) You've promised us a boating accident.

KERMADOC: Yes.

LAVROYER: But I'm afraid, you're not the most reliable of men. So, as a precaution, we'll give you someone to help you.

KERMADOC: And take half of my money?

LUDOVIC: No. Your share will remain intact.

LAVROYER: Anyway, you know him. It's Jaouen.

KERMADOC: But he drinks even more than I do!

LAVROYER: Possibly, but he's young and even when he drinks, he keeps his head.

(*Inside, Marie Anne goes to listen*)

KERMADOC: Fine.

LAVROYER: So go back in.

LUDOVIC: Should we go and check on the children?

LAVROYER: I doubt our presence will reassure them.

(*Kermadoc enters the shack and closes the door behind him*)

KERMADOC (*to Marie-Anne*): Ah, you heard us. Yes, I have even more gold—see! (*she wants to take the money*)Get your grubby paws off! I am the head of the family! (*he drinks*) Listen, we can drink, but never together. The kids might escape. No brandy for you until I wake up.

LAVROYER (*to Ludovic*): Get Jaouen.

(*Ludovic lights a cigar, then moves towards the back and returns with Jaouen*)

JAOUEN: Why'd you bother me? I was about to go to sleep. You spoke to me already. I understand what I'm supposed to do.

LUDOVIC: Then it won't do any harm for you to tell us what you understood.

JAOUEN: I understood that if the two kids were to die at sea, I'd get 500 big ones. And I can drink all I want. (*hums a tune*)

LUDOVIC: That's not all. Kermadoc is old. You're young and strong.

LAVROYER: So you must help him do the job. No pain, no gain, my lad.

JAOUEN: You want me to…?

LUDOVIC: You're afraid?

JAOUEN: Me? I ain't afraid of nothin'!

LUDOVIC: Do you need some money now?

JAOUEN: Thanks. When I'm the Saint-Claude's heir, I'll have as much money as I could want.

LUDOVIC: I don't think he's as much of an idiot as you said.

LAVROYER: We're counting on you, Jaouen.

JAOUEN: Don't worry.

(*Lavroyer and Ludovic leave. Jaouen raps on the door of the shack*)

MARIE-ANNE: Who is it?

JAOUEN: It's me, Jaouen.

MARIE-ANNE (*to Karmadoc*): Should I open?

KARMADOC (*half-asleep*): Yes, open. He knows about it. He's coming to help us. (*he goes back to sleep*)

JAOUEN: I was going to knock the door in, Marie-Anne. Ah, the kids are awake.

ÉMILE: Oh, look, Tina, what a red face that one's got.

JAOUEN: Eh, so what? Are they mistreating you here?

ÉMILE: No, Monsieur.

JAOUEN: Hey! You're calling me "Monsieur"!

TINA: They took my necklace with the portrait.

MARIE-ANNE: It wasn't me, it was him (*pointing to the snoring Kermadoc*) my husband.

JAOUEN (*low to Marie-Anne*): What a brute, His pockets are loaded with money and he steals a necklace from this kid. Just making her suspicious. You know where he hid it?
MARIE-ANNE: Yes.
JAOUEN: Give it to me.

(*Marie-Anne finds the necklace and gives it to Jaouen who returns it to Tina*)

JAOUEN: Here! Hide this under your corsage.
TINA (hiding it) You see, Émile, he gave me back my necklace.
JAOUEN: Now, go back to sleep, kids.
MARIE-ANNE (*low to Jaouen*): I don't like this. The boy reminds me of my son. You must save them.

(*Jaouen says nothing. The children start to doze off. After a while, Jaouen wakes Kermadoc with a series of small kicks*)

KERMADOC: What is it?
JAOUEN: You don't need to get up. They told you, right?
KERMADOC: Yeah. You're coming with me tonight?
JAOUEN: At eleven. I'll have a boat. You still have time to snore. Till tonight.

(*He leaves*)

KERMADOC (*to Marie-Anne*): Lock the door and give me the key.

(*She obeys. Karmadoc takes the key and falls back to sleep. She drinks a little and lies down beside him.*)

(*Outside, Jaouen leans on a rock, pensive. Mathurine appears*)

MATHURINE: Ah, there you are!

JAOUEN: What do you want, Mathurine? You're always around. Why?

MATHURINE: Me? I'm just curious. Is it here you wait for your *gast*?[7] (*reaction by Jaouen*) Yes, that beautiful Parisian woman that I saw you talking to yesterday.

JAOUEN: Why are you such a meddling, busy-body?

MATHURINE: It's funny, isn't it? All the local girls turn you down, but this Princess falls into your arms.

JAOUEN: Shut up!

MATHURINE: You know, she isn't far. I saw her on the other path. I bet she's looking for you.

JAOUEN: Get out, or else…

MATHURINE: You'd hit an old woman?

JAOUEN: And twice on Sunday! (*shaking his fist at her*)

MATHURINE: The drunk and the slut. Hoot! Hoot!

(*Mathurine leaves. Soon after, Zizi appears*)

ZIZI: Jaouen! Why aren't you at your shack?

JAOUEN: Because I was with these two men…

ZIZI: Ah! The children are dead!

JAOUEN: No.

ZIZI: Are you sure?

JAOUEN: Yes. I just saw them. They're planning to drown them at a spot about 120 leagues deep.

ZIZI: How do you know that?

JAOUEN: I know because I'm the one they recruited to help old Kermadoc.

ZIZI: You're not lying to me, Jaouen?

JAOUEN: How could I lie to you?

ZIZI: So you say you saw the children?

JAOUEN: Yes. They're inside that shack. (*pointing to the shack*)

ZIZI: What if they hear us?

---

[7] Promiscuous woman in Breton.

JAOUEN: Kermadoc and his wife are dead drunk, and the children are asleep.

ZIZI: Can I see them?

JAOUEN: They're both asleep.

ZIZI: Let me look at them through the window.

JAOUEN: Stand on that rock. But be careful.

ZIZI: The window is very high. Support me. (*he does*) Why are you trembling?

JAOUEN: You know why.

ZIZI: Come on, Jaouen. You know I just want to save them. If you committed this awful murder, the authorities would catch you and you'd be guillotined.

JAOUEN: Are you threatening me?

ZIZI: Worse—you would be cursed before God!

JAOUEN: Bah! I don't believe in God.

ZIZI: Then you cannot swear that you've told me the truth!

JAOUEN: I don't need to swear, because I love you.

ZIZI: Jaouen!

JAOUEN: Tell me what you want me to do?

ZIZI: There's an American with a yacht anchored in the bay. You'll put the children on board.

JAOUEN: Easy enough.

ZIZI: But I want everybody else except you to think the children are dead. Especially, these two men.

JAOUEN: The one called Ludovic?

ZIZI: Especially him.

JAOUEN: From what I heard, he loves you too.

ZIZI: And I hate him. After you've saved the children, this man will be ruined.

JAOUEN: I will force myself to act in accordance with your will.

ZIZI: I am rich, Jaouen. I will give you all the money you want.

JAOUEN (*laughing*): Ah, ah! But don't you know? I am the bastard son of the last of the Saint-Claudes. The whole fortune will belong to me.

ZIZI: Who told you that—Ludovic?

JAOUEN: Yes.

ZIZI: And you believed him?

JAOUEN: I believed him. But what difference does it make? If what you asked of me costed me a hundred million, that still wouldn't matter. There's no need to speak of money between us. (*A silence*)

ZIZI: What do you really want?

JAOUEN: You know very well what I want. You are beautiful. More beautiful than all my solitary dreams. You've driven me crazy. I can't sleep anymore. I didn't know there were women like you. I see plainly you mock my despair. What I want is you. (*he comes toward her, his large hands stretched to embrace her*)

ZIZI (*looking at him as she would her tigers*): I forbid you to touch me. (*after hesitating, he steps back*) Why are you recoiling?

JAOUEN: Because your eyes scare me.

ZIZI: As for me, I'm not afraid of you.

JAOUEN: I'm strong. But with you…

ZIZI: On your knees. (*he kneels down*) Ask my pardon!

JAOUEN: Pardon! Pardon!

ZIZI: Now do what I've told you.

JAOUEN: Give me something of yours.

(*she gives him her scarf; he kisses it passionately and vanishes into the rocks*)

ZIZI Will he keep his word?

CURTAIN

## SCENE VII

Moonlight. The ocean. Rocks on the right and left. Jaouen's boat is at anchor.

AT RISE, Kermadoc shows up as Jaouen emerges from the boat. Marie-Jeanne and the two children stand in a corner.

JAOUEN: Kermadoc.

KERMADOC: We're waiting for you.

JAOUEN: I brought my boat. It's anchored. I've got two big rocks to attach to the kids' feet.

KERMADOC (*pointing*): They're there. They came without resistance. They're very scared.

JAOUEN: You seem less drunk than usual, Kermadoc.

KERMADOC: I haven't had anything to drink since this morning.

JAOUEN: That was a mistake. When you do something like this, you need the courage that only comes from a bottle. Here's yours. (*Jaouen gives Kermadoc a bottle. Kermadoc drinks but Jaouen discreetly pours his out*)

JAOUEN: Who's crying over there?

KERMADOC: My old lady. (*drinks*)

JAOUEN (to Marie-Anne): Why are you crying, Marie-Anne?

MARIE-ANNE: Save them, Jaouen! Save them!

JAOUEN: Hum.

MARIE-ANNE: Save them! I'll give you all the money we have. Why aren't you listening to me?

KERMADOC (*half-drunk already*): What's she saying?

MARIE-ANNE: I don't like it. I'll call out! I'll scream!

JAOUEN: The storm will scream louder than you.

KERMADOC (*to Marie-Anne*): Get out! Enough! You are good for nothing! Go home! Go to bed, and wait for me!

MARIE-ANNE: I don't want to.

KERMADOC: Obey or I'll whack you good.

MARIE-ANNE (*crossing the rocks*): You're going to drown them.

KERMADOC (*laughing*): She's lost her head.

JAOUEN: You haven't drunk enough, Kermadoc. Look, my bottle has half what you have. To our health, and our fortune! (*Jaouen only pretends to drink*)

KERMADOC: Got to gag the children.

JAOUEN: Leave it to me. (*gives the children a flask*) You must drink this.
ÉMILE: Is it poison?
JAOUEN: No. It will help you sleep.
TINA: Better drink it, Émile.
JAOUEN: You won't suffer, kids, I promise you.

(*Tina drinks, eyes fixed on Jaouen. Then she gives the flask to Émile*)

TINA: Since we are going to die, say a prayer.
ÉMILE: Holy Virgin Mary, we are orphans and no one loves us. They're going to kill us. Takes us with you to Heaven.
KERMADOC (turning over his bottle): It's empty? Ah, ah, ah, it's empty already.
JAOUEN: Hurry up! The sea's still calm. I'm going to put the kids in the boat. (he *carries the sleeping children into the boat*) Come on!
KERMADOC (staggering onto the boat): I think I see a green light in the water.
JAOUEN: You're crazy. It's the lighthouse. You're three sheets to the wind. Come on, I'll give you a hand!

(*He helps Kermadoc into the boat. They get in and the boat moves out. Then Silence.*

(*Ludovic appears with a battery operated lamp*)

LUDOVIC: I heard the noise of oars. They aren't going far… After tonight, Jaouen will be the last legitimate heir. He's the only person between me and this fortune. An unnecessary murder, Lavroyer said, but he's wrong. Hark! I hear the boat returning.

(*The boat returns*)

JAOUEN: Just in time. The storm is almost here. Hey, Papa Kermadoc, are you asleep? A little water will wake you up. (*he wakes Kermadoc up splashing some water on his face and puts him ashore*)
KERMADOC: Where are we? Where are the kids?
JAOUEN: Don't make me laugh, old boy. You're the one who tossed them overboard.
KERMADOC: Ah, yes, I remember... The ropes, the weights.
JAOUEN: Still, without me, you would never have done it.
KERMADOC: True.
JAOUEN: Come on. Go home and keep your mouth shut. The two of us are rich now.
KERMADOC: Till tomorrow.

(*He staggers out; Ludovic lights his lamp*)

JAOUEN: Who's that? (*sees Ludovic*) Ah, it's you, Monsieur Ludovic.
LUDOVIC: You know my name?
JAOUEN: Your friend said it this morning.
LUDOVIC: Ah yes, I remember.
JAOUEN: Now I'm a millionaire. The work is over.
LUDOVIC: Not yet.

(*He stabs Jaouen with a knife and vanishes.*

(*Jaouen screams and falls. Zizi enters*)

ZIZI (*calling*): Jaouen! (*in a flash of lightning, she sees him*) Jaouen! You saved them, didn't you? Didn't you?

(*Jaouen, unable to speak, utters a last moan and rolls dead at her feet*)

CURTAIN

## SCENE VII

A Spartan room. The sea can be seen at the rear. There's a table with two chairs at the right.

AT RISE, Zizi and Oudja, both sitting, are talking.

ZIZI: Oudja, I'm deadly anxious. I have no news of Georges. He's dead, perhaps.
OUDJA: Oh, no, no.
ZIZI: No news of the children, either, for thirty-six hours. I saw the green light from Holmcroft's yacht. He should have sent me a telegram by now. Nothing. Could Jaouen have killed them?

(*Enter Rouscoubon*)

ROUSCOUBON: Ah! I thought I'd never find you.
ZIZI: What about Georges?
ROUSCOUBON: He's alive, but very weak. He'll be here soon.
ZIZI: Oh, thank you!
ROUSCOUBON: What about the children?
ZIZI: I don't know. I'm dying of anxiety.
ROUSCOUBON: And the other heir? The bastard son?
ZIZI: You mean, Jaouen? He was going to save them, but he's dead. I don't know if he kept his promise.
ROUSCOUBON: Dead?
ZIZI: Yes, he died before my very eyes. Without being able to tell me anything.

(*M. Renault, the Investigating Magistrate, enters*)

RENAULT: You are Mademoiselle Zizi?
ZIZI: Yes, Monsieur.
RENAULT: I'm the Investigating Magistrate Renault. What is your real name?

236

ZIZI: Zinz Datti.

RENAULT: And your profession?

ZIZI: I work as a tiger-tamer at the Circus Dirko.

RENAULT: As, yes! I recall that terrible accident two months ago.

ROUSCOUBON: Her wounds are completely healed.

RENAULT: I wasn't speaking to you, Monsieur.

ROUSCOUBON: I'm Baptistin Rouscoubon, former professor of philosophy and moral sciences, at…

RENAULT: Please wait your turn to be questioned. (*to Zizi*) This affair concerns the possible murder of two children, alleged to be the heirs of the great fortune of the Saint-Claudes.

ZIZI: Oh, I beg you to tell me the fate of these children if you know it.

RENAULT: I know nothing except that, a few days ago, they were at Saint-Malo, and that they have vanished.

ZIZI: My God!

RENAULT: There is a witness however. Thomas!

(*A policeman enters*)

RENAULT: Call Mathurine in.

THOMAS: Yeas, Monsieur le Juge.

(*Thomas goes out and returns with Mathurine*)

RENAULT: Your name?

MATHURINE: Mathurine Colet.

RENAULT: Your profession?

MATHURINE: Fisherwoman

RENAULT: Tell us what you know.

MATHURINE (*looking accusingly towards Zizi*): When this woman came here, she had a secret appointment with Jaouen. I saw them. I even saw him kiss her hand.

RENAULT: Tell us about the children.

MATHURINE: One night, I was, er, wandering about Old Man Kermadoc's shack.

RENAULT: Why were you "wandering about," as you put it?

MATHURINE: To find out what was going on. I'd heard kids crying inside. The next day, Jaouen came to see Papa Kermadoc, and in the night, the children disappeared. That's not all. That same night, I saw that woman out in the storm. She was near Angels' Point. That's where they found Jaouen's body, stabbed near his boat, which had been broken by the waves.

RENAULT (*to Zizi*): What do you say to this?

ZIZI: Yes, I met Jaouen. I spoke to him. I asked him to save the children that these wretches wanted to kill. I'd give my life to know what has become of them.

MATHURINE: She's the one who killed Jaouen.

ZIZI: Me? I did not!

RENAULT (*to Mathurine*): You may leave now.

MATHURINE: But you've got her, the filthy slut! Don't let her get away with it!

(*The policeman drags Mathurine away*)

RENAULT: Thomas, bring in Maître Patelot.

(*Thomas goes out and returns with Maître Patelot, a Notary*)

RENAULT: Your name?

PATELOT: Ernest Patelot.

RENAULT: Your Profession?

PATELOT: Notary at Saint-Malo.

RENAULT: Maître, tell us what you know.

PATELOT: Today, on the 15th of October, before the President of the Court, I opened the Last Will and Testament of the Marquis Armand de Saint-Claude, who passed away in America. I shall now give you a summary description of its contents. The Estate of Monsieur de Saint-Claude, who sired no children, goes to his nephews and nieces...

RENAULT: These are the children of whom we are speaking?

PATELOT: Yes. Émile and Valentina de Saint-Claude. However, if they are deceased, then the aforesaid estate goes to Jaouen Tusseric, the bastard son of the aforesaid Monsieur de Saint-Claude.

ZIZI: And, if he, too, is deceased, to Monsieur Ludovic de Roche-Aiglon.

RENAULT (*to Zizi*): Ah. You know this will?

ZIZI: Yes, I do.

RENAULT: In that case, you had no motive to prevent Jaouen Tusseric, a local lad who was infatuated with you, and who today would be a millionaire, from receiving his inheritance. Thomas, bring in Kermadoc.

(*The policeman returns with Kermadoc in handcuffs*)

RENAULT: He's still drunk. Remove the cuffs.

(*The policeman removes the handcuffs*)

RENAULT: Monsieur Kermadoc, yesterday, you were seen paying for your drinks with gold coins in several local cabarets. You even gave one to a beggar, something unheard of coming from a skinflint like you. This morning, I found several more coins in your hut. Where did you get this money?

KERMADOC: That's my savings.

RENAULT: Do you know anyone here?

KERMADOC (*after looking around suspiciously*): No.

RENAULT: Two children were staying with you.

KERMADOC: What children?

RENAULT: Your wife didn't deny it. It's true, however, that she went mad the night of your crime.

KERMADOC: What crime?

RENAULT: It's obvious you were but a tool. Confess, give us the name of your employer, and it will go better for you.

KERMADOC: I have nothing to confess.

RENAULT: If you lie, your head will roll. And you'll go to Hell where you'll burn for eternity.

239

KERMADOC: Eternity? By the Name of God, I don't like that! (he makes the sign of the cross.)
RENAULT: Like what?
KERMADOC: I don't want to burn for eternity.
RENAULT: Then you'd better talk.
KERMADOC: Fine. Two nights ago, Jaouen and me, we took the children out in his boat to drown them in the bay. We put lead weights on their feet. When we came back, they were gone.
ZIZI (*collapsing*): Ah! They are dead! They are dead!
ROUSCOUBON: Monsieur le Juge, I know who is behind this.
RENAULT: In that case, tell us.

(Noises outside)

ROUSCOUBON: No need. Here they come. I sent them a telegram signed Zizi.

(*Ludovic enters without noticing the police. He's in his driving attire*)

LUDOVIC: My dear Zizi, I came as soon as I got your telegram.

(*Lavroyer enters, also dressed in driving attire*)

ROUSCOUBON: Hello, old boy. (*presenting Ludovic to the Magistrate*) Monsieur le Juge, this is Monsieur Ludovic de la Roche-Aiglon.
RENAULT: Ah-ha! So you're the heir to the Saint-Claude fortune.
ROUSCOUBON (*to Ludovic*): And this is His Honor Monsieur Renault, Investigating Magistrate.
LUDOVIC (*to Zizi*): What's all this?

ZIZI: I was mad to trust Jaouen. It was on your order, Ludovic, that these two children were murdered. And you killed Jaouen too.

RENAULT: Do you happen to know these two men, Monsieur Kermadoc? Speak.

KERMADOC: One day, they came…

LAVROYER: Pay no attention to what this drunk says. Here are their death certificates issued by the Russian authorities. (*places death certificates on the table*)

(*Georges enters*)

GEORGES: He's lying!

ZIZI: Georges!

LUDOVIC: Georges—alive !

GEORGES (*to Lavroyer*): You dare to claim that these children died in Russia with their father when I saw them alive, with my own eyes, with you, only a week ago in Mayenne! (*he staggers, Zizi supports him*)

RENAULT: And who are you, Monsieur?

GEORGES: Georges de la Roche-Aiglon.

ROUSCOUBON: Who was stabbed by…

GEORGES: Shut up, Rouscoubon!

ROUSCOUBON: …By his brother, here present. As for the excellent Monsieur Lavroyer, he gave me a crack in the head that nearly killed me.

GEORGES (*to Zizi*): Rouscoubon told me everything. What about the children?

ZIZI: I don't know. They're probably dead.

(*Holmcroft enters*)

ZIZI: Mister Holmcroft…

HOLMCROFT: The children are fine, Miss Zizi! Jaouen had time to transfer them abroad my yacht.

(*Émile and Tina enter*)

HOLMCROFT: Go hug Miss Zizi who saved you, kids.

(*As they do, Holmcroft goes to the Magistrate*)

HOLMCROFT: Sorry to be so late, sir, but that storm knocked out the telegraph system all along the coast.
LUDOVIC (*to Zizi*): You snake! You betrayed me!

(*He rushes at Zizi with his knife. Holmcroft pulls out a gun and shoots him dead in his tracks. Lavroyer rushes Holmcroft who turns around and coolly blows the man's brains out*)

HOLMCROFT: Ah, double or nothing. Now, that's American style justice.
RENAULT: Now, look here, Monsieur…
HOLMCROFT (*blowing smoke off his pistol*): Yes, Your Honor, I know I'm a bit quick on the draw, but I'm at your disposal.

CURTAIN